Old Dog . . . New Tricks

The deputy thumbed back the hammers on the scattergun and poked the barrels into Stillman's back.

Not so much thinking as reacting, Stillman knocked the shotgun aside with his right elbow, both barrels exploding into the door. With the same motion he drew his Colt, turned, and slammed the butt against the deputy's head.

The big man fell like a sack of grain, bouncing off the wall and making the whole room jump.

"Who in the hell do you think you are?" bellowed the red-faced Englishman.

"Ben Stillman, deputy U.S. marshal, retired . . ."

ONCE A MARSHAL

Peter Brandvold

BERKLEY BOOKS, NEW YORK

ONCE A MARSHAL

A Berkley Book / published by arrangement with
the author

PRINTING HISTORY
Berkley edition / November 1998

The Penguin Putnam Inc. World Wide Web site address is
http://www.penguinputnam.com

ISBN: 0-425-16622-8

BERKLEY®
Berkley Books are published by The Berkley Publishing Group,
a member of Penguin Putnam Inc.,
375 Hudson Street, New York, New York 10014.
BERKLEY and the "B" logo
are trademarks belonging to Berkley Publishing Corporation.

PRINTED IN THE UNITED STATES OF AMERICA

10 9 8 7 6 5 4 3 2 1

For Gena and Old Shep—
remembering our adventures
on the Hi-Line

A savage place, as holy and enchanted
As e'er beneath a waning moon . . .

—Samuel Taylor Coleridge, "Kubla Khan"

PROLOGUE

Stout as a fence post, the diamondback coiled around a tuft of buffalo grass, raised its head, and tested the air with its long, forked tongue.

Jody Harmon was relieving himself behind a fir tree, taking a break from his work. Lost in his thoughts, he didn't realize the fallen branch he was pissing on was a snake. When the rattles shook, he gave a start, splashing his boots and trouser cuffs.

"... Ho, now," he said tightly.

His pants hung open, exposing him to the viper's scrutiny. He wanted to cover himself but feared that if he so much as twitched, the critter would leap forward and sink its two-inch tines into his bare flesh.

The snake investigated the scuffed toe of his boot, pulled back, and increased its rattle. Jody flinched.

"Just hold still," a quiet voice said.

"I'm not goin' anywhere."

"Just . . . hold . . . still."

From the sound of his father's voice Jody knew he was trying to get a bead on the snake, probably propping his old Sharps rifle on the windmill tower they'd been horsing together out of square-cut pine logs felled and dragged from the surrounding ridges that had turned a smoky blue green in the late-afternoon light.

The snake's arrow-shaped head glided sideways. Its rattle stuck straight up in the air. One of the horses whinnied.

"Pa . . ."

"Hold still."

The snake's mouth opened. The needle teeth shone. The coil sprang, and the viper shot upward as if propelled from a cannon.

Jody jumped, tripped, and landed in a juniper bush. Had he heard the Sharps's boom? He looked down.

The big snake lay in his lap with its fangs striking con-vulsively against his jeans, a hole the size of a silver dollar in its neck.

"Oh, jeez!"

He flung the beast away and scrambled to pull up his pants. The rattler lay in the grass with its wrinkled, white belly heaving, its smoky eyes open, its jaws working. Its body spasmed, whipping its tail.

"Right through the neck." Bill Harmon smiled, walking forward with his smoking rifle slung over his shoulder—a big, grinning bear of a man in baggy coveralls and a sugar-loaf sombrero shading his bearded face. "Still got all your parts?"

Jody wiped his hands on his jeans and scowled. "Think it's funny, do you? You mighta shot sooner."

"What fun would that o' been? I was memorizing the picture of you standin' there offerin' your noodle to that viper so's I could detail it for my grandchildren."

The elder Harmon hooted and held the snake's blindly striking head down with his boot. The tail whipped his pants several times before the death spasms slowed.

Bill bent down, grabbed the snake by the neck, and held

the long, curving body up for inspection. "That's a hog, there! I'll fry him up for supper."

"I ain't eating that."

"You'll eat skunk but you won't eat rattler?"

"I haven't ate skunk."

The elder Harmon gave a mischievous smile. "Sure ya have. That rabbit you had the other night was a skunk I trapped under the icehouse."

"That's disgusting! You sure as hell didn't get that out of Ma's recipe box."

Harmon guffawed.

Jody shook his head. He pulled on his gloves and walked back to where the windmill tower lay near a freshly dug stock well. "If you're through funnin', let's get this job finished. I got plans later."

Letting his laughter cool to a slow boil, the elder Harmon took the snake and his rifle to the tool wagon hitched to a stout, hip-shot gelding. "Those plans happen to be named Crystal Johnson?"

"They might."

"What you got goin'?"

"Dance over at the Bitter Creek School."

"Sounds serious. You better head on back to the ranch and get cleaned up. It's pret' near four."

Jody shook his head and talked around the nails in his mouth. "You'll never get this done yourself by nightfall."

Harmon smiled at his son. The dark eyes and taut, determined jaw reminded him of his wife, Jody's mother, a Canadian Cree named Tah-Kwah-I-Mi-Nah-Nah. The name meant "chokecherry" in English; she'd been born during the Moon of the Ripening Chokecherries.

A humble, bighearted woman whose easy nature and life joy had equaled that of her father, Chief Stick, she'd been a hard worker to boot. Bill remembered years ago waking at three in the morning and watching her sew moccasins by firelight in her hide-bottom chair while humming the ancient songs she'd learned from her grandmothers.

Jody didn't have her sense of humor, but he had her vigor and her practicality, not to mention her soulful eyes, sleek, coal-black hair, and quiet dignity.

"Who says we have to have it done by nightfall, anyway?" Harmon said. "Like I always told my old huntin' buddy, Ben Stillman—you're dead a long time."

Jody gave the final licks to a nail and sat back on his haunches. "Ben Stillman again. Pa, you're living in the past."

"Ben Stillman is not the past. He's alive and kicking—though I ain't seen him in twenty years."

"How do you know he's alive, then?"

"They used to tell about him in the Great Falls paper. But it's been a while. Might be dead now, I'll admit. The likes of me and Ben, we don't live long."

He paused, studying the ground in contemplative silence. Jody watched him, wishing he could read the old hide hunter's mind.

"Anyway," Bill said, slapping the boy's knee, "this tower isn't going anywhere, and we got some time before the serious powder flies, so you head back to the cabin and get gussied up for your girl."

"Let's both cash it in, then."

Bill shook his head. "Nah, I'll dally here, hammer a few more nails, and enjoy the sun goin' down. When you're scrapin' fifty and don't have women waiting for you anymore, you start appreciatin' things like the sun goin' down. Pathetic, ain't it?"

"You sure, Pa?"

"Sure as your noodle was just about snake supper!"

"Will you quit?" Jody set his hammer in the tool wagon

and rolled down his shirtsleeves. "Well, don't try to do too much and irritate your shoulder."

"Don't worry about me, youngun. You just worry about keepin' that little woman happy so she doesn't fall for one of those Dutchmen in Hungry Hollow." Harmon's dark blond beard broadened with a smile; his eyes glittered.

"Little chance o' that," Jody said. "Crystal Johnson likes her Dutch spiced with Injun." Grinning, he mounted his horse while his father held the bridle.

Jody nodded, giving his buckskin the spurs. "See you back at the cabin."

Harmon watched him ride off down the two-track wagon trail narrowing between fir-covered ridges, disappearing around a hill. Dust and the sound of his hoofbeats lingered in the still September air.

That was quite a boy he and Cherry had raised. Bill wished she could see him now, practically a man. She'd died of pneumonia four years ago, and he'd wrapped her in deerskins and laid her in a tree on Mount Baldy, offering her back to Mother Earth and Father Sky.

He wondered if Ben Stillman was gone now, too. The prospect of it filled him with nostalgia, and he got out his Bull Durham and indulged in a smoke.

When the sun had burnished the southern ridgetop, filling the valley with cool, blue shade, he ground the butt with his boot heel, donned his gloves, adjusted his hat, and picked up his hammer.

He was lost in his work when the gelding whinnied and shook its mane. He looked up to see a rider at the high end of the valley following the trail out from the pinewoods and curling around a tawny knoll studded with rocks.

The old, gray mule came on slowly, swinging its forelegs as though they were lead. Its head hung down, its ears twitched, its back sagged with the weight of the burly rider.

Harmon recognized the man's floppy, dark hat and the heavy, rounded shoulders. His head bobbed as though his neck were broken.

As the mule neared, Harmon saw the rider was packing a rifle, the butt snugged against his thigh. With the hand holding the reins, he took pulls from a quart jar.

Harmon continued hammering nails until he heard the mule pull up behind the tool cart. The gelding blew and whinnied.

"Easy, Chester," Harmon said to the draft horse. "Afternoon, Johnson."

The man's voice was slow and thick. "Howdy."

"Doin' a little huntin', are ya?"

"A little."

"What's the quarry—coyotes, rabbits, or longhorn elk?" Harmon laughed and hammered another nail.

"Anything that moves. If I can hit it, I'm gonna kill it."

Bill considered the man uneasily, and Johnson parted his lips, grinning.

He was known throughout the Two Bear Mountains as a drunk and a laggard ten months out of twelve. He left his ranch chores to his five children and long-suffering wife and rode around the mountains drinking and taking potshots at fence posts and deer. Harmon's regard for the wretched soul wavered between loathing and sympathy.

Bill crawled off the tower and retrieved another log from the pile by the tool wagon. "Shootin' and drinkin' don't mix too well," he said, positioning the log over the tower legs. "You're liable to mistake your foot for a rabbit and shoot it plum off!"

Johnson ignored the warning. He smelled of liquor and rancid sweat. Staring dully at Harmon, his nose bulbous and purple-veined, his eyes red and swollen, he growled, "Where's your boy, Bill?"

"What's that?"

"Where's your boy?"

Rolling his leathery cheeks up under his eyes, his stomach tightening as though he'd swallowed sour goat's milk, Bill met the man's glowering stare. "Why do you ask?"

"He was seen with my daughter again."

Harmon glanced off, setting his jaw tight as a wedge. So that's what Johnson's visit was all about. He'd had a feeling it was more than a social call. "Let's not get into all that again, Warren," he said despondently.

"Where is he?"

Harmon plucked a nail from the pouch around his waist and positioned it over the log. "None o' your business." He held the nail and tried to steady the hammer.

"If it involves my daughter, it's my business sure enough."

"Your daughter is old enough to decide who she wants to see, and so is my son." Harmon gave the nail a tentative rap. "We have to stay out of it."

Johnson leaned precariously from the saddle, thrusting out his blunt face like a sledgehammer. "I told him to stay away from Crystal. I don't want him seein' her no more. It was one thing when they were kids, but they ain't kids no more."

Harmon gave the nail two solid raps and eased his anger back to a simmer, gritting his teeth. "The wars are over, Warren. We have to put 'em behind us."

"They ain't over," said the veteran of Beecher Island, shaking his head. "They ain't ever gonna *be* over."

"My Cree wife delivered all five of your children—*including* Crystal," Bill reminded the rancher.

"You're muddyin' the issue!"

Harmon raised his hands and shook his head in defeat. He knew from experience there was no reasoning with the

man. "Okay, Warren. I'll remind him how you feel about
it." He turned back to his work.

"No, I'll remind him how I feel about it. Where is he?"

Harmon looked at the rifle riding Johnson's knee—an
old Springfield with a stock as gray and splintered as sea-
soned cordwood—and wagged his hammer at it. "You
ain't goin' nowhere near my son packin' that iron."

"He at the cabin?" Johnson asked, wrinkling his red
nose.

Harmon's chest rose with restrained anger. "You turn
that animal around and go home," he said tightly.

Johnson scoffed and spurred the old mule. Bill grabbed
the bridle with an arm as big and weathered as an old cedar
post, nearly pulling the beast over sideways. "You hard o'
hearing?"

Johnson brought the rifle down level with Harmon's
eyes. "Let go that bridle, you squaw-screwin' bastard son
of a bitch!"

Harmon grabbed the rifle by the barrel and threw it away.
Then he grabbed Johnson by the collar and flung him to
the ground. The drunk rancher landed with a grunt as the
mule spooked off, snorting and kicking.

Harmon stepped over the man, balling his hands into
fists. "If you go anywhere near my boy, Johnson, I'll cut
your heart out and feed it to the *crows*!"

Wincing at the pain in his back, Johnson pulled a .31-
caliber pocket pistol from his coat and wielded it uncertainly. He peeled back the hammer, blinked, steadied the
barrel, and squeezed the trigger.

The pistol cracked like a branch snapping.

Harmon staggered backward as the bullet creased his
shoulder. He looked at the tear in his shirt, amazed. "You
son of a bitch!"

He glanced around for Johnson's rifle. Not seeing the

carbine in the tall grass, he moved toward the tool wagon for his own Sharps.

The pistol cracked again. Harmon straightened at the impact of the bullet just above his kidney. Another crack and the feeling of a bee sting in the back of his thigh.

He took one heavy step toward the tool wagon before his knees gave. He sank to the grass, planted his fists. He turned to see Johnson getting to his feet, grunting and wheezing through gritted teeth, spittle stringing from his chin.

The man approached with his shoulders hunched, one hand on his back, the stubby pistol extended in a quivering fist. He swallowed, his Adam's apple bobbing in his thin, swarthy neck. "Shoulda done this a long time ago, you old squaw dog."

The gun cracked, and a bullet tore into Harmon's chest, knocking him back with a grunt. He took a breath and lifted his head to watch Johnson move toward him, peeling back the hammer and firing another round.

Bill flinched, but the bullet whistled past his ear and slapped the grass. Knowing the miss was accidental, he suddenly realized he was going to die.

Between ragged breaths, he said, "You . . . stay away . . . from my son . . . you sick . . ."

Ten feet away, Johnson raised the pistol, grinned, and cocked the hammer. He pulled the trigger. The hammer slapped the firing pin with a metallic click. He looked at the weapon, frowning, then pulled the trigger three more times.

The five-shooter was empty.

Harmon pushed himself onto his elbows, blood pouring from his chest and over the hand, trying to hold the wound closed. He heaved up onto his knees, twisted around, and crawled to the wagon, his knees smearing blood in the grass.

Behind him, Johnson stumbled toward him. Harmon reached into the wagon box for his rifle. His hand found the cold barrel.

Johnson tripped in the grass and fell, landing on his Springfield. He jacked a shell into the breech as Harmon turned from the wagon with his Sharps.

Johnson aimed and fired before Harmon could poke his finger through the trigger guard. The bullet ripped through Bill's neck. "Ahh," he grunted, and fell back against the wagon.

He sighed, feeling a chill, fighting to remain conscious. He smelled the alcohol and sweat, felt the shadow of the man standing over him. "You ... stay away from my boy."

Then his eyes closed and he sank sideways into the grass.

When he opened them again, Warren Johnson was gone and the sun was only a salmon wash over the western ridges. The first stars winked in the east.

He saw in a waking dream his son riding down the inverted V of the darkening valley away from him, the lad's body diminishing with each step of his horse.

Bill wanted to call a warning. He wanted to save his son as he had not been able to save his dear Cherry.

But he could manage only a grunt, a labored, raspy whisper. "Jody ..."

Then the boy was gone.

1

Deputy U.S. Marshal Ben Stillman had tangled with some of the deadliest badmen north of the Big Horn Mountains, going eighteen years without more than a flesh wound. Then a bullet fired by a drunk whore pierced his back in a Virginia City brothel.

Three years later, he parted the batwings of the Mint Saloon in Great Falls, Montana, and winced at the steady throb in his head.

From the fall of September light on the passing buckboards and lumber drays, he judged it was nearly noon. That meant his poker game had consumed eighteen hours. Thinking back, he thought he'd probably averaged one drink an hour, and his aching head and cottony mouth corroborated the tally.

He flicked his cigarette into the dusty street and stood on the boardwalk, steadying himself in the swirl of time. At this hour four years ago he was probably returning to town from a predawn excursion after cattle thieves or whiskey runners, with three or four owlhoots and a corpse or two in tow.

Now, amazed at how swiftly a man's life can sour, he moved up the boardwalk through the midday bustle, feeling as ramshackle as a landfallen sailor, and stopped at the post office for his mail.

The postmaster lifted his green eyeshades and hawk nose over the mahogany counter and sized up the ex-lawman's demeanor. "Made another night of it, did ya, Ben?"

Stillman scowled at the Windsor stove filling the office with eye-watering coal smoke. "Why don't you get your damper fixed?"

"Too many government forms to fill out."

The man plucked mail from a pigeonhole and handed Stillman a *Police Gazette* and a catalog of poultry supplies from Chicago. He lifted his chin. "That cowpoke find you?"

"What cowpoke?"

"The one that was lookin' for you. Didn't tell me his name. I told him you always stopped for your mail but never at the same time. All depends on the night before." The man gave a self-satisfied chuckle and snapped his dentures. "He waited an hour, then went to lunch."

"You didn't tell him where I live, did you, Jug?"

"I didn't want him sitting around here all day, Ben. I have work to do."

Stillman lifted his hat and ran a hand over his tender head with a sigh. "What did he look like?"

"Stetson hat, jeans. Cowpoke."

"Armed?"

The postman nodded.

"Thanks for nothin', Jug."

Stillman wished he had more than the derringer strapped to his leg, but he hadn't carried a real gun in several months. After a year with no one coming for him, he had finally relaxed, thinking he'd at last been forgotten by those he once hunted.

But now the old tension sprang anew.

He made his way through the backstreets where trash burned, dogs ran, and a lady in a soiled cotton dress and scarf beat a rug hanging from an open shed door with a willow switch. Stillman scrutinized every bindle stiff and saddlebum he met, looking for a killer's eyes.

When he came to his rented three-room shack a block from the stockyards, he pulled the pistol, stepped quietly onto the stoop, and tried his front door. Still locked. He opened it quickly and stepped inside, pulling back the pistol's hammer until the curved trigger clicked down to his finger.

Everything appeared as he'd left it—the threadbare settee, the hide-bottom chair, the elk antler rocker around which newspapers and magazines were stacked and playing cards were scattered.

When he'd checked the other two rooms, he stepped out back to check the chicken coop, a converted buggy shed sitting under a cottonwood. In the cavelike dark, his barred rock hens ruffled their feathers, cooing plaintively.

"Hello, ladies," he said, noting the empty feeder. "Sorry about that. The old man got suckered again."

He scooped corn from the bin with a coffee can while the hens dropped from their roosts in a flurry of black and white, then headed for the gate. He walked back to the house, put the peashooter in a cookie jar, and retrieved his double-barrel Greener from under the bed.

Soon a fire burned in the cookstove perking a pot of coffee while Ben Stillman sat patiently in the elk antler rocker facing the front door, the Greener across the arms of his chair.

He lifted his eyes to the cracked plaster wall over the settee, where a beautiful young woman with dark French features smiled from a gilt frame. "Oh, Miss Beaumont," he said tiredly. ''Why didn't I marry you when I had the chance?''

His eyes glazed with memories of good wine, golden afternoons along the Yellowstone River, the silky warmth of her naked body next to his. How long had it been since he'd seen her . . . touched her? Seven years. It felt longer.

Sometimes he wished he'd never met her that summer on her father's ranch near Milestown, never been stupid enough to propose . . . never been enamored enough to believe her father, the great Alexander Beaumont, would have let his fine-blooded daughter marry the likes of a Western lawman. It would have been like studding a mustang range horse to a Kentucky Thoroughbred. It simply wasn't done.

But then, she must have known that. Maybe that's why she'd accepted his proposal. She'd known her father would turn it down for her. He squinted his eyes against the pain of the old question: had she really loved him?

''Go ahead and beat yourself silly,'' he told himself. ''You know you'll never know the answer to that question.''

The light flickered in the window. Boots thumped on the porch. Someone knocked.

Stillman thumbed back the rabbit-eared hammers on the two-bore to full cock. ''It's open.''

A young man entered.

His jeans and cotton shirt hung on his thin frame, and a flat-brimmed hat nearly covered his eyes. His narrow, wind-burned face was clean and olive-colored, suggesting some Indian or Mexican blood. When his eyes settled on Stillman's shotgun, he jumped as though he'd spooked a rattler in a woodpile.

''Ho, now!''

''Ho, now yourself! Reach for the rafters and state your name and business before I grease the walls with you.'' His eyes dropped to the gun hanging low on the kid's hip—an old Walker Colt with worn walnut grips.

"My name is Jody Harmon from the Two Bear Mountains on the Hi-Line," the young man said to the shotgun, his hands held high. "Are you Ben Stillman?"

"What if I was?"

"I'd like to talk to you, that's all."

"What about?"

"I'm Bill Harmon's son."

Stillman's eyes played over the lad once more, recalling his old friend. "How do I know Bill has a son?"

"How do you know he don't?"

"Don't sass me, boy!"

The lad squirmed under Stillman's impassive gaze. "When's the last time you seen him?"

Stillman rubbed his chin. "Must be near twenty years now."

"Well, I'm seventeen," the boy said. "I'd be happy to hand you my six-shooter so you can point that scattergun in a different direction."

"Do it. Slow."

When Stillman had the gun, he released the Greener's hammers and set it across his lap. "Milk River Bill is fair-skinned," he challenged. "You appear to have some Indian blood."

"My mother was a Cree from Canada."

"Why 'was'?"

"She died four years ago."

Stillman unfurled his eyebrows and gestured to the worn settee to his right. "Have a seat."

The kid removed his hat and sat down, giving a nervous laugh. "Boy, for a minute I thought you were really going to grease me."

"So did I. An ex-lawman gets all kinds coming around.

For all I know, you're a pipsqueak trying to win a bet.''

He retrieved a flask from a pile of newspapers beside his chair, splashed some whiskey into his coffee cup, and offered the flask to the boy. ''You imbibe yet?''

''No, sir.'' The young man's eyes slid from the ex-lawman's wavy mane of dark brown hair flecked with gray, his big, weathered face with sky-blue eyes and untrimmed mustache, to his bull chest, trim waist, and legs, slightly bowed and hard as oak.

''What you lookin' at?''

''I ain't never seen a famous lawman before,'' the lad said, flushing. '' 'Cept in books.''

''What did you expect? Wyatt Earp?''

''I reckon.''

''Sorry to disappoint you.''

Stillman sipped the whiskey and savored the burn. He found himself liking young Harmon, in whose features he saw his old hunting pal Milk River Bill, so named for his fondness for Montana's Milk River country up on the Hi-Line.

''How's your old man?''

''He's dead, sir. That's why I'm here.''

Stillman sighed heavily, looking pained. Milk River Bill was a friend from Stillman's old soldiering and hunting days, when grizzlies still haunted the plains, wolves panted around campfires, Indians prowled, and a stouthearted friend like Bill could make the difference between life and death.

''What happened?''

''Two weeks ago we were building a windmill in a draw on our winter range. I quit early, and when Pa never followed me home, I rode out and found him dead by the tool wagon.''

''Rustlers?''

"Prob'ly—we been hit before—but I didn't find any steers gone this time."

"See any tracks?"

Harmon nodded. "One rider. He rode up the ravine to Hobbs's range. I lost him after that. I'm not much of a tracker, I'm afraid."

"Who's Hobbs?"

"Rich prick from England. He homesteaded a hundred and sixty acres in the Two Bears, but calls the whole Clear Creek Valley his own—and all the water runnin' into it. He kicked our cows out and fenced it off three years ago, in eighty-four. He has good stock, mostly shorthorns from Oregon bred up with a couple bulls he brought over from England.

"They eat a lot of grass and drink a lot of water. The drought two years ago scared him. That's when he started tryin' to buy out all us smaller operators grazing our long-horns on creeks feeding the Clear. Some sold and some didn't. For those that didn't, shit started rainin'; men came cursin' us and threatenin' to burn us out."

Stillman steepled his fingers under his chin, nodding. "He calls the public domain his own, does he?" It was one of the oldest, bloodiest conflicts in the West.

A quiet blaze burned in Jody's eyes. "All us ranchers homesteaded our sections fair and square. We graze our cattle together in the Two Bear Pool. Now he's tryin' to break us up and run us out 'cause he has the money, power, and guns to do it. I think he sent one of his men—probably Weed Cole—to kill Pa, hopin' the rest would turn tail and run."

Stillman frowned. "Who's Cole?"

"Hobbs's ramrodder. He's come to our place before to cuss us out and threaten to burn our buildings if we didn't leave."

"What's the county sheriff's position on all this?"

Jody shrugged. "Doesn't have one. He's scared. Hobbs is too big a bear for old Ed Lewis to tangle with, I'm afraid. Oh, he came out when Pa was killed, mumbled somethin' about findin' his killer, but I haven't seen hide nor hair of him since. Didn't expect to, and I don't, neither."

Stillman sipped his coffee. Slowly his thoughts turned to Milk River Bill, his lips forming a smile.

He chuckled, said, "One time, when me and your pa were ridin' back to Fort Keogh after a huntin' trip, we spied a horse in a buffalo herd. It had a frayed rope around its neck, but your old man cut it from the herd and kept it. It turned out to be a top cavalry mount. Only he told everybody he'd bought it from a trapper along the Marias River."

Stillman paused, remembering. "After a while he couldn't afford to keep me quiet anymore, so he sold the horse to a man on the Sun River for two hundred and fifty greenbacks." He guffawed and looked at the boy, hoping to cheer him. "But even for that, ol' Bill was only getting back half what the horse cost him in drinks."

Young Harmon smiled weakly. "Mr. Stillman, I ain't sellin' out to Hobbs. Pa, Ma, and me, we built that house from raw timber. That's where I was raised. I'll be eighteen come spring, and I aim to marry a girl from up the creek."

He regarded the palm he was polishing with a fist. "Pa once said you were faster on the draw than anyone, and you weren't afraid of nobody."

"Bill was exaggeratin'," Stillman said with false modesty. "How did you know where to find me?"

"Pa kept up with you in the newspapers. Was always bragging about how he was friends with the mighty Ben Stillman."

Stillman sipped his whiskey, sloshed it around in his

mouth, and swallowed. "As you can see, I'm not so mighty anymore, son. And I'm no longer a lawman."

"I ain't askin' you to arrest anybody."

His face expressionless, Stillman said, "You want me to find your pa's killer and deal some frontier justice, that it?"

The boy pulled a scribbled note from his jeans. "Here's an IOU for five hundred dollars. I wasn't gonna sell any steers this year 'cause the prices are down, but I'll sell as many as it takes to make this good."

"Five hundred dollars ain't much for taking a man's life, son," Stillman said.

"It's all I got."

"Keep it." Stillman rose and walked to the window. "I don't know what books you've been reading, but I'm not Wyatt Earp or Doc Holliday or any of the like. I'm just an old retired lawman with a crippled back and whiskey-shot nerves."

After a long silence the boy said weakly, "Pa said—"

"I haven't seen your pa in twenty years," Stillman snapped. "The Ben Stillman he knew died three years ago on the floor of a Virginia City brothel. I don't trouble anybody, and I don't want anybody troublin' me. You've worn out your welcome."

Young Harmon got up slowly and walked to the door. Stillman's voice stopped him. "Take it to the territorial marshal in Helena. He'll find who killed your pa."

The lad's voice was dull with disappointment. "He won't do nothin'. The Hi-Line's too far from Helena, and my old man was just a ten-cow cattleman with an Indian wife and a half-breed son."

Stillman lowered his head and ran his hands through his salt-and-pepper mane in frustration. He was forty-four, and he hadn't ridden the owlhoot trail in three years. Though he hadn't left it willingly, he couldn't go back now, even for young Harmon. Not only could his back go out on him, laying him up for days, but—he hated to admit it—he'd grown soft from whiskey, women, cards, and too many hours glued to his rocker reading newspapers and dime novels and smoking one cigarette after another.

"I'm sorry, son," he said with a pained expression, meaning it.

But Jody Harmon had already left.

2

Jody Harmon left Great Falls after seeing Stillman and camped that night in a cottonwood grove along the Missouri River, several miles downstream from Fort Benton.

The next day he followed Birch Creek north through the Two Bear Mountains, making White-Tail Creek an hour before dusk. At twilight he halted the pony on a rise overlooking the ranch that was now his alone.

On the velvet meadow, he'd half expected to see lamplight, smoke curling from the cabin's chimney, and his old man sitting atop the peeled-log corral fence smoking a post-supper cigarette with his sleeves rolled up his big, corded arms and his hat tipped back on his head.

But the small log shack with a lean-to pantry was quiet and dark. No smell of pine carried from the chimney. His father was not smoking a cigarette on the fence or wrestling a wagon jack in the yard or cursing his mules in the pasture.

Moving his eyes up meadow, Jody saw the mound and the rough wood cross of his father's grave. He shivered against the cold loneliness greeting him here and clucked his buckskin down the rise toward the solemn ranchstead.

A dog barked, and Jody was warmed by the familiar sound of his dog, Duff. He'd made ten yards when three shots rang out in quick succession, the first thudding into the butte behind him and the third ripping his hat from his head and throwing him off the horse.

The buckskin reared and ran toward the safety of the barn. Jody was trying to get to his feet and run for cover when he heard, "Oh, my God."

It was a familiar voice. Jody stopped.

"Crystal!" he yelled. "Stop shooting, goddammit!"

"You hit?" A shadow in the night, she moved toward him up the rise, breathing heavily, the dog at her heels. When the dog saw Jody, its whole body went to work, wagging its tail.

"I don't think so," he said, wincing against the pain in the shoulder he'd landed on. "What the hell you shootin' at, for chrissakes?"

"I thought you were a rustler."

"Well, I ain't. Duff, git now!"

"What were you doin' lurkin' around in the dark?" she asked, holding her lever-action Colt in one hand and pulling the dog away with the other.

"I live here. What are you doin', lurking around in the dark and taking potshots at folks?"

"I fed the horses and was about to head for my sister's when I heard Duff barking and saw a rider on the hill. What was I supposed to think?"

"Oh, don't think, girl. Just start shootin'. Is Dex hit?"

"He didn't act like it. When I saw him, I knew it was you."

"S'pose you woulda polished me off otherwise, you bushwacker," he said, getting to his feet and retrieving his hat.

"That's the thanks I get for doing your barn chores!" She turned and stalked down the hill.

He appraised the hole through the crown of his hat and

turned to follow her. "You're the only woman I know who can dry-gulch a man and make *him* feel guilty."

"Why are you home so soon?" she asked when he caught up with her.

"I wasn't in the mood for dallyin' around Great Falls."

"Did you see Stillman?"

"Yep."

"Well, what did he say?"

"He said no." Jody approached the buckskin standing by the corral with its reins dangling, and inspected the animal for bullet wounds. "He said no, but I don't believe him."

She frowned. "What?"

"He's broken some—there's no doubt about that. But there's a fire in his eyes. Reminds me of Pa." Leading the horse into the barn, he said, "I got a silver dollar says the mighty Ben Stillman hops the stage to Big Sandy."

Crystal laughed. "The stage?"

"I don't think he'd ride this far in the leather. He's got a bullet in his back. But he'll come. He'll be here."

Jody lit an oil lamp and hung it on the wall. He started at a pigeon flying against the rafters—always jumpy since finding his father in the ravine by the stock well, his clothes soaked in blood.

Then he unsaddled the buckskin, inspected its shoes for loose nails, and began rubbing it down with straw. Crystal perched on a stall with her boot heels hooked over a plank and her rifle across her knees, watching him work.

"I think it's awful, hiring a man to kill another," she said.

Jody shot her a grim look. "If Cole killed Pa, Crystal, he deserves what he gets. I'd kill him myself if it was anybody else."

She remembered how he'd cried the day he'd buried his father, and smiled regretfully.

Jody asked after a while, "What's been going on around here?"

She shrugged. "Nothin'."

"Nothin'," he mocked. "Miss me?"

"Uh-uh," she said coyly.

He turned to her and dropped the straw. He liked the way she looked this time of day, with her tired eyes, her strong Scandinavian cheekbones flushed, her wiry blond hair wisping out from her homemade rabbit hat with ear-flaps. She'd made the hat herself, shooting two jacks last winter, scraping and drying the skins, fitting them to her pattern, and sewing them together with waxed thread.

"Yeah, you did. You missed your Injun beau." He took her rifle and stood it against the wall, leaned down, and kissed her, nudging her hat off.

"No, I didn't," she said, lacing her hands around his neck and touching her forehead to his.

He kissed her again, and she opened her mouth for him. He liked the feel of her full lips against his, the sweet, nectary smell of her mixed with horse and leather. He gently pulled her from her perch and into a straw mound, where he kissed her and nuzzled her neck.

She laughed.

At length his fingers drifted to the buttons on her man's cotton shirt. He'd undone half of them and was moving his hand toward a breast when she pulled away, scolding, "Okay, soldier. Throw some water on it."

"Come on, baby," he complained. "You missed me."

"Don't 'baby' me, Jody Harmon. If you're looking for a quick poke, go to town."

"Crystal!"

She rose, brushing hay from her clothes and buttoning

her shirt. Her hair was prettily disheveled and flecked with hay. "Come on. I'll fix your supper before I head to Marie's."

He grabbed her hand. "Wait."

"What?"

He stared at her with eager eyes, searching for the eloquence he'd practiced over and over on the trail home from Great Falls. It had been snuffed out by the passion of the moment, replaced with: "Let's get married."

He knew that loneliness and fear of the future had hastened the proposal, but he also knew he loved this girl and had never wanted to be with anyone else. Having grown up together on neighboring ranches, they were friends as well as lovers.

She looked down at him, feigning an air of consideration.

"As soon as I get on my feet," he added. "It might take me a few months, but Pa taught me most all there is to know about runnin' a spread, and Mr. Hall in town has promised me credit through the winter. Besides, when Stillman comes, things are gonna change around here."

"He'd have to do more than kill Weed Cole to change things around here," Crystal said.

"Yeah, but that's a start. Getting rid of Cole will show Hobbs we ain't playin' by his rules."

"I think you're banking kind of heavy on a broken-down ex-lawman," she warned.

"Crystal," he said, his voice rising with frustration, "will you or no?"

"Will I what?"

"Forget it." He got up angrily and brushed off his pants. "I ain't begging you to marry me, Crystal Johnson. There's plenty more where you came from." He led the buckskin outside and turned toward the corral.

"Oh, don't get so huffy. I'll marry you, I guess," she said to his back. "But you're not just trying to get a poke, are you?"

"Crystal!"

3

Three days later the stage rolled into Great Falls at eight in the morning, its steel-rimmed wheels churning street dust and scattering dogs and chickens on Central Avenue. It pulled into the corral behind the stage office, where two hostlers switched teams while the epithet-spewing driver berated them to hurry.

Eight minutes later it rolled out of the corral behind fresh horses chomping at the traces, and rocked to a stop before Ben Stillman waiting on the boardwalk with a war bag, bedroll, and hand-tooled rifle boot containing his Henry rifle, the stock boasting an inlaid pearl bull's head.

"All aboard!" yelled the driver, a bulldog of a man with a round, sunburned face and a cheek swollen with tobacco. He grinned broadly at Stillman, the sole passenger. "Where you headed, Ben?"

Stillman was dressed for travel in a brown corduroy jacket, string tie, and ten-gallon Stetson, a buckskin mackinaw draped over his arm in anticipation of the coming cold. He wore his long-barrel Army Colt in a soft leather holster high on his hip, and he was puffing a stogie.

"Up to the Hi-Line."

"The Hi-Line! There ain't nothin' on the Hi-Line but tracklayers and peckerwoods."

"Well, my monkey calls it home."

The driver frowned. "Monkey?"

"The one on my back," Stillman said. "Take it easy on the downgrades, will you, Morris? I get stage fright."

The driver laughed at the old joke. Stillman tipped his hat, stuck his stogie between his teeth, and climbed aboard. The stage started at a brisk pace, heading north out of Great Falls along the Missouri River.

As the wagon rocked and rattled and the driver's whip cracked like a pistol, Stillman watched the Highwood Mountains rising and falling through the dust out the west-facing window.

It had been nearly three years since he'd taken to the trail—officially or unofficially—and he suddenly felt like a homesick child. He'd asked Mrs. Sullivan to look after the house and the chickens, for she was reliable if a bit persnickety, but he found himself longing for his hens and for the old rocker he spent so many hours in, drinking coffee spiked with whiskey and playing endless games of solitaire. Still, he enjoyed the spicy smell of sage through the window, and all the trail memories it conjured.

He produced a travel flask from a coat pocket and sipped, forgetting that in a bold moment he'd filled it with water. Crestfallen, he sipped the flat, tepid liquid, which did nothing to ease the morning pain in his back, and marveled, as always, at the irony of his fate.

His career as a deputy U.S. marshal for the court of Justice Henry K. Bishop in Helena had ended in 1884, when he'd arrested a gambler in a Virginia City brothel. The man had been breaking tables and chairs and mouthing off to the blackjack dealer. He was too stewed to resist arrest, but as Stillman escorted him to the door a woman behind him shouted, "Just you wait, Marshal! That bastard owes me for three nights runnin'!"

"He'll pay you tomorrow," Stillman had told her, leading the gambler toward the batwings.

"Oh, no, he won't!" the woman bawled in a drunken rage. " 'Cause he's gonna be *dead* tomorrow!"

Before Stillman could turn around, he felt a sudden pressure in his back, like a quick shove by a powerful hand. A quarter second later he heard the crack of a pistol. He staggered forward, confused, feeling his knees turn to putty. When he hit the floor, he twisted around and saw the bartender wrestling a gun out of the screaming woman's hand.

As if to confirm what Stillman had suddenly realized, the barman yelled, "Jesus Christ, lady, you shot the marshal!"

The bullet, breaking several ribs, had lodged so close to his spine that the doctors had not dared remove it, and insisted he retire his badge. If the bullet jarred his spine, it could cripple him. Nevertheless, he was a lucky man, they tried to assure him. If the slug had entered a quarter inch farther right, he'd have been in a wheelchair. A half inch more, he'd have been in a box.

"But a half inch farther left, and I'd still be wearin' my badge," he muttered to himself.

Big Sandy lay four stage stops and a river crossing north of Great Falls. A bustling little burg since the opening of the Assiniboin Indian Reservation to homesteading, its solid brick and rickety wood-frame buildings and pole corrals sat on a high bench that unrolled like a sagebrush carpet from the slopes of the Two Bear Mountains.

The plankboard walks were crowded with a polyglot group of rugged immigrant railroaders in coveralls and cowboys in chaps and jangling spurs. Loading pens hugged the Great Northern depot and water tank a half mile north.

Standing beside the stage office, Stillman gave his gaze to the McNamara and Marlow general store, where buck-

boards stood behind gelded mules and a tabby cat lounged
on a porch rail. Beyond, where the town straggled off into
prairie, a stoop-shouldered farmer was doggedly clearing
breast-high sagebrush with a grub hoe. Another Iowan
suckered by Jim Hill's promise of a dry-farmer's paradise,
Stillman speculated.

The country was not new to the ex-lawman, who had
hunted the last great bison herds here with Bill Harmon
when they were little more than green twigs and thatches
of hair. Except for the vanished buffalo and all-but-
disappeared Sioux and Blackfeet, little had changed in
twenty years. A semiarid prairie punctuated by small, iso-
lated mountain ranges catching the moisture rolling off the
Rockies, it was a big, open country swallowed by sky. For
reasons he could not explain, it gave him comfort.

He looked up at the fir-covered ridges of the Two Bear
Mountains, marked here and there by streaks of red rock
and patches of turning aspens. Then he brought his eyes to
a high, shale-topped butte, trying to recall the name.

"That's Old Baldy," came a female voice from behind
him. "Highest point in the Two Bears."

He turned to the girl standing in the shadow of the stage
office. She stood well over five feet, with long, sun-
bleached hair falling out of a homemade rabbit hat. Trim,
tan, and well muscled, she looked like hardy frontier stock
in her man's calico shirt, elk hide vest, faded denim
breeches, and high-topped Wellingtons. She even had a
short-barreled Smith & Wesson and a wide cartridge belt
strapped around her waist.

Moving toward him, she asked, "Are you Ben Stillman?"

"That's right."

She held out her hand. "I'm Crystal Johnson, Jody Harmon's fiancée."

"Nice to meet you, miss," he said, shaking her long, firm hand. "But I'm confused . . . ."

"When Jody got your cable sayin' you were coming, he sent me to fetch you out to his ranch."

"You're Jody's girl from up the creek."

"That's right."

He turned to the two horses standing at the hitching post—a roan filly with a Colt rifle in the saddleboot and a big bay with a dun mane and a spotted rump. "The bay is for you, Mr. Stillman. It was Mr. Harmon's favorite."

Stillman stepped forward to appraise the gelding, running his hand down its long, straight neck and mane, talking softly, acquainting the animal with his scent and the sound of his voice.

"He got a name?"

"Sweets."

"Any pitch?"

"You wouldn't want a horse without a little pitch in him, would you, Mr. Stillman?"

Stillman returned her smile and secured his rifle, bedroll, and war bag to the saddled bay. He produced spurs and a wide leather brace from his saddlebags, donned the spurs, wrapped the brace around his waist, and cinched it.

"Compliments of a young lady in Virginia City," he answered Crystal's curious stare.

He mounted slowly, the saddle feeling hard and ungiving beneath him. With one hand on the cantle, the other on the horn, he scrunched around on the seat as if to soften it.

Crystal said shyly, "If you don't mind me asking, how many men have you killed, Mr. Stillman?"

He laughed, liking her. "Oh . . . twenty or thirty."

"Is that a lot?"

"It's right up there with Earp and Masterson."

He and Crystal Johnson spurred eastward out of Big

Sandy, toward the Two Bear Mountains, turning green gold in the hazy afternoon light.

Stillman had seen a lot of the West, but he'd never seen mountains as lovely as the Two Bears. A series of old volcanoes, rounded by time, covered with grass, and capped with rocky shelves, they'd been named by the Assiniboins, who thought from a distance they resembled two fighting bears.

Springs bubbled in storybook valleys, deer grazed on shaggy slopes, and brush-lined draws were thick with berries and cattle. Wide meadows, deep with grama and buffalo grass, rose to aspen groves and rocky dikes peppered with ponderosa pines and wind-stunted firs.

"Beautiful country," he said as the horses forded a creek. "I can see why some men would consider it worth fighting for."

Crystal nodded. "The plains are so dry. Nothing grows but prickly pear and sage. That's why everyone wants a stake in the Two Bears."

After a thoughtful pause she said, "I know Jody wants you to kill Weed Cole, Mr. Stillman. And if ever there was a man in need of killing, that man is Cole. But killing him won't be the end of our troubles. Donovan Hobbs can hire other gunmen."

"I didn't come to kill Cole. Like I told Jody, I'm not a hired gun. It ain't right for one man to play judge, jury, and executioner. I aim to gauge the situation and cable the territorial marshal in Helena. He'll send a passel of deputies to see to Hobbs and his crew."

"That'll be the day."

Stillman glanced at her. "How many men does Hobbs have on his roll, anyway?"

She shrugged. "I'd guess fifteen or twenty. But Weed Cole is like ten men himself."

"How's that?"

"Didn't Jody tell you? He's a regulator. They say he used to run with the Milton bunch down in Oklahoma."

Stillman's heart skipped a beat. He remembered the name now. Cole was an outlaw from down in the Cherokee Nation. The last Stillman had heard of him, he'd killed a Texas ranger and disappeared in Colorado. He was the only one of the Milton bunch who'd managed to stay ahead of the law, and he was known as the squirreliest and deadliest of the group.

Stillman closed one eye, cocked his head, and looked at her across his shoulder. "I guess this ain't gonna be no strip-and-go-naked picnic, is it, Miss Johnson?"

4

They rode into a shaded canyon where a log-and-sod road-house and corral fronted a creek. Stillman noted the chill air and thought they must have risen at least a thousand feet since leaving Big Sandy.

The wind was blowing, and the sky was raining aspen leaves.

"This is Olson's Roadhouse," Crystal said, dismounting. "We can rest our horses here and get a bite to eat." She turned to the low-slung cabin and yelled, "Have any of that venison left, Iver?"

A thin man with high-water pants and face like a relief map of the Missouri River breaks appeared in the doorway, wiping his hands on a filthy apron.

"Come and get it, Crystal," he said around the corncob pipe in his mouth.

He turned inside and said something, and a towheaded boy of about ten ran out to feed and water their horses.

"Treat 'em right, sprout," Stillman ordered, tossing the boy a nickel.

He followed Crystal inside, where it was dark and warm and the cookstove puffed cedar smoke. Two riders sat at one end of the long plank table, eating in silence. Their eyes followed the newcomers.

"Hello, Crystal," the bigger of the two said, tipping his hat.

He gave his partner a furtive glance that was not lost on Stillman, who secured the holster at his side.

Crystal mumbled a tight hello.

Iver Olson brought two steaming plates, and Stillman dug into the venison stew with garden vegetables with delight, for he hadn't eaten since breakfast. Five minutes later he mopped his plate with a biscuit and held out his coffee cup for the boy to refill from a blue enamel pot.

"Where's your half-breed boyfriend, Miss Crystal?"

It was the same rider who had greeted her. A big, shaggy man in his twenties, he had little round eyes, a bushy red beard, and freckled, pink cheeks.

Crystal reddened and glanced at Stillman. "If you mean Jody, he's home. Working."

"He's home—working," the man mocked, sharing a grin with his partner. "I thought maybe you got yourself a white man. A little old for ya, but at least he's your color, huh?"

Crystal leaned toward Stillman. "That's Delwyn Sleighbough and his brother, Kenny. They work for Hobbs."

"Why don't you introduce us proper?" Delwyn Sleighbough stood and stepped away from the table.

Stillman did the same. "What do you say we put a stop to this before it gets started?"

"Just wanted to introduce myself," the rider said, spreading his hands innocently.

He wore gaudy, hand-tooled boots and a low-crowned hat trimmed with hawk feathers. His frizzy red hair fell over his shirt collar, peppered with seeds and trail dust. An ivory-handled Colt hung low on his beefy thigh, and he smelled like he'd been wrestling a mink.

"I'm Delwyn Sleighbough and this is my brother, Kenny. Like she says, we ride for Mr. Hobbs. He doesn't like strangers this close to his range, especially with rustlers about. Who might you be and where you headed?''

"I'm just a friend of Miss Johnson here, a poor chicken farmer lookin' for a claim," Stillman said with a conciliatory smile.

"There's no claims to stake in these parts, so you best move on."

"It's a free territory, Del," Crystal said. "A man can ride where he wants."

"Hush your mouth, Crystal Johnson!"

"Hush your own, you filthy dog!"

The room fell silent. Delwyn turned to Crystal, his face flushed, a fire in his eyes. His voice came pinched between gritted teeth. "You Indian-lovin' whore."

He moved stiffly toward her. Stillman froze, unable to intervene, his features a mask of confusion. It was all happening so fast, and the quarters were so tight. Where was Olson? The boy? If guns were drawn, one of them or Crystal might take a bullet.

He wasn't prepared, and the old instincts weren't kicking in.

Approaching the girl, whose face stiffened with defiance and fear, the rider clenched his fist and cocked his arm. Crystal gave a clipped scream, recoiling. Her hat fell and her hair flew.

At the last moment Stillman grabbed the man's fist. Kenny Sleighbough reached for his pistol. Stillman's Colt barked, and the slug tore through Kenny's chest and into the cabin wall with a puff of dust and splinters. Kenny dropped his pistol and looked at his chest, where frothy blood sprayed.

"Kenny!" Delwyn Sleighbough screamed.

Kenny staggered backward and fell like a windmill toppled by a gale. He cupped the wound in his hands. His head propped by a chair, he looked from his bleeding chest to his brother with an expression of fear and wonder.

"Kenny!"

Kenny's arms dropped, then his chin. His head nodded twice, convulsively.

"You killed my brother, you old bastard!" Delwyn reached for his gun. He stopped when he felt the business end of Stillman's Colt poke his forehead.

"That's enough, Delwyn." From the kitchen door, Iver Olson aimed a 30-30 with an octagonal barrel. The tow-headed boy peeked out from behind him.

Delwyn turned to the old man and stared at him for a long time. "He killed my brother."

"I know. Mister, I reckon you and Crystal better leave."

Stillman dropped two silver dollars on the table. "Let's go."

"My God," Crystal whispered.

They didn't speak again until they were a long ways up the trail. The horses had resigned themselves after slowing down from a gallop. Stillman took the reins in his teeth, got out his makings pouch, and built a smoke, spilling as much tobacco as he rolled. His hands were shaking. Five years of whiskey and poker had turned his nerves to jelly.

"I didn't even see you draw your gun," Crystal said.

"Didn't know myself until I done it."

"I'm sorry, Mr. Stillman. I should have kept my mouth shut."

"Yes, you should have. You'll want to watch your back now. That's one chafed tomcat."

"And he better watch his. If I catch him shadowin' me, I'm liable to dry-gulch the son of a bitch. Pardon my French."

Stillman smiled, believing she would at that.

•   •   •

Near dusk, they topped a rise, and Crystal reined her horse to a stop.

"This is the Harmon place," she said.

Stillman pulled up beside her and cuffed his hat back on his head. A log house, an unchinked barn, and several out-buildings and pole corrals spread out below them, rosy in the last light. The ranchstead was flanked by a high, grassy ridge topped with ponderosa pines. A creek meandered through willows. Shadows had pooled, and the smell of timothy lofted on the cool mountain air.

They spurred their horses down the hill and into the ranchyard, where Jody Harmon was forking hay to the four horses in the corral. A yellow dog growled at Stillman from behind a wagon wheel.

Crystal said, "Oh, Duff—quit." The dog wagged its tail and whined, but its eyes remained with the stranger.

"Hello, Mr. Stillman," Jody said. "Nice to see you again." He removed a glove and stuck out his hand for Stillman to shake.

"Same here, young Harmon."

"Let me take your horse for ya."

" 'Preciate that." Stillman swung out of the leather and bent his knees to work the kinks out.

"I s'pose I have to take care of my own mount," Crystal said with mock scorn.

"You ain't company," Jody replied in the same vein, leading Stillman's bay to the barn. "In fact, I was hopin' you'd make supper. I'd hate to subject Mr. Stillman to my cookin' so early in his visit."

"We ain't even married yet, Mr. Stillman, and he's already got me cookin' for him."

"Smart man," Stillman said with a wink in Jody's direction.

"I guess you're in luck, bucko. I told sis I might be late tonight."

Stillman gave them a quizzical look.

"My father's against Jody and me," Crystal explained. "On account of Jody's half-Indian. So I live with my sister Marie and her husband Ivan mostly. They live two miles over east."

Stillman chewed the information for a bit. "That's going to make gettin' hitched a little hard, ain't it?"

Crystal hefted the saddle from her horse and started toward the tack room. "We'll burn that bridge when we come to it."

When the horses were rubbed down and turned in to the corral, the three retired to the cabin.

"We got trouble with Delwyn Sleighbough, Jody," Crystal said, striking a match to light the kitchen range.

"What kind of trouble?"

"I killed his brother at Olson's Roadhouse," Stillman said.

"It was my fault," Crystal said. "He goaded me into name-callin', and Mr. Stillman had to intervene before I broke his jaw for him. Kenny drew and Mr. Stillman blew him out of his boots faster'n lightning."

Jody looked at him, smiling. "I told you he was fast."

Stillman couldn't help basking in the admiration. It had been three years since he'd considered himself anything but a has-been, a Great Falls curiosity staggering from one saloon to the next, ignoring the mocking eyes of cardsharps and the rueful advertence of bartenders and pleasure girls.

He said, "Yeah, well, it won't matter who's fast or who's slow when Delwyn Sleighbough comes calling, because he sure as hell won't be alone, and he won't warn us beforehand."

"He rides for Hobbs, you know," Jody said.

"I know."

"What are we gonna do?"

"Well, since I was with Crystal, he's no doubt figured where I am, so we better assume that he and several others are right now getting good and drunk and mean and making a beeline for this ranch. I doubt he'll come this soon, but we'll have to take turns keeping watch."

"That son of a bitch," Jody said.

"From what I've seen and heard so far, it seems these lovely mountains are just ripe with sonso'bitches."

They checked their weapons, setting rifles near the door and windows, then each took a turn at the washbasin on the range, cleaning up. During supper Jody asked Stillman about the old days, and Stillman talked of buffalo hunts and tracking parties, all-night rides and dawn Indian raids. About good people and bad, and how hard it was at times to tell which was which.

"Your old man was one of the very best," he told Jody. "There was never any doubt about that."

"He said the same about you," Jody said, taking Stillman's empty plate to a washtub simmering on the stove and refilling their coffee cups.

Stillman's eyes gained a thoughtful cast as he watched the boy and thought of Bill. "One spring on the Sun River we stopped at this farm where a woman lived with her five kids—two of 'em toddlers. The spring before, the woman's husband had drowned in the river back o' their house trying to unbog a calf. Well, the woman's predicament fairly haunted Bill, who was the softest touch of anyone I ever knew."

Stillman shook his head and slapped the table in mock exasperation. "I swear every damn hunting trip for the next three years took us by that cabin—no matter how far out of the way it was—and we'd have to spend a few days there, carvin' up meat for the woman and fixin' up the place. Bill even taught the oldest boy how to shoot and trap so he could fend for the family."

Stillman paused thoughtfully, blew on his coffee. "God-damned softest touch I ever saw," he grumbled, blinking.

Jody, who'd stood over Stillman listening to the story, returned the coffeepot to the range, scrounged around in a cupboard, and came back to the table with a corked bottle.

"This here's Pa's own Kentucky whiskey. I know he'd want you to have a drink on him."

Stillman smiled and held the half-full bottle out to the firelight, admiring the rich amber whiskey. "A drink from Bill Harmon's bottle—well, I do believe I came to the right place, after all."

He uncorked the bottle, sniffed the lip, savoring the oak-and-honey aroma of the malted liquor. "Ah . . . Bill always was partial to good spirits," he said. He winced and wagged his head. "But I think I'll pass. If I climb into that bottle, I'm liable not to crawl out again till mornin'."

Stillman corked the bottle and, summoning all his strength, shoved it across the table.

Studying him with her chin in her hand, Crystal said thoughtfully, "You have the fever."

"What's that?"

"For the bottle. My father has it, too."

"Lord help him," Stillman said.

"I doubt even the Lord could help my father," Crystal said.

Jody shoved a spoon around on the table. "Tell me, Mr. Stillman—what made you decide to come?"

Stillman held the coffee mug in his big hands and shrugged. "Lord knows I tracked the killers of lesser men than your pa."

He knew that was only half the reason. The other half

had more to do with Jody than his father. Stillman didn't want to disappoint the young man.

He peered into his coffee. When he glanced up, he saw Jody staring at the rifle Stillman had propped against the wall behind his chair.

"That sure is a fine-lookin' rifle," the young man said.

Stillman slid his chair back and shucked the Henry from its boot. He handed the .44 rimfire across the table to Jody, who handled it carefully, running his hands down the walnut magazine and gold-plated, factory-engraved receiver to the pearl inlaid bull's head and brass butt plate.

He whistled and looked at Stillman admiringly. "Where'd you get such a thing?"

"That there's a gift from the late Johnny Dawson, marshal of Dakota Territory. He sent it to me my tenth anniversary on the job. Been with me ever since."

Jody hefted it to his shoulder, aimed at the ceiling corner. "It's light."

"Only nine pounds, that sixteen-shooter is. Just hope I don't have to use it tonight." He sipped his coffee. "You two better get to sleep. I'll take the first watch."

"No, Mr. Stillman," Jody said, returning the Henry to its boot. "You've had a long trip. We'll take the first two watches."

"In that case, I'll turn in."

"You can have Pa's bed, if you don't mind. . . ."

"I'm not superstitious."

He went outside and relieved himself, then came back in, picked up his rifle, and retired to the bedroom off the kitchen. There was an old iron bed sagging in the middle, a ladder-back chair, and a pine bureau, its drawers spilling denim overalls, wool sweaters, gloves, and winter mittens—all, Stillman imagined, as Bill had left them. It was strange, entering a dead man's life.

He removed the back brace and undressed. His legs and buttocks were sore from the ride, but not as sore as he'd expected. He slumped into bed and covered himself with a wool blanket. His hands behind his head, he thought for a long time about Bill Harmon, remembering the adventures they'd shared in another life. How young they were then, and wild. He'd always planned on looking up his old friend—next week, next month, next year. Now that big, brawling, exuberant man was gone, and Stillman would never see him again.

He sighed at the strangeness of life. Then he closed his eyes, relaxed his muscles, and willed himself asleep.

5

On the porch, with the Henry across his lap and his mackinaw buttoned to his throat, Stillman watched the next day dawn cool and clear. Blackbirds and chickadees quarreled in the trees along the ridges.

There'd been no sign of trouble, which wasn't necessarily good. Often, the longer it brewed, the harder it went down.

After a breakfast of steak, eggs, and potatoes, Jody led the former lawman to his father's grave, a mound of fresh dirt in an aspen grove near the creek. Stillman wanted to pay his respects.

"This was Pa's favorite fishing spot," Jody said.

"I bet he pulled some lunkers out of there."

"This summer he caught a five-pound trout on half a grasshopper."

"I know it might be hard, but I'd like you to show me where you found him," Stillman said when they were walking back to their horses. "I doubt if there'd be any tracks, but there might be something."

"Yes, sir."

"Was he shot from the front or the back?"

"Both."

"Both . . . ?" Stillman stopped and faced Jody. "What caliber gun do you think?"

Jody shrugged. "There were four small holes in his chest and thigh, then there was one big hole—" His voice caught. He winced. "There was a big hole in his neck."

Stillman squeezed the boy's shoulder. "Any powder burns?"

"I wasn't looking for none, but I believe there were."

The ex-lawman took his chin between thumb and index finger. "Well, we know he wasn't bushwacked, then."

"Weed Cole's the only one around with gall enough to walk right up to a man and shoot him over and over again—with two different guns. Like he was funnin' with him."

"Possibly," Stillman allowed. They stood in silence for a while, listening to the birds and the morning breeze ruffling the grass. Stillman asked presently, "Where's your ma buried, son?"

Jody pointed his chin southward, where the broad, dark cone of Old Baldy rose in the ridge-relieved distance. "We built a scaffold for her in a tree on Baldy. It's sacred ground to the Crees."

"She teach you the old ways?"

"Bits of language and such. When I was little she took me to pick sweetgrass, and I sweated with her some. She was always a little funny about it, though, like she was teachin' me somethin' dangerous, somethin' it was best I didn't learn."

"I 'spect she was tryin' to save you from the fate of her people."

"The only way she could o' done that was change the color o' my skin."

Stillman pursed his lips and nodded. They heard hoofbeats and turned to watch a rider gallop into the Harmon ranchstead and hit the ground running toward the house.

"That's Bud Harrington," Jody said. "Smoke Harrington's son. I wonder what burr's under his blanket."

He and Stillman swung into their saddles and rode into the ranchyard as the neighbor boy, finding the house vacant, ran off the porch and pushed one boot through a stirrup.

Crystal ran from the barn. "Bud, what's the trouble?" she yelled.

Bud Harrington was maybe fourteen, short and stocky, with a pug nose and sandy hair curling out of a threadbare watch cap and coppery down on his upper lip. He wore his gun in an army holster turned so that the butt snugged up against his rib cage. His face was red with exasperation.

"Someone cut our fence last night. They made off with nine steers. Pa's trackin' 'em now."

"Where's he at?" Jody said as he and Stillman trotted up.

"He said he'd be at the old Phelps place at eight o'clock."

Jody turned to Stillman. "What do you think, Mr. Stillman?"

"I'll ride with the boy. You and Crystal stay here and keep an eye out for Sleighbough."

After nearly an hour he and Bud Harrington came upon a falling-down ranchstead tucked against a low, wooded hill. A lone rider sat in a clearing atop the hill, surveying the countryside through a spyglass. When Smoke Harrington saw them, he rode down on his dun.

"Who's this?"

"Ben Stillman, Jody's pa's friend," Bud replied.

Smoke Harrington was a dark-haired, soft-bellied man with a perpetual grimace. He wore his hat brim funneled down in front, shading his eyes, and a canvas coat and jeans and a Dragoon pistol in a worn Montgomery Ward & Company holster. His teeth shone white against his sun-darkened face as he smiled derisively.

"Oh—you're the one young Harmon collected to do our dirty work for us."

"I came to help find Bill Harmon's killer, if that's what you mean." Judging by his first impression, Stillman didn't like the man. The boy, Bud, seemed antsy in his father's presence, truckling without saying anything.

"No offense, Stillman, but after listenin' to young Harmon tell about you, I was expectin' someone more in the Wyatt Earp line."

"Buffed me up some, did he? Any sign of your beef?"

"I lost it on the other side of this hill."

"Let's take a look."

After a half hour of searching, he found the tracks of eleven hooves—two shod—on the other side of a marshy swale. He and the Harringtons followed the tracks up a slow rise to a rocky saddle studded with firs. As they started down the other side something tore the air between them.

A rifle cracked.

Bud Harrington yelped and fell backward off his mount. Stillman jumped from his horse as more lead spanged around them. One foot caught in the stirrup and the bay dragged him several feet before he worked loose.

He crawled over the saddle as bullets spit gravel in his face, then scrambled for cover behind a rock and a fir tree and picked a prickly-pear thorn from his cheek, feeling foolish. Intermittent rifle fire punctuated the whine of ricocheting lead.

Turning, he saw Bud Harrington sitting against a rock and holding a bloody hand to his forehead.

"How bad's he hit?" Stillman called to the boy's father.

Harrington thumbed back the hammer on his pistol and moved to return fire. "Just grazed his forehead. He'll live.

How 'bout yourself?'' There was more disdain than concern in the inquiry.

Stillman nodded.

While Harrington shot back with his ancient Dragoon pistol, Stillman peered around the rock and surveyed the ground sloping southwestward to a patch of stunt willows. Two gunmen lay behind a grassy lip a hundred yards before the grove, about seventy yards below the saddle.

Glancing around, Stillman saw Sweets fifty yards down the grade behind him with the other two horses. He ran to him stiffly and returned to the rock with his Henry rifle.

After checking the breech, he lifted the target sight, and moved into position between the rock and a wind-twisted fir. He waited to see a head and a puff of smoke, and fired. The 260-grain round landed several feet shy of its mark, blowing up dust from the tawny grass.

"Shit," he muttered, ejecting the brass.

"Why don't you let me try?" Harrington yelled. The bushwackers were out of range for his pistol.

Ignoring the rancher, Stillman fired twice more, trying to get the feel of the gun again. What had it been—four years?

He fired, cursed, and ejected the smoking shell, the smell of burned gunpowder filling his nose. The next shot struck a rifle barrel with a muffled ping.

The gunman cursed, and the shooting stopped. Several moments later both bushwackers appeared running across the meadow below the lip, heading for the willows.

"Let me try a shot!" Harrington yelled.

Gritting his teeth, Stillman levered another bullet into the breech, leveled the sight a foot above a retreating gunman, and squeezed the trigger. About a second and a half after the carbine barked, the gunman toppled forward into the grass, arms and hat flying.

The other stopped, hesitated, did a two-step, and ran on.

He disappeared in the trees before Stillman could lay the sights on him.

"You finally got one," Bud Harrington said, glancing at his father for approval. The right side of his face and forehead were covered with blood, his eye squeezed shut.

"With that sixteen-shooter, I don't see how he could miss."

When they'd retrieved their horses, they rode out to the man lying belly-down in the grass. He was tall and thin, balding on top, with long hair on the back and sides, and an untrimmed beard. A dark, wet hole gaped in his back just below his shoulder blade. Blood trickled at the corner of his mouth where a silver tooth glinted in the morning sun.

Looking down from his horse, Smoke Harrington said, "Connie Dwire."

"Who'd he work for?"

"Hobbs, I reckon."

"He worked for just about ever'body in the mountains, one time or 'nother," Bud Harrington said. "Just a drunk, ain't that right, Pa?"

Harrington ignored the boy. "I figured he was dead or drifted out of the country."

"Well, he's dead now," Stillman said. "I'll take him to the sheriff in Clantick, explain the situation."

"Say what?" Harrington was exasperated. "I say we hang him from a branch on Hobbs's range, set an example!"

"I didn't come here to set examples. I came to help straighten out this mess."

"Then you came to kill Donovan Hobbs and Weed Cole!"

Stillman shook his head. "I ain't the law, and we don't know they're responsible."

"Who the hell else?"

"That's what we find out." Stillman gave the rancher a hard look. "Now the law's been broke here, so we give the sheriff a chance to fix it. If he don't fix it, then we call in the marshal in Helena, and he fixes it."

Harrington stared at him, then shook his head, resignedly. "Come on, Bud," he said to his son. "Let's fetch our steers and get your head stitched before you bleed to death."

6

Stillman followed Whitetail Creek north to Clantick with the body of Connie Dwire tied behind his saddle.

Harrington's reaction to his strategy chafed him, as did nearly everything else about the man. The rancher was the breed who shot first and asked questions later.

Stillman had stood at the perimeters of enough land disputes to know that such men blurred the distinction between guilt and innocence. They often made such a mess of things that when the smoke cleared and the dust settled, you couldn't tell what was what nor who was who.

On Clantick's main street, paralleling the Great Northern tracks, he rode past blanketed Indians selling polished buffalo bones and beaded belts on boardwalks stacked with kegs and shipping crates. The landless Indians stared indifferently at the corpse of Connie Dwire, whose stiffening legs stuck out awkwardly from the right side of the ex-lawman's horse.

Stillman stopped at the jail and found the door locked and the lights out. He continued to Auld's Livery on Third Avenue. The hostler was mucking out a stall in high-topped rubbers. Stillman asked if he could leave the corpse.

"The corpse will cost you extra." Auld was a big

German with a blond beard, high forehead, and a free-ranging left eye with a white scar above and below it.

"I'll stall him with my horse."

"Still cost you extra."

"You're a hard man, Mr. Auld."

"I ain't an undertaker."

When he'd turned the bay over to Auld and laid out the corpse, Stillman walked two blocks to the Windsor Hotel. It was getting too late to ride back to the Harmon ranch. Jody and Crystal could watch the place. Stillman thought he might be able to learn more about Hobbs in town, then get an early start in the morning tracking the rustled herds.

Sunburned bullwhackers and derby-hatted drummers sat on the veranda, kicked back in their chairs with soapy beer mugs clenched in their fists.

Stillman nodded on his way up the steps.

He registered in the lobby, took his war bag and rifles upstairs to his room, and produced a water flask, taking several long pulls in lieu of the rye he'd been imagining for the last five miles. He brushed the dust from his clothes, combed his hair in the chipped mirror over the bureau, and took another pull from the flask.

Downstairs, he asked the desk clerk where he'd find the sheriff this time of day and on his direction headed for Howell's Saloon.

At the back of the narrow, smoky room a man in a pin-striped shirt and suspenders was playing "The Blue Danube" on an accordion while several cowboys played poker and a pleasure girl filed her nails. Seeing no one with a badge, Stillman stepped up to the mahogany bar and inquired with the apron.

The man blinked at him and gave his waxed mustache an idle twist. "Back room upstairs. But they won't let you in."

"They?"

"He's playin' poker with Hobbs and some others."

Stillman's stomach took a spin. He knew he'd have to confront Hobbs at some point. "Give me a glass of water in a shot glass."

The man looked at him strangely. He took a shot glass from under the bar and filled it from a glass decanter. Looking insulted, he set the shot glass on the counter.

Stillman knocked it back and dropped a coin on the bar. "Thanks."

Upstairs, he knocked on a door at the end of the hall. The conversation within ceased.

A chair scraped the floor, the sound of footsteps on squeaky floorboards grew, and the door was opened by a dull-eyed brute with a deputy's star. He was holding a double-barrel shotgun in massive, tattooed arms.

"This here's a closed game, friend."

Stillman blocked the door open with his boot. "I'm opening it."

The man's face mottled with rage. "You need your ears cleaned, old man?"

"I'm looking for Sheriff Lewis," Stillman said.

"Who in the hell *is* that, Todd?" came the voice of an angry Brit.

Stillman brushed past the deputy. He faced a square table where four men sat around a whiskey bottle, poker chips, and a pile of playing cards. The burnished glow of an oil lamp swept late-afternoon shadows into the corners.

"You Lewis?" Stillman asked the man with the sheriff's star.

"That's right. Who wants to know?" He was old and gray and his eyes were rheumy blue behind thick-lensed spectacles.

"Ben Stillman. I want to report a rustlin'."

"You do, do ya?"

"I brought the body of Connie Dwire to town. He was moving stolen cows and I shot him."

A small man in a boiled shirt, cravat, black suit, and waistcoat removed a pencil-thin cigar from his mouth and said casually, "Todd, take this man back to the jail. The sheriff will see to him later—when he's broke."

The deputy thumbed back the hammers on the scattergun and poked the barrels into Stillman's back.

Not so much thinking as reacting, Stillman knocked the shotgun aside with his right elbow, both barrels exploding into the door. With the same motion he drew his Colt, turned, and slammed the butt against the deputy's head.

The big man fell like a sack of grain, bouncing off the wall and making the whole room jump.

"Who in the hell do you think you are?" bellowed the red-faced Englishman.

"Ben Stillman, deputy U.S. marshal, retired. You Hobbs?"

The man didn't say anything.

There was a grim cast to his wide, pear-shaped face as he stared evenly at Stillman. Judging from the goatee and the straw-yellow locks falling to his shoulders, he fancied himself another Bill Hickok or George Custer. But the small, round paunch bubbling his waistcoat where a gold watch fob shone—and the smooth hands and face, the uncertain eyes, and the melon-ripe articulation—betrayed just another high-headed Brit. Stillman knew when all the Western grass was gone, he and his brethren would return fat and happy to merry ol' England and their blooded hunting dogs.

Sheriff Lewis said to Stillman, "I thought you was dead."

"Not yet."

"You know this man?" Hobbs said, turning to the sheriff.

Lewis shrugged. "I heard of him. Had quite the reputation in his day. Drunk whore shot him, as I recall. Ain't that right, Stillman?"

"Wasn't my night."

"What do you want?" Hobbs said.

"You gentlemen hard-of-hearing? I'm reporting the rustlin' of Smoke Harrington's steers and the death of Connie Dwire. There was another rider, but my aim was off."

"You didn't come to the Hi-Line to track cattle rustlers," Hobbs said.

"My old friend Bill Harmon disappeared off his range two weeks ago and turned up dead," Stillman said in a low, gravelly voice that contrasted with the high, stuffy speech of the Brit. "I came to see what the sheriff was doing about finding his killer."

"I thought you said you was retired," the sheriff said.

"I'm still a taxpayer."

Hobbs retrieved his cigar from an ashtray and took a short drag from the side of his mouth, smiling at Lewis. He was enjoying this. "Well, Ed?"

Lewis fidgeted. "I'm workin' on it."

"Any leads?"

"Nothin' yet."

Hobbs turned to Stillman. "There you have it."

"You don't have any idea who'd want to kill my friend Bill Harmon, do you, Mr. Hobbs?"

"You're not accusing me, are you, Mr. Stillman?"

"Some say you've taken illegal possession of some twenty thousand acres in the public domain and fenced it off from outsiders. They say you want more, and you're trying to clear out all the ten-cow operators in the Clear Creek Valley."

Hobbs lifted his head and blew a narrow stream of blue cigar smoke at the ceiling. "I've lost twenty-five head of market-ready steers myself, Mr. Stillman."

"Who hired Weed Cole?"

"Who's Weed Cole?" Hobbs waited for a reply.

None came.

"The small outfits around me are doing the rustling. They're jealous of me for my land and money. They're too lazy to work for what they want, so they steal from me and call me the thief."

"You find your cattle on their ranges?"

"Bunches."

"Who do you think killed Bill Harmon?"

"One of them."

"Why?"

"How would I know? I'm not one of them."

Stillman sighed, scratched his head. "Well, I don't mean to interfere, Sheriff, but I think I'll dally here awhile, see what I can come up with."

"You ain't a lawman no more, mister. You said so yourself."

Stillman ignored this, continued his thought. "But I have a feeling that if we find the guy who got away from me today, we'll only be a step or two away from my friend's killer."

Hobbs said, "You might have the drop on him now, Stillman. But the sheriff must arrest you for assaulting his deputy there."

The sheriff cut a worried glance at Hobbs. The deputy was sitting on the floor, his back to the wall, rubbing the purple goose egg growing on his temple.

"Sounds to me you're afraid of what I might find," Stillman said to the rancher.

"Not at all. But the Hi-Line is not like other places. It's

not as *civilized* yet, thank heavens. We'll deal with this problem ourselves, in our own way. That's the way it's always been.''

''Well, I hate ridin' roughshod on tradition, but I'm going to find out who killed Bill Harmon one way or another. Now, the sheriff can arrest me or shoot me, but I've wired my successor, Dale True, in Helena. If he doesn't hear from me, he's going to send a whole passel of deputies to knock down barns and turn up sod.''

He stopped to evaluate Hobbs's reaction to his bluff. There was none.

He turned to Lewis. ''Connie Dwire's stalled with my horse over at Auld's. You'll want to fetch him before Auld feeds him to his hogs.''

The he stepped over the deputy's feet and left.

7

In the Sam Wa Café across from the Broadwater and Pepin general store on Main, Stillman cut into an overdone sirloin while soldiers at the next table shared bawdy anecdotes about a girl named Mattie. A dour Chinese woman in a purple smock ghosted around the room, lighting the lamps.

Stillman ate without relish. His mood was low, his nerves jangled. He'd been hoping to gauge the situation here as anonymously as possible, then light out for home, leaving the rough stuff to the boys with the badges.

But already he'd killed a man, had one tracking him, and antagonized the local law—not to mention Donovan Hobbs.

Fine piece of work, he chided himself. You should have stayed home with your chickens.

He paid for his meal and went up the boardwalk, threading his way past dogs and drunk night owls. Piano music and raucous laughter spilled from saloons and gambling halls. Three bindle stiffs in oversized coats were camped under a hay wagon, passing a bottle around and waiting for the next train.

"Hey, mister, you want some fun?" asked a petite girl of about fourteen in a slow, Southern drawl.

Her pink dress, stuffed with tissue paper, was lumpy around the oversized bosom. Leaning against a saloon front and chewing gum, she tilted her head to one side and smiled, showing a chipped front tooth and a gray bruise around her left eye.

Feeling old and feeble, Stillman turned the corner and continued toward his hotel. Two blocks before he got there, he heard footsteps behind him. He stopped and glanced over his shoulder.

No one was there. He continued on until he felt eyes burning a hole through his back, heard muffled footsteps on the boardwalk.

Turning, he released his trigger thong and pulled his gun. A woman in a dark dress and a shawl stepped into the shadows of the storefronts a half block behind him. Then, apparently unsatisfied with her hiding place, she moved, half running, back down the boardwalk.

"Hey!" Stillman called.

He ran to catch her. She was wearing heels, and he caught her before she made it to the next street. He grabbed her arm and swung her around, immediately recognizing the wide, brown eyes and smooth, chiseled cheeks of the only woman he'd ever loved.

"Fay!"

"Oh, Ben—let me go!"

She pulled away and ran, skirts swirling. He watched her disappear around the corner. He stood there, heart pounding, unable to move.

Finally he walked back down the alley as though in a dream. In the hotel lobby, he picked up his room key automatically and returned to his room. A set of bedsprings were getting a workout next door, but he barely heard. He stripped, sat on the edge of the bed in his long johns, and drank from his travel flask. Moral courage flagging, he yearned for a high glass of Tennessee Mountain and a bottle of Blatz.

He ran a hand over his head and studied the warped pine boards between his feet. He kept replaying the scene in the alley, over and over, until his brain went numb. Had he really seen Fay Beaumont? What was she doing in Clantick?

He sighed and capped the flask and set it on the bedside table next to his pistol. He turned down the wick on the lamp and crawled into bed and stared at the ceiling, listening to a drunk Irishman singing ballads in the room above and seeing Fay Beaumont again in the dark dress and the shawl.

Oh, Ben—let me go!

Physical and mental exhaustion had nearly overcome him when someone knocked. "Hold on."

He lit the lamp and pulled his pants over his long johns. Grabbing his Colt, he opened the door. Fay stood before him, head tipped forward, lustrous brown eyes demure. She clutched a beaded purse with both hands and held her night cape closed below her bosom.

"Hello, Ben."

"Good Lord—it *was* you."

She glanced at the Colt, and smiled. "Can I come in?"

"Wait, I ain't dressed." He closed the door and scrambled into his shirt, socks, and boots. When he'd buttoned his pants and ran his hands through his hair, he opened the door. "Sorry, come in."

She hesitated, then, stiffly, she moved past him into the room. Stillman closed the door and set the pistol on the marble-topped washbasin. She stood shyly holding her purse, and the flickering lamplight played across her beautiful face, lightly flushed, eyes cast down.

"Fay . . ." Stillman tried, searching for words.

Bringing her delicate chin up, the soft brown eyes, she said, "I'm sorry I ran. You caught me by surprise."

He knew he was staring, but as always with her, he couldn't help himself. She was even more lovely than he remembered, a lithe, coltish wonder with ivory skin, almond-shaped eyes, and raven hair swept back under a feathered hat. Her full bust, accentuated by a low-cut bodice, tapered to a narrow waist and slender hips.

Everything about her, from her huskily feminine voice to her perfume, bespoke her French aristocratic lineage tempered by a touch of the Western tomboy; she'd been raised on Racine and horses.

He smiled, shook his head. "You're a sight for sore eyes, Miss Beaumont."

"You, too, for a man with a bullet in his back."

"You heard?"

She nodded. "I'm sorry you had to retire. I know how much marshaling meant to you."

He motioned her to a chair, and she moved to it stiffly, fingering the tassels on her cape. He wanted to wrap his arms around her, but an invisible boundary held him back.

He laughed, cheered by her presence just the same. He'd thought he'd never see her again. "What in hell are you doing here, Fay?"

She fidgeted a ring on her left hand. "I live here. My husband and I were dining at the Decker when he mentioned an ex-lawman from Helena had interrupted his card game."

Stillman's smile altered to a searching gravity.

"I married Donovan Hobbs three years ago."

He scowled, blinked his eyes, staring. He let several seconds pass, hoping he'd misunderstood. "You're not joking, are you?"

She seemed not to hear him. "When he went back to his

poker, I decided to go sleuthing,'' she said. She paused, then laughed dryly. "I guess I don't have to ask you what you think of him.''

"Hobbs?" The name stuck like a bone in his throat.

She turned a hard gaze to him sharply. "Sure." Then she turned away and studied the shadows in the corners of the tawdry little room, as though searching for something.

"I met him four years ago,'' she said at length, slowly. "My father introduced us. They met at the Montana Club in Miles City. Donovan had just come from England to operate the spread on the Hi-Line his father had bought." She stopped. An ironic smile pulled at her full lips. "Of course, he'd never even seen a cow, but that didn't stop Donovan.''

She watched him, her lustrous eyes filling with cool reproach. "You have no right to look at me like that. You broke my heart.''

He wheeled to the window, nodding.

Her presence sent memories scattering in all directions within him. There was a cottonwood grove by an oval green meadow humped with ancient burial mounds. The tall grass danced in the wind, the bluebells swayed, the wild irises blazed among the blossoms of the balsamroot.

Just beyond the woods lay the Yellowstone River in a wide stony bed littered with driftwood, a flock of Canada geese barking on the shore, a great blue heron laboring upward through a shaft of morning sun.

Voices were speaking, saying foolish, lovely things— soft voices, happy voices embedded in the moment. There was teasing and laughter and two laughing lovers running through trees. The meadow and woods and geese and heron—the teasing and laughter—all faded behind a single sentence: "Marry me, Fay.''

Her words reached him as a barely audible whisper. "Why are you here, Ben?"

Stillman turned back to her. He gripped a corner of the armoire and stared gloomily off into space. "Someone murdered an old friend of mine—Bill Harmon. His boy asked me to help find the killer."

"And you suspect Donovan?"

He nodded.

She pursed her lips and looked at her hands. "Well, I wouldn't put it past him."

The old lawman's habit returned as if to save him. "Have you seen Weed Cole on your place?"

"I've seen lots of men on our place, from a distance. Donovan won't let me near them, nor them near me. To say my husband is a jealous man is like saying Judas was a tattler."

"Why don't you leave? Go back to your father?"

"He's dead," she said matter-of-factly. "Two horrible winters broke him—financially, mentally, physically. My mother returned to St. Louis to live with her sister."

She folded her hands in her lap and sighed. "There's nowhere for me to go. Besides, Donovan would kill me." She looked at him as if at a stranger, and he wished she'd left him with his memories. "Don't interrogate me, Ben. Go home. If Donovan's involved, there's nothing you can do about it."

"He that big?"

She raised her eyebrows. "He regularly dines with the governor; does that tell you anything?"

She got up and crossed the room to the door. She moved like a woman who'd been beaten down to hard defiance, to whom everyone was suspect. Even he. It hurt to see her like this. Where was the bright, sassy twenty-year-old he'd fallen in love with?

She stood there a moment, then laughed, her eyes filling with tears.

"What's so funny?"

"When I first heard you were in town, I thought you were here for me."

He stared at her, unable to find the words.

Suddenly she threw her arms around his neck and hugged him desperately. He held her, ran his hands down her slender back, feeling her tremble with suppressed sobs, and yearning for the past when they were together and happy and their lives were before them, full of promise and love.

"I'm sorry, Fay," he said, gently holding her face in both hands and wiping away the tears with his thumbs. "I should have—"

"Don't." She wrestled away from him. "Don't do that to me now. You've done enough." She wiped her eyes with the back of her hand and looked at him imploringly for several seconds. "Leave here."

Before he could respond, she turned and left.

He stood for a long time, staring at the door.

8

Fay Hobbs held her night cape closed at her throat as the top buggy clattered through the chill night. Stars shone in the bare branches of the trees along the road. The seat springs creaked and the air smelled tinny.

"Are you cold?" Donovan Hobbs asked her.

"No, I'm fine."

"There's a robe under the seat."

"I'm not cold."

"Well, why are you so bloody quiet?"

She tried a smile. "Am I quiet? I guess I didn't realize."

Hobbs snorted. "Didn't realize it, eh?"

He clucked to the harnessed sorrel, agitated. It was nothing new, this maddening secrecy of hers. He knew it was this way with all women, but it chafed him just the same. Sometimes he thought he should have remained a bachelor, relying on Clantick's surprisingly innovative hurdy-gurdy houses for his pleasure.

But there was the matter of progeny, and only a fool would not have pursued the lovely daughter of Alexander Beaumont when presented the chance.

"Where's the muslin?" he asked.

"What?"

"I thought you went to inquire at the mercantile for a length of muslin?"

Her heart skipped a beat. "Oh. Yes. They were closed, after all."

The sorrel kicked a stone into the buggy's path. The right wheel hit it, and the carriage bounced. Hobbs cursed. "That's all I need—a cracked wheel!"

He drove the buggy in troubled silence, then looked at her, frowning. "You haven't been *naughty,* have you, Mrs. Hobbs?"

She stared at him, feeling a constriction in her chest. What a fool she'd been, visiting Ben's hotel! Any number of people might have seen her. Donovan might have seen her. But she hadn't been able to stop herself.

She said, "What do you mean?"

Then Hobbs smiled, turning it into a joke. He reached over and gave her knee a squeeze, then pulled a cigar from the breast pocket of his frock coat and lit it, puffing. She started breathing again.

As she rode there beside her husband she thought of Ben Stillman—his wry sense of humor, his gentle spirit, his big, handsome face and broad, muscled shoulders. How different he was from the man she'd tried to snuff his memory with.

She remembered the oddly cold letter he'd sent her when he'd left Miles City. *Fay,* it had begun, *I have been reassigned to the Flathead Reservation to look into a criminal faction that has organized there to distribute liquor to the Indians. It will be a two-month job at least. I am afraid I will not be back to Miles City, Fay. After many nights without sleep, I have decided our marrying is not right. You need a good man with money who will not keep you waiting for him when he might not ever return. I am sorry, my love.*

If you do not understand now, I am confident you will soon.
Trust me. As always, Ben.

Remembering the lines she knew by heart, she felt the
old anger grow. How dare he make decisions for both of
them! She was a woman, not a girl; he was her lover, not
her father. It saddened, angered, and confused her, for it
had not been at all like the Ben Stillman she had come to
know and love.

Now a voice called from the darkness. "Who goes
there?"

"Hobbs."

"Evenin', Mr. Hobbs." A rider approached, a carbine in
his arms. His seal-brown gelding expelled jets of steamy
breath into the starlit night. Hobbs reined the sorrel to a
halt.

Fay recognized the man only as one of her husband's
many riders. She didn't know names. Like the others, he
was crude, dirty, and dangerously stupid.

"All quiet?" Hobbs said.

"Yes, sir. We've got most of the steers moved down to
the winter pastures, and those we're movin' out—well,
they're ready to move out."

"Good. I shall meet you men at first light." Hobbs was
about to flick the reins when the rider cleared his throat.

"Mr. Hobbs, someone shot my brother."

"Who?"

"Don't know his name. A stranger. We came upon him
at Olson's. We just asked him who he be and where he
come from, and he pulled his pistol and shot Kenny through
the heart." The man's voice was heavy with restrained
emotion. "My poor mother's tending to the body now so
we can bury him in the morning."

Hobbs frowned. "Big man? Ten-gallon Stetson? Salt-
and-pepper mustache?"

"That's the bastard. Pardon my language, ma'am."

"You'll get your chance at him, Del. I assure you."

"Thank you, Mr. Hobbs."

"Go bury your brother and be back at the ranch by to-morrow afternoon."

"Yes, sir."

Hobbs clucked the sorrel into motion, angered by the loss of a hand, though he figured Kenny had probably deserved it. He'd wanted to put a bullet through that repugnant beast's head several times himself.

As the buggy clattered away Fay turned to watch the rider disappear in the darkness, her hands clenched together in her lap.

When Hobbs pulled up to the barn, the old stable hand Grubber Early came from the bunkhouse, yawning and pulling up his suspenders and grumbling under his breath about the lateness of the hour. By a coal-oil lantern, he unhitched the sorrel as Hobbs and Fay started for the house.

A big, clapboard barrack with massive stone chimneys abutting both ends, it sat a hundred yards from the bunk-house, barns, and corrals, in a little grove of transplanted trees and shrubs.

A light burned in Hobbs's office window at the house's right end. Having left it dark, he stopped and eyed it suspiciously.

Glancing up, he saw that the light was out in the upstairs bedroom of his servants, Ernesto and Julia Bodio. It was nearly midnight, and they were surely asleep.

"Grubber, who's in the house?"

"Search me, boss," Early said as he led the sorrel to the corral. "You want me to have some of the boys check it out?"

"No, I'll take care of it. Fay, you stay here until I call

for you." He'd feel foolish if he awakened two trouble-shooters and it turned out to be nothing.

"Maybe they should check it out," she said without thinking.

Through gritted teeth, he hissed, "Did you hear what I said?"

Not taking any chances, he drew his nickel-plated Bisley and advanced stealthily toward the window and crouched.

He heard footfalls inside. Someone was moving around in his office, opening and closing drawers and, from the sound of clinking glass, drinking his Spanish brandy.

He peered under the shade and cursed. The man inside was square-jawed and dull-eyed. His nose, blunt and slightly crooked, bore the appearance of several fractures. His short, dark brown hair lay close against his skull, and his thick, cracked lips bore a shit-eating grin.

He sat down carelessly in Hobbs's steer-horn chair and set Hobbs's brandy snifter on Hobbs's mahogany desk, where one of Hobbs's cigars—one of the two dozen that arrived last week from the governor—burned in Hobbs's favorite nickel-plated ashtray.

Hobbs turned away from the window. "It's all right, Fay," he said as he walked around to the porch.

Not waiting for her, he walked through the front door and down the short, cedar-paneled hall to his office. He gave the door an angry push and walked in.

"Cole, what . . ."

The chair sat three feet away from the desk—empty. Hobbs turned to survey the rest of the room when an arm whipped around his neck from behind, jerking his chin up and pinching off his wind. The cold steel of a pistol pressed against his temple.

Flailing helplessly at the arm and unable to breathe,

Hobbs rasped through gritted teeth, "Cole . . . god-damn . . ."

"Oh. Sorry, Mr. Hobbs."

The wiry, long-muscled arm released its grip. The pistol dropped, leaving the barrel's cold tattoo on Hobbs's temple.

Hobbs turned to see Weed Cole grinning at him, mocking, the gunman's Fu Manchu mustache looking like a sick bird. "You shouldn't go sneakin' up on a man, Mr. Hobbs."

"This is my house, you idiot! What the hell are you doing here?"

The gunman, still grinning, shrugged with infuriating insouciance. "Just stopped by for a drink, Mr. Hobbs. When I saw you weren't home, I figgered I'd wait, have a little brandy. Didn't think you'd mind."

"Didn't think I'd mind? You break into my house and you don't think I'd mind?" Hobbs snorted and rolled his head around, checking for neck damage. "Where are the Bodios?"

"Upstairs, sleepin' like little wop babies. You should get a new lock on your door. It's real easy to pick."

Bare feet padded in the hall. The faint aroma of orange blossoms entered the room. The sound and the smell seemed to entrance Cole, who moved to the door like a puppet.

Passing with a lantern, Fay glanced in at them.

She'd undressed before the sitting-room fire, as was her habit on cold nights, and pulled on an old buffalo robe for the journey to her bedroom. The robe had been a childhood gift from her grandfather.

She continued down the hall, her velvety hair puffing out from her neck and cascading down her back in long, chocolate curls. Her pink, slender feet looked especially delicate and feminine under the hem of the old robe.

Cole watched her until she'd disappeared in the shadows.

Hobbs slammed the door. "That's my wife you're leering at, Mr. Cole."

Cole inhaled deeply and held it, savoring her smell, then slowly exhaled. "I guess you know what she's wearin' under that robe."

"Mr. Cole," Hobbs hissed, "let's get back to what you're doing here."

Cole licked his lips. "Nothin', I bet. Am I right?"

Hobbs's gaze turned so cold it snuffed the light from even Weed Cole's eyes. "Let me tell you something, Cole. You might be able to shoot ten men in the time it takes me to sneeze, but if you ever go near my wife, I'll have you hunted down and quartered like a Bastille Day pig. You understand?"

"Hey, I was just—"

"Do you understand?"

Cole shrugged, turned away, and dropped into a stuffed leather chair. He fidgeted, hiked a boot onto his knee, looked around the room for a place to settle his eyes. Then he met Hobbs's gaze and held it, blinked, and smiled that maddening smile. "Sure."

Perturbed, Hobbs moved stiffly around the room, drawing the heavy curtains and lighting another lamp. Meanwhile Cole retrieved his cigar from an ashtray and refilled his brandy glass.

"That deserves a finer palate than yours," Hobbs remarked.

Knowing he'd just been insulted but not exactly how— "palate"?—Cole returned to his chair and dropped into it with a grunt.

Hobbs smiled, satisfied the upper hand was again his.

He poured himself a brandy and sat in his steer-horn chair behind his big mahogany desk. The chair, fashioned from Texas leather and Patagonian steer horns, was a wedding present from his father in Bristol.

"As long as you're here, I might as well tell you we're moving twenty-five head to town tomorrow, and another twenty-five over east. Goodnight will meet you at the river with his men."

"Why don't I go to town with the others? I'm due to stomp with my tail up."

"Because if we get trouble, we'll meet it with the southern twenty-five."

Cole considered his brandy. "Pshaw—who's gonna mess with you, Mr. Hobbs?"

"You'd be surprised. On your way back, I want you to get that crazy Van Orsdel out of that hollow. Do whatever you have to do, but don't kill him. We've an ex-lawman skulking around here because you went and killed Bill Harmon."

Cole looked at him with one eye closed. "Who?"

"Who?" Hobbs mocked.

"I didn't kill no Harmon."

Hobbs looked him over. He prided himself on knowing when a man was lying to him, a trait he'd acquired as a major in India. Cole had the witless look of honesty.

"Well, who did, then?"

"Hell if I know."

Hobbs turned his head and scratched his ear. "Shit!" he shrilled, voice cracking, golden locks bouncing on his shoulders. "What a bloody mess."

9

Stillman woke early when a door slammed in the room above him and high heels clattered down the hall. It hadn't been a restful night, anyway. The bed was too soft, and, having, as a lawman, taught himself to sleep lightly, every sound in the crowded hotel had made him reach for his revolver.

He dressed and shaved, squinting in the dim light penetrating the window shade. He wrapped the brace around his waist and placed his ten-gallon Stetson carefully on his surprisingly clear head. Life without liquor had its upside, namely mornings.

After checking his Army Colt for brass, he left his room, stepped across the drunk cowboy passed out on the stairs, and crossed the dark lobby to the street.

He paused on the boardwalk, taking in the grungy little cow town still sleeping off last night's drunk. He heard someone sweeping the boardwalk down the street, and noticed a blacksmith was already at work nearby, the sound of the bellows rising on the cool morning air. A dog barked. Meadowlarks cooed. A barn door scraped on a rusty track.

Over east, eroded buttes were capped in morning pink.

Stillman followed the smell of fried bacon down the

street to Sam Wa's. The proprietor parted the kitchen's lou-
vered doors, bowing and smiling. He was a short, heavyset
man with a round face and protruding eyes. A goatee lent
a somewhat mystical touch.

Stillman ordered two eggs, once over, with potatoes and
bacon, and the Chinaman nodded and smiled and shuffled
back to the kitchen.

The former lawman had an edge this morning, a deep
funk despite his abstinence from alcohol and gambling. He
couldn't get Fay off his mind. He'd seen too many cow
towns—Mandan, Billings, Miles City—bowing and scraping to the English money of men like Donovan Hobbs, for
whom every person, every animal, every acre, every tree,
and meandering creek—every Miles City beauty—meant
only the bottom-line tally in a ledger book.

He remembered the night he'd met her.

Fay's father, whom Stillman had met at a dinner at Judge
Bishop's Helena mansion, had invited him out to their
ranch. He was struck by the beauty of the young woman
who'd interrupted their premeal brandy and cigars with
news that one of the horses had taken ill.

She later joined them for dinner in the stone-walled dining room with its apple-wood fire, French chandeliers, and
enough silver to fill a mine. He avoided her gaze, fearing
one look would lead to a stare. Later, when he was walking
back to the corral for his horse, she snuck up behind him
in the dark and stuck a wet finger in his ear. She was wearing an old buffalo robe over a pair of shapeless jeans, and
her hair was tussled.

"You were ignoring me," she said, pouting. "Why were
you ignoring me?"

He felt like a tongue-tied schoolboy. "Was I?"

"You know you were. Why?"

He indulged in a stare. "You're beautiful."

Unfazed by the compliment, she said, "How long will you be in the country?"

He was on temporary assignment, helping the Miles City sheriff during a potentially explosive court trial involving vigilantes. "Until the trial's over."

"Do you like to ride?"

He smiled. "Yeah, I like to ride."

"Saturday at noon, meet me at Parker Butte. We'll go riding."

Before he could respond, she'd turned in her buffalo robe and walked away in the darkness.

Now he wiped the remaining yolk from his plate with toast and walked outside. The sun had lifted above the eastern buttes and the swallows twittered atop the false fronts of Main. He saw the shingle for Jensen's Tonsorial Parlor and headed that way.

Jensen was a quiet Swede who walked with a limp. He led Stillman into a paneled back room where a red-hot stove sat with several boilers of steaming water. He filled an oak tub, mumbling in Swedish.

Stillman undressed, poked a foot in the water, and gestured for another bucket.

"Two buckets, two beets," the Swede said.

Stillman handed the man two bits from his pants, and Jensen limped off. Stillman sank slowly into the water, wincing against the heat but feeling the muscles soften in his back.

"Aha," he sighed.

He was stretched out in the tub enjoying the silky feel of the castile soap against his lye-burned skin when the Swede situated another man in the tub next to him.

"You're Ben Stillman, ain't you?" the man asked when the Swede had left again.

"I'm Stillman."

"Sophus Anderson."

The man held out a soapy hand. He had a narrow brown face and bushy gray eyebrows flared up at the ends. His large eyes were sunken and squinty, and the sides of his nose were spectacle-marred. He shaped a big, toothy smile. "I own the bank and the big house on the hill."

Stillman shook the man's hand. "You braggin', sir?"

Anderson shook his head, smile fading. His tone turned grim. "Nothin' to brag about. Donovan Hobbs has the paper on all of it, me included."

"How's that?"

"Back east I heard this was the next great cattle range, which indeed it is. I came here with a little nest egg, and Hobbs hatched it for me."

"So he plays and you sing," Stillman said with a nod.

"I guess you could say that, yes." The banker's eyebrows lifted a wistful grin. "Who strums your chords?"

"I do."

"You sure?"

Stillman frowned, offended. "Is this goin' somewhere?"

"You hear of Amiel Mundt?"

"He ranches out near the Harmons, I'm told."

"That's right. Amiel was my first friend out here in the Big Lonesome."

"Go on."

Anderson studied his bathwater for a moment, troubled. "I think he's going to disappear."

"Like Bill Harmon?"

Anderson nodded.

"How do you know?"

"Ain't sayin'." The banker cast a glance at the door. "But I'd appreciate your riding out there. I haven't seen hide nor hair of Amiel or Mary in several weeks."

"I'm heading that way this morning. I'll take a look."

"Appreciate it." Anderson scrubbed under his arm and gave Stillman a curious look. "You're the one shot by a whore, aren't you?"

"That's right."

"Ain't that the way it goes?" the banker said, giving his head a quick shake. "I reckon I'll get drunk and bet the farm one of these days, and they'll plant me in a pauper's grave."

"Just be careful whose fiddle you dance to."

"I reckon." Anderson grew thoughtful. He rubbed his nose and narrowed a nearsighted gaze at Stillman. "I'd appreciate your not mentioning this conversation to anyone. Nothing personal, but I think you made some enemies last night."

"No doubt."

"Word of advice?"

"Let's have it."

"Don't be invitin' Hobbs's lovely wife to your hotel room anymore."

10

The mid-morning sun slanted down on the tawny grass, rippled by a vagrant wind. A low line of hills trimmed in shade marked the course of a distant creek. To the south the Two Bear Mountains rose above the shimmering prairie.

Stillman brushed a grasshopper from his cheek and rested his chin on his rifle butt.

After his bath at the Swede's, he'd picked up his horse at the livery barn and left Clantick, coming upon an antelope herd eight miles south of town. The pronghorn had moved ahead of him for half an hour, unriled but keeping their distance, relying on their keen eyes and noses to warn them of danger.

Now they grazed indifferently, unaware of Stillman lying at the lip of an old buffalo wallow, his bare head concealed in a sage clump.

The wind fishtailed and the heat waves danced, suspending the pronghorn in a mirage several feet from the ground. Stillman pulled back the rifle's hammer and snugged a shoulder against the butt plate.

He separated a big-rumped doe grazing on a rise about two hundred yards away, drew a breath, and let out half.

He closed his right hand around the stock's neck and touched the first joint of his index finger to the trigger and slowly tightened it as the doe swam into the sights. The animal suddenly lifted its muzzle and turned as if sensing the bead drawn on the muscled flesh above its shoulder.

An ear twitched. Flies swirled around its head. The muscles on its white rump contracted as it began to move, alerting the herd.

Before it took a step, Stillman's gloved finger took up its slack. The Henry boomed. At the same moment as dust and sod flew at the doe's feet, she jerked sideways and ran.

The echo of the shot was swallowed by the huge sky, and the acrid smell of burned powder was swept away on the wind.

"Goddammit."

Stillman got up stiffly and ejected the spent brass. He looked toward the pronghorns. Most had disappeared, bounding toward the distant buttes to the west. A small group broke off and curled south.

He stood there a moment, liking the weight of the rifle again in his arms and the smell of the late-summer prairie, the arch of the sky over the mountains.

He remembered when he was nineteen and trailing the buffalo between the Musselshell and the Milk, he and Bill Harmon trading hides for whiskey and roasting buffalo tongue over open flames with wolves and coyotes howling and the stars hanging low over the buttes.

He carried the Henry to his horse, ground-hitched nearby. An hour later he topped a ridge and smelled the creek hidden in the brush below. He rode down the ridge and followed the willow-choked canyon into a clearing where a slab shed sat before a grassy knob.

"Stop where you are."

The voice came from the cabin door. Stillman reined the bay to a halt.

"Who you ridin' for?"

"Myself. Name's Stillman. Are you Amiel Mundt?"

The man didn't say anything. His face was shaded by the cabin's overhang.

"Sophus Anderson sent me."

The man spat to one side. "He did, did he?"

"He wanted me to make sure you and your wife were all right."

"Tender of him, after calling my banknote due. Him and Hobbs send you?"

"I came here from Great Falls to find out who killed Bill Harmon. He was a friend of mine from the old days."

The man stepped out from the doorway, squinting and holding a carbine. He was tall but whittled down to bone and hard muscle.

Stillman guessed he was around forty-five, though years in the saddle had made him look older. He had a thin patch of black hair behind a sharp widow's peak, and cautious, deep-sunk eyes. His chin stuck out like a cancer.

"Sophus Anderson was a friend of mine," he said. "I borrowed money from him for years, and I always made good on it. Now he says I'm too big a risk."

The man's eyes were wide, his back taut. "I'm a respectable man. I pay my bills. All I want is a piece o' land and some cattle to graze, and now people I thought were my friends want me out."

"Who's at the root of it? Hobbs?"

Another voice said, "Who the hell else?"

Stillman looked at the outhouse on the cabin's left flank, where a man appeared pointing an old Springfield rifle in Stillman's direction.

The man planted the rifle butt on his hip and walked

toward Stillman, who nodded. "I'm Ben Stillman."

"Warren Johnson," the man mumbled. He blinked and stared warily.

He appeared mid to late fifties, short and swarthy, with forearms the size of tree trunks and a big, pockmarked face. His red-rimmed eyes and knob nose webbed with blue veins bespoke a drinking man. Stillman saw little resemblance to his daughter Crystal.

"Don't just stand there blabberin', Amiel," a woman called from inside the house. "Bring 'em in."

"You heard the boss," Mundt said. "Leave your hardware and come on."

He and Johnson walked into the house. Stillman followed after hitching his horse and taking a drink from a pipe running from a hillside spring.

The cabin was small and ramshackle, with homemade furniture, a two-burner stove, and curtains made from flour sacks. It smelled like old bear rugs and boiled meat. The head of a mountain lion snarled over the fireplace. For a feminine touch, a blue parakeet twittered in a wire cage next to the stove, and a red geranium bloomed in the kitchen window.

"Mary, this is Mr. Stillman," Amiel told his wife. "He was a friend of Bill's."

"Pleased to meet you, Mr. Stillman."

"Likewise, ma'am."

"I'm sorry about Bill. He was a friend of ours, too. He played his fiddle for us winters."

A thin but stalwart-looking woman with deep lines around her eyes, she set an extra plate and cup at the scrubbed-pine table. Her hands were as gnarled and callused as any man's.

"Sit up," she said. "Like I told Warren, it's not much,

but I wasn't expecting company." Stillman knew it was an explanation, not a reproach.

During dinner, Mundt said, "Sorry about the greetin' we gave you, but we can't be too careful around here. And when I saw the Harmon brand on that bay, well . . ."

"I understand," Stillman said, cutting the tough, stringy beef. He guessed it was the shoulder of an old bull Mundt had dragged from a draw. "It's just too bad such pretty country has to be molested by cattle rustlers and hired guns."

"Didn't used to be that way," Mundt said. "We all used to get along around here—all through the Two Bears. When a man's fence was down and he didn't know it, his neighbor'd fix it for him. His cows got out, his neighbors helped get 'em in. We worked together, like one big spread. Then Hobbs got greedy and decided he needed more land."

He bit into a sourdough roll and chewed, wagging his head with disgust.

Johnson studied his plate with a frown. "I don't know, Amiel. Sometimes I think we oughta just sell out, try our luck elsewhere."

"You're no more in favor of that than I am, Warren."

"Why not sell?" Stillman asked. "If Hobbs wants your land that bad, maybe he'd give you a good price for it."

"He offered half what it's worth."

"You can't dicker with him?"

Mary Mundt cleared her throat. "Hobbs can offer all the gold in heaven, but I won't leave my boy."

"Boy?" Stillman asked.

A hush fell. Johnson drank his coffee.

Mundt sighed. "We had a thirteen-year-old son. He died two years ago."

"I'm sorry," Stillman said with a wince. "Was it the flu?"

"At first I thought so," Mary Mundt said. "But he was fox-bit."

"Rabid fox," her husband added.

"He's buried on that hill there where he used to play," Mary said, nodding out the window. She turned to Stillman, her eyes hard. "I won't leave him here alone."

There was another silence. Then Mundt's voice rose several octaves, changing the subject. "Warren here's been hit by Hobbs, too, haven't you, Warren?"

Johnson snorted and sipped his coffee. "They took six of my year-olds last week."

"Cut your fence?" Stillman asked.

Johnson nodded, chuffed a curious laugh. "Left enough tracks for a rodeo yard."

"Did you report it?"

"Why bother?"

Mundt jumped in. "The law around here is owned by Hobbs."

Stillman studied Johnson. Fidgety and flushed, he was a curious old sot. Was he conniving or just shy? "Did you get a look at any of the riders?" Stillman asked him.

Johnson pursed his lips and shook his head, not meeting Stillman's gaze. "Happened at night."

Mundt cleared his throat and absently brushed crumbs around the table with a large, callused hand. "We don't need to see who's stealing our cows. We know it's Hobbs. Hell, I've seen his men herding stolen beef at high noon! If I see 'em again, I'm gonna get Johnson here and a few others, and start shootin'."

"Why don't you let me look into it for a day or two before you declare war?" Stillman said. "If I can find proof it was Hobbs or his men who killed Bill Harmon, we'd have enough cause to wire the territorial marshal in Helena.

If murder's involved, he'll make this dispute a priority. He'll send deputies.''

"What kind of proof you need?" Johnson asked.

"Well, we're not going to get anything solid because there were no witnesses, and I doubt there are any tracks left. But if we can find who's stealing cattle, odds are we'll find Bill's killer. If we find his cows, too, the killers will swing for sure."

Mundt looked at Johnson. "Nothin's for sure around here, is it, Warren?"

The blood vessels in Johnson's nose expanded. He scowled and shook his head, mumbling, "Nothin'—that's right."

Stillman caught himself staring at Johnson and wondering why the old goat seemed so edgy, and quickly covered it with a sigh. "I'll ride south and see if I can't track those herds," he said.

He had Mundt draw him a map of all possible rustling corridors leading toward the Missouri River breaks. He mopped gravy from his plate with a roll and finished his coffee.

Rising, he said, "Ma'am, I'm much obliged for that wonderful spread."

But Mary Mundt was still staring out the window at her boy's grave.

Stillman rode south, following Mundt's map through brushy ravines and draws, anywhere a rustled herd might be driven. For two hours he saw little but game trails, line shacks, eagle's nests, and occasional abandoned home-steader cabins—Hobbs's influence, no doubt.

His heart quickened when he came across a cattle trail pocking a wide ravine. He followed it up and down the coulees for close to an hour before realizing it was taking

him back toward town. Doubting that even the dullest-
witted rustlers would head their stolen beef toward Clantick, where they'd be easily noticed, he stopped in a glen
to water his horse and shape a cigarette. Licking the paper,
he glanced northward.

Two columns of black smoke curled over the grassy
hills.

He'd seen enough brushfires to know it wasn't brush
burning. He looked around. Getting his bearings from the
peak he'd been keying on, he stared at the smoke again,
furling his eyebrows.

Buildings were burning.

As much from the sick feeling coming over him as from
the distance and direction of the smoke, he knew that the
Mundt cabin was on fire.

11

Rounding the last curve in the trail before the Mundt ranch-stead, Stillman smelled wood smoke laced with kerosene. Then the trees opened and he saw the fire-engulfed barn and cabin and felt the hot wind spawned by the flames.

"Mundt!" he yelled above the fire's roar, looking around through the heavy black smoke while holding the fright-ened horse's reins taut. "Amiel! Mary!"

Dismounting, he saw Mundt lying beside a corral post and ran over to find blood pouring from the man's chest and head. After checking for a pulse and finding none, he looked around for Mary and discovered her sprawled by the water trough before the cabin, one bullet through her wrist, another through her chest, and an oval daguerreotype of a grinning, towheaded boy of about twelve clasped in her hand.

Stillman pulled the bodies under a tree.

Glancing around for a sign, he discovered two shell cas-ings by the corral, and foot- and hoofprints near the cabin. He separated the tracks his own horse had left earlier from a single set of two.

There was another set—probably Warren Johnson's—leading north. Stillman frowned at the tracks, wondering whether luck or cunning had saved the rancher. Had he set up his neighbors then slipped out before the blood flowed?

Stillman swung into the saddle and followed the two horsemen east through woods, across White-Tail Creek, and up the steep, grassy slope of a shaley dike. At the base of a tall rock he discovered a freshly discarded kerosene can.

At the dike's crest he saw that the riders had stopped, probably to blow their horses and look behind them. Knowing he could have been spotted from there, Stillman warned himself of a possible ambush. But he was soon so caught up in his tracking that he didn't see the rider on the ridge above him until smoke puffed from the man's carbine.

The bullet whined past the bay's ear. Startled, the horse threw its head sideways and bucked, and Stillman hit the ground on his butt. He reached for the reins, but the bay tore off down the trail, kicking, until it disappeared around a hill.

Hunched in the grass, Stillman looked around. The rider was coming down the ridge. Another approached from the trail behind him. He had nowhere to go but into the brush on the other side of the trail.

He ran hard and fast, keeping his head down, dodging deadfall limbs and hawthorn spikes. He pushed through willow thickets and cattails, jumped a deadfall log, and high-stepped through a knee-deep creek.

Gaining the opposite bank, he burrowed through the willows and lay several yards from the water on his belly, trying to quell the labored rasp of his breathing.

He listened.

He could hear fleeing deer snapping twigs and thrashing brush, the scratching of the reeds around him, the distant screech of a hawk. A beaver slapped the creek. Then he heard voices—men's voices in the distance.

They were moving closer.

". . . can't see a damn thing in this brush . . ."

"Keep lookin'. I know he's in here."

"Shit, he coulda—damn!"

"What?"

"Nothin'. I flushed some ducks."

"Keep lookin'."

"You don't have to tell me to keep lookin'. That's the bastard that shot Kenny."

Stillman lay quietly, his face to the ground, soaked from the waist down. Gradually the voices faded.

Then he heard a horse approaching. It came from a long ways off to stand only a few feet away in the willows. Stillman smelled the rider's cigarette and the sweet-musky smell of mink. He lifted his chin and craned his head to take a look.

Through the swaying weed tops he saw the head and shoulders of Delwyn Sleighbough.

He carefully thumbed back the hammer on his Army Colt and turned to face the man. He suppressed the urge to shoot him, for the shot would bring the other and who knew how many more? But if he needed a shot, he wanted a clean one.

Sleighbough sat his mount, looking around and smoking. The hawk feather in his hatband nodded in the wind, and his frizzy red hair flapped on his collar. His brown horse stared at Stillman, rolling its eyes and nibbling its bit. Stillman's heart drummed in his ears.

He jumped when Sleighbough shouted, "He musta moved on up the creek!"

There was no reply.

"Shit," Sleighbough muttered. He reined his horse and rode off through the weeds. Stillman sighed and depressed the hammer.

He waited there for two hours, until the sun was halfway down the sky. Then he moved, one step at a time, through the weed-choked wash carved by the creek. It took him a long time to make the bottom of the low, wooded hills rising on the wash's far side.

He found a draw with a feeder creek running perpendicular to the main bed and followed it until it ended at a rock wall. He sipped from a spring pushing up through mossy stones, backtracked, and started up the side of the draw along a winding deer trail, pausing for breath behind scattered clusters of ponderosa pine.

As winded as an old nag, he chided himself for his three-year debauch. His heart pounded and his ears rang, making his head hurt. At the peak, he collapsed on his hands and knees, fighting for air.

He felt the cold steel of a pistol barrel press against his forehead.

"Howdy, Mr. Chicken Farmer," Delwyn Sleighbough said. "You're a dead man."

"You gonna talk about it, or you gonna do it?" drawled another.

Stillman looked between Sleighbough's knees and saw a cowboy sitting against a tree in a broad-brimmed hat, cream duster, woolly chaps, and a brace of mismatched pistols.

His wrists resting on his knees, he casually chewed a long grass stem. He had a nose like a weathered ax handle and eyes as hard as granite. His Fu Manchu mustache hadn't been trimmed in months.

Stillman squinted. "You Weed Cole?"

"None of your fuggin' business."

"I'm gonna shoot you now, you old bastard," Sleighbough said, pulling Stillman's pistol from his holster. "What do you think of that?"

"You two kill Bill Harmon?" The wind blew up the draw and whistled in the trees.

Cole looked at him, working a wad of tobacco in his cheek, a slow smile pulling at the dark brown mustache curving around his mouth. "Yeah, we killed Harmon."

"What for?"

The gunman shrugged, spit a line of chew in the grass next to Stillman's face. "Fun."

Sleighbough cut the man a look. "What are you talking about, Cole?"

Stillman took the opportunity to wrap his arms around the big rider's knees and flip him over backward.

The gun fired into the air. Stillman grabbed it from Sleighbough's hand and turned to shoot Cole, his thumb peeling back the hammer. As it locked, Cole, standing, blew the pistol out of Stillman's hand, ripping two inches of skin from his middle finger.

Cole yelled, "Del, you moron!"

Sleighbough stood and retrieved his hat, his face flushed with rage. "You're gonna pay, Mr. Chicken Farmer. You're gonna pay."

He spat dirt, snugged his hat on his bushy head, and stalked over to his horse standing in the trees. He returned with a lariat and a bullwhip. Cole watched him, amused.

Sleighbough's eyes were like embers. His jaw was set in a hard line. "Take your coat off."

"It's chilly."

Sleighbough brought up his pistol.

Stillman shrugged, slipped out of his mackinaw, and tossed it to the ground.

Sleighbough twirled a loop around Stillman's waist and drew it tight. He pulled him to a tree and tied him there. Then he produced a knife from his belt and cut a line down the back of Stillman's shirt and underwear, tearing with his

free hand, laying the white, rounded shoulders bare. The
sudden exposure raised goose bumps.

Sleighbough stepped back and twirled the bullwhip.
"This is for Kenny, chicken farmer." He lunged forward
and slammed the leather against Stillman's back.

The pain skewered like a hot sword. "You bastard!"
Stillman grunted.

"Did you like that?" Sleighbough snarled. "Well, here,
have another!" He grunted as he pulled back the whip,
whistling it through the air in a wide arc and heaving it
forward to crack into Stillman's naked back with a report
like pistol fire.

Stillman winced, cursing and seeing red. He pressed his
cheek against the tree, bracing himself for the next blow.

Sleighbough stepped back and dropped the whip. He was
angry and wild but calculating.

He took off his filthy buckskin jacket and rolled his shirtsleeves up his big, freckled arms. Then he picked up the
whip and stepped up to the tree where Stillman hung like
a carcass.

The ex-lawman could hear Sleighbough breathing
through his nose. He could smell him, the mink odor min-
gled now with sweat.

"You ready? Here it comes, chicken farmer!"

With a high whistle and a sharp crack, Sleighbough tattooed another welt to Stillman's back. Stillman's agonized,
involuntary grunts and curses followed the bullwhip's whistles and cracks for several minutes. They echoed off the
ridges, sending birds screaming from the trees.

Weed Cole grinned and shook his head and spit tobacco
at Sleighbough's boots.

Then the grunts fell to a murmur. Then they died.

And all that echoed were the whistles and cracks of the
bullwhip.

"You have enough?" Sleighbough said at length.

There was no reply. Stillman hung against the tree, un-moving, half kneeling, his arms lashed to a limb above his head. His chin sagged to his chest, his salt-and-pepper hair lifting in the breeze. His back was as red as a side of beef.

Sleighbough chuckled, breathing hard, and wiped the sweat from his forehead. "I know *I* have. I'm plumb wore out!"

Weed Cole stood and drew his pistol.

"No. He's mine," Sleighbough said.

He untied Stillman and returned the rope and whip to his saddlebag. Turning from his horse, he drew his pistol, and fired at the tree where Stillman lay slumped against the bark.

12

Jody Harmon cantered his buckboard down **Main Street** in Clantick and pulled up at Hall's Mercantile. He set the brake, stepped onto the loading dock, **and pushed through** the shop's double doors.

"Boy, those buggies get fancier every year," he said, regarding the top buggies hanging upside down from the high, tin ceiling.

"Don't they?" said Mrs. Hall, a big, gray-haired woman in a blue calico dress with white lace.

She stood behind the counter cutting wedges out of a wheel of yellow cheese with a butcher knife. "The salesman claims they'll be running all by themselves before long. Won't even need a horse."

"That's salesmen for you."

"What can I do for you?"

Jody pulled a long piece of notepaper from his pocket and set it on the counter. "Here's my list. I'll run over to the blacksmith, then load up the wagon on my way back to the ranch."

Mrs. Hall pressed the wrinkles out of the paper and looked at it, tentative. "Oh my," she said, her big, high-pitched voice quaking. "This is quite a list."

"Something wrong?"

"No. It's just . . . well, I think I'll have Mr. Hall talk to you, Jody." Flushed, heavy brow furrowed, she turned and started for the back room.

Jody frowned, tipped his dusty hat back on his head. "If it's my credit you're worried about, Mr. Hall told me he'd stake me through the winter."

She looked at him, hesitant and nervous, her big bosom heaving. "I'd better get George." She turned clumsily through the curtains at the end of the counter.

Mr. Hall appeared several minutes later, chewing his lunch and looking flushed. A male version of his wife, he was a big, round man with fine, gray hair swirling around the pink crown of his head and eyes the soft blue of spring ice.

He wiped his hands on his apron and said tightly, "Hello, Jody."

"What's the problem, Mr. Hall? You said you'd stake me through the winter. You know I'm good for it."

"I know you're good for it, Jody." He set his elbows on the counter and leaned forward, clasping his small, pale hands together. "Here's the deal. I'm not good for it. I'm the one. Business—well, it's been tough lately. And . . . well . . ."

He shrugged his big shoulders and scowled at the tobacco tins under the glass countertop before lifting his eyes to Jody's. "Times are tough."

"At Pa's funeral, you said you'd help me any way you could. Well, I said you could help me out by extending my credit. I'd pay you back in spades and be a steady customer for you, Mr. Hall—just like my pa always was."

"Your pa was a loyal customer, that's true. Everyone liked Bill. But dammit, Jody, business is business."

"You're about to lose your shirt here, huh?" Jody said,

glancing around at the merchandise stacked on shelves and on the floor and hanging from the ceiling.

The bell over the door rang, and Sophus Anderson walked in.

"Hi, Jody."

"Mr. Anderson."

"How's things out at the ranch?"

"Tough, and they just got tougher."

Anderson set one elbow on the counter and sucked a tooth, the overhanging lamps glinting in his spectacles. "Well, business is tough, Jody. The mercantile business, the banking business, and the ranching business. It's all tough."

"This sounds like the same chat I was just having with Mr. Hall. Ain't that a coincidence?"

"You know how many young men your age can ranch alone and turn a profit?" Anderson said.

"I know one that can."

"Jody, why don't you sell that place? Maybe cowboy for a while. Sock away some money. Or at least try it somewhere it's not so damn tough, and you don't need so damn much land to profit."

Jody squinted his eyes, crossed his arms, and sighed. "You're calling my banknote due, ain't you, Mr. Anderson?"

Anderson and Hall shared a glance. "Jody . . ." Anderson said.

" 'Jody' yourself," Jody snapped. "I know when I'm getting greased for the pan. Hobbs has put the screws to you both to cut my credit and drive me out."

Hall's big face colored to the crown of his head. He looked at Anderson, then at Jody, his soft blue eyes sheepish and agitated. "Jody, that isn't true."

"He killed my pa, not expectin' I'd take over for him.

Now he's getting you two to cut my credit and drive me out.''

Hall shook his head, looking at Anderson for help. "That's just not true," he said unconvincingly.

"What's he gonna do next—have Weed Cole shoot me like he did Pa? . . . Don't tell me it ain't true when I know it's true. Why else would you cut my credit only two weeks after extending it? You're knuckling under to Hobbs because he's got an interest in this store and because you got as much spine as a pile of dogshit."

"Now, listen here," Hall warned, pushing himself off the counter and taking a defensive stance.

Jody ignored him. Turning to Anderson, he said, "When's my note due?"

Anderson dropped his eyes. "One month, the first of November."

Jody glared at him, said in a pinched voice, "You son of a bitch."

Hall roared, "I won't have that kind of talk in my store, Mr. Harmon!"

"You're a son of a bitch, too, Hall. A fat, lyin', cheatin' son of a bitch! You both got my pa's blood on your hands!"

"Get out! Get out!"

Anderson only stood there, looking down through the glass countertop.

Jody edged away, his face flushed with anger, darting harsh glances between the two men. "You both need a horsewhippin'!"

Just then, Sheriff Ed Lewis walked in with a deputy Jody recognized as a part-time drover known for beating up women in the local hog pens. They both carried shotguns.

"That's enough, young Harmon. What's all the yellin' about?" Lewis said. His white Stetson came up only to the deputy's shoulder. As if to advertise his authority, he pulled back one side of his suit coat to reveal his badge pinned to a wool vest.

"This is between me and these two businessmen here, Sheriff."

"Doesn't sound like business to me. Sounds like you're makin' threats about horsewhippin'. That's assault." Lewis looked at Anderson and Hall. "Would you men like to press charges?"

Jody snorted, incredulous. "Charges!"

"Not if he leaves now," Hall said.

Anderson didn't say anything. He was still looking down through the glass countertop.

"Todd, escort Harmon to his wagon," the sheriff said. "Make sure he leaves town. If he comes back within a week, arrest him."

"It'd be my pleasure, Sheriff," the deputy drawled, a light in his eyes. "Come on, you dirty Injun."

Jody knew it would be a mistake to do anything but walk out of there, climb into his wagon, and drive home. But when the deputy jerked his arm behind his back and pushed him toward the door, screwing his wrist until his arm nearly popped from its socket, the lid blew off.

Jody ripped his arm from the deputy's grasp and smashed his right fist into the man's jaw. Todd staggered back as Jody swung again, catching him square in his unguarded stomach. The man dropped his shotgun and hit the floor cursing, bringing a display of soaps and colognes down on top of him.

"You half-breed son of a bitch!"

Jody had just turned to the other men, poised for an assault, when the sheriff poked him in the head with the butt of his shotgun.

"Take him over to the jail and lock him up."

The deputy got up biting his lower lip and blowing through his nose, his face as red as a branding iron. With one hand he dragged Jody to the door like a sack of grain.

"You think you're smart, don't ya?" he snarled. "But you're just another dumb Injun to me."

He maneuvered one of the two doors open and jerked Jody onto the boardwalk.

The sheriff, Hall, and Anderson stood in silence after the door closed, staring out at the street.

"Well, that's that." Lewis sighed.

"Let him go," Anderson said.

Lewis looked at him. "What?"

"Let him go."

Lewis looked at Hall. Hall pursed his lips and nodded.

Arching his eyebrows and shrugging, Lewis said, "If you say so." Then he wandered out.

"Well, he had one thing right," Anderson said to Hall at length.

"What's that?"

"We are sorry sons of bitches."

13

That afternoon, Crystal Johnson rode into her sister and brother-in-law's ranchstead and found Marie lugging a full water bucket across the yard toward a bonfire burning by the chicken coop.

"Marie, what on earth?" Crystal said, reining her horse to a halt beside her sister, a somber, hardworking woman five years Crystal's senior.

Oval-faced, with long, straight blond hair in need of washing, she had Crystal's green eyes but little of her spirit.

"Hi, Stormy," she said in her dreamy, singsong voice.

Crystal slid out of the leather and grabbed the bucket. "Give me that. You're seven months pregnant, Marie!"

"Oh, Stormy, I'm not helpless."

"Do you want to lose another one?"

Marie put her hands on her hips and straightened her back, trying to ease the strain of the child in her belly, putting her face to the afternoon sun. "These chickens need butchering before it snows. You know how fast that can happen around here."

"Where's Ivan?"

"He and Zachary are herding their steers to town. I thought I'd surprise them by getting the flock butchered and dressed. You know how tired Ivan gets after a day in the saddle.''

"Oh, Marie!''

Crystal hung the bucket on the rod-iron frame over the fire and turned to her sister. "You sit down on that stump over there, and I'll butcher the chickens.''

Marie obeyed and gave Crystal a nervous smile. "Stormy, Dad's here.''

Crystal shot a look at the corral, where Warren Johnson's gray mule stood twitching its ears at flies.

"What's he want?''

"He wants to see you.''

"Well, I don't want to see him.''

Marie stretched out her legs and arched her back, wincing. "He came this afternoon, just after Ivan and Zach left with the steers. He's been sitting at the kitchen table for the last hour, talking to himself and crying. He's been saying your name over and over. Maybe you should talk to him.''

"He's drinking, isn't he?''

Marie nodded solemnly and looked off in her dreamy way.

"I have nothing to say to the man.''

Marie turned to her slowly and retrieved a windblown lock of hair from her face. "He's your father, Stormy.''

"He's never been a father to me or to you or to any of us.''

"He's weak, Stormy, that's all. Weak and scared.''

"You used to tell me that with bruises covering your face.'' Crystal pulled the ax off the chopping block and inspected the blade. "Has this been sharpened?''

"Yes.''

Crystal chucked the ax back into the stump and walked to the chicken coop, returning with a red rooster. She swung the screaming chicken's head onto the block and chopped it off with one quick swipe of the ax, then held the bird by its feet while it jerked and flapped its wings. Blood like red string stained the ground.

"I don't understand you, sis. How many times can you forgive him?"

"Sometimes it's not a matter of forgiveness. Sometimes it's just a matter of understanding."

"And you understand him?" Crystal regarded her sister uncomprehendingly as the rooster's death spasms subsided. "Is that why you married a man just like him?"

Marie's eyes dimmed and filled with tears. She put her hands on her pregnant belly and sobbed.

Crystal sighed and dropped the chicken. She knelt down and clasped her sister's hand. "I'm sorry."

Marie took her hand and held it to her cheek. Then she saw something behind Crystal and gave a start.

"What's goin' on?" The voice was deep and muffled, like distant thunder.

Warren Johnson stood over them, hatless, his hair matted, a faded cotton shirt sticking out of his torn jeans, a tin cup in his hand. His eyes were red-rimmed and swollen. Crystal could smell the pungent corn whiskey on his breath.

"We're just talkin', Daddy," Marie said in her little-girl voice. "Just catchin' up."

"Hello, daughter," he said to Crystal.

"Hello."

"What's new?"

"Nothin's new."

"That's no way to talk to your old man."

Crystal didn't say anything. Kneeling there beside her sister, she stared at the hard-packed ground dusted with oats and straw.

Marie said, glancing at the sun, "Lordy, look what time

it is. I bet Daddy's ready for his afternoon coffee, aren't ya, Daddy?'' She heaved herself up from the stump and slinked off to the house.

Warren Johnson adjusted his crotch and sat on the stump. He sipped from the cup and swallowed, pinching his face. "Hellfire, Ivan's mash tastes worse than the stuff we used to sell to the Injuns!"

"What are you drinking it for, then?" Crystal said with disgust.

She walked into the chicken coop, found another chicken, returned to the stump, and lopped its head off. Her father watched her with a dour, drunk expression on his pockmarked face.

She tried to ignore him, dunking the spasming bird in the scalding water, laying it on the rough plank table used for butchering, and going to work on its feathers.

Johnson cleared his throat, said thickly, "Hey? I was hopin' I could talk to ya."

"What about?"

He stared at his cup. "I want you to come home."

"No."

"I'm askin' you now, polite-like. I ain't tellin' you. I know how you take to bein' told."

"Thanks for asking, but I'm staying here."

He fell silent, a brooding, angry look on his face. Watching her expert fingers plucking the chicken and dropping the feathers in the empty nail keg beside the table, his eyes suddenly turned rheumy. His chest heaved.

"Crystal, I feel bad," he said to his cup.

"What do you feel bad about?"

" 'Cause you don't care about me. None of my kids care about me. You won't come home, and I can't do nothin' with ya. Everything I say gets twisted and throwed back in my face, like I'm the bad one, I'm the only bad one."

She rolled her eyes and didn't say anything. When she finished with the chicken, she went and got another. He stayed there, sipping thoughtfully from the cup.

Why don't you just leave? she wanted to shout. *Please, please, please—just go away!*

"It ain't like I ain't done nothin' wrong. I know I done wrong by ya. I done wrong by lots o' folks. I ain't a saint, and I'm sitting here now with my hat in my hands askin' if you'll forgive your old dad."

Crystal looked at him curiously. Somehow he sounded more contrite than usual. She frowned. "Who else have you done wrong by, Pa? Anyone in particular?"

His features froze. He turned away, troubled. "No, I . . . I just know I done wrong, that's all. . . ." His voice trailed off.

"Okay, you're forgiven," she said finally. "Now, I've got lots of work to do here, and it's getting late. . . ."

She wondered how many times she'd told him she forgave him without forgiving him. It was like a game.

He cleared his throat. "So what do you say? Will you make up with your old dad and come home?" He tried a smile.

"No." Here it comes, she thought. She felt her muscles clench, as if warding off a blow.

She remembered the night he'd come home from town after learning she'd started seeing Jody Harmon. Sitting at the supper table with her mother and brothers and sisters, she could tell by the staring, angry look he gave her through the meal that he'd learned about her and Jody from his gambling and drinking buddies, who had no doubt rubbed his face in it.

Still, she wasn't prepared when, as she cleared the table, he suddenly grabbed her hair, jerked her to the floor screaming, and dragged her to the door amid the sounds of breaking dishes and the screams and cries of her brothers and sisters.

"What did I tell you about sleepin' with Injuns, girl!" he roared, throwing her into the muddy yard. "Maybe this'll learn ya."

Then he'd slammed the door and didn't open it again until morning. She'd slept, cold and wet and muddy, under an old cattle blanket in the barn.

He stared at her now for a full five minutes without saying anything. It was the stony stare he'd given her the night he'd found out about her and Jody, and which always sent goose bumps down her back.

"It's that half-breed, ain't it? You're shacking up with him now."

She didn't respond.

"Is that right? Am I right? You shacking up with Harmon's half-breed buck?"

She plucked the feathers along a wing and bit her cheek until her eyes watered.

"Hey? I'm askin' you a question." He reached out and grabbed the half-plucked chicken away from her, his eyes challenging, wanting a fight.

She turned and stalked back to the chicken coop, staring at the ground and fighting back tears of anger and heartbreak. When she returned, he was still there, staring at her with those strange, lightless eyes.

He watched her dress the chicken for about two minutes. Then he reached out, grabbed her by a belt loop, and swung her to the ground, yelling, "I don't want you screwin' that goddamn Injun, girl!"

"I don't care what you want!" she screamed, jumping to her feet and fisting her hands. "I don't care!"

She felt the dam of her anger break as she poised to defend herself.

He moved toward her on wobbly legs, the cup still in his left hand, clenching his right fist and drawing it back. She could tell from the thin smile wrinkling his grizzled cheeks that he didn't expect her to defend herself.

When she slapped the hand holding the cup, splashing his face with corn liquor, he inhaled hoarsely, shaking his head, and looked at her uncomprehendingly. Then the light of recognition shone in his eyes. The smile returned, only bigger.

"You bitch!"

She ducked away from his first swing, spinning him around, but the next one connected with her forehead, sending her to the ground on her shoulder and knocking the wind from her lungs.

Marie ran from the house, screaming, "Daddy!"

From the ground, Crystal said, fighting for air, "Go back to the house, Marie."

But Marie kept coming. "Stop it! Stop it!"

"Marie, go back to the house!" Crystal yelled again.

Marie stepped between them, begging them to stop. He pushed her away and she stumbled backward and fell.

"Marie!" Crystal yelled.

She started toward her sister, but Johnson caught her by the hair and swung her around. She drew her fist back and let him have it squarely on the eye. As he staggered back, he grabbed her collar, and they fell together in a heap by the chopping block.

Rising to an elbow, he glanced at the ax. She lunged for the chopping block and grabbed the ax before he got there.

He growled, "You think you can kill me, girl?" He smiled ominously. "Better. You better." His voice was low and eager and teeming with challenge.

She scampered back on her butt, pushing with her feet and holding the ax in both hands, her lips quivering and tears streaming down her face. "I will. I'll do it if you don't leave."

Still grinning, he retrieved his .31-caliber pocket pistol from his left boot and heaved himself up, his head swimming with alcohol and adrenaline, his mouth foaming like a rabid dog's.

Crystal looked at the gun, watched her father's thumb pull back the hammer.

"Daddy!" she screamed.

"Just savin' you from that savage, girl—that's all I'm doin'," Johnson said tightly, raising the gun.

Crystal screamed again and dropped the ax, reflexively drawing her own six-shooter from its holster, cocking it, and pulling the trigger. The slug hit Johnson's gun with a metallic bark, blowing it from Johnson's grip.

There was a silence.

Johnson stared at the fresh blood pooling between his boots, awestruck. He lifted his hand and saw the two fingers shot away at the second knuckle. Another finger hung by a thread. Blood stringed to the ground.

Johnson's mouth opened, his lungs filled with air, his head went back, and he bellowed like a foundering bull. It was a godlike scream of agony.

The corralled horses looked up from their oats, ears twitching.

He held the wounded hand to his belly, blood spraying on his shirt and jeans and face, his eyes wide with shock and pain and disbelief, his screams echoing around the barnyard.

Inside the cabin, a baby cried. Two dogs came running from behind the woodshed, looking guarded and sheepish.

Crystal reholstered the Smith & Wesson and ran to Marie, who'd gotten to her knees, holding her stomach.

"Are you all right?" Crystal yelled.

Marie nodded, swallowing, her hair in her face. "I'm all right. You go."

"I won't leave you."

"I'll be all right. Go. *Go!*"

Crystal glanced at her father, who lay curled on the ground, knees drawn up to his belly, crying and cursing and holding his bloody hand to his chest.

"I'll be at Jody's," she told her sister. "I'll be back."

She ran to her horse, climbed clumsily into the saddle, and galloped away.

Behind her, Johnson's animal wails echoed.

14

When Stillman rode up to the stables at the Beaumont ranch, Fay was saddling her pinto pony in wool riding slacks and light cotton blouse with a tabby cat named Scoundrel wrapped around her neck. Her hair curled down her shoulders beneath a black felt hat, and her perfume smelled like citrus.

Several hired men were loitering around the stables, bashful and hesitant. They wandered over to the corrals when Stillman showed up, casting jealous glances behind them.

"Where we going?" he asked her.

She peeled the cat off her neck and kissed its nose. She looked up at him coquettishly, brown eyes flashing. "You'll see."

They rode for an hour in the eroded, yucca-bristled buttes along the Yellowstone River. The summer sun was warm against his face, and the sage peppered his nose. A rattler poked out from behind a gnarled hawthorn, spooking their horses.

"I lost a good mare here when I was twelve," Fay said, when they rode onto a grassy shelf made hazardous by several large holes—some twenty feet in diameter—where cave ceilings had fallen in. "Father took away my riding privileges for a month. Then he bought me a Tennessee Thoroughbred for my birthday."

"I'm so sorry," he said ironically.

She led the way down a steep path that wound through pillars and dikes and leveled out amid river rubble where prehistoric bison bones and arrowheads winked in cutbanks.

He followed her into a cave. The air was cool, and a golden shaft of afternoon sun slanted through the open ceiling, where cliff swallows cooed and squawked. There were sand drifts moist from the previous rain. Boulders lined the chalky walls where roots webbed. The air smelled clean and earthy.

They dismounted and tied their reins to the roots. From her saddlebags Fay produced ham sandwiches wrapped in paper, apples wrapped in cloth, and a wedge of cheese she carved with an ivory-handled pocketknife. Handing him a bottle and a corkscrew, she said, "Open please?"

"What's this?"

"Wine I swiped from Father's cellar."

"How old?"

"Older than both of us put together," she said with a husky laugh.

They ate and talked on the floor of the cave. Then she took him exploring the paths where she'd played as a child—an only child whose sole companions were the conjurings of a vibrant imagination and animals.

"That's an old dinosaur tooth," she said, pointing out a large, wedge-shaped object in a sandstone wall.

Her eyes were bright and girlish and full of awe, her face flushed. He was amazed at how quickly she could go from being a woman to a girl and back again. "I looked it up in my science books."

He smiled, touched by her earthy beauty and spirit.

"I used to pretend I was an orphaned Indian girl surviving on my own—just my horse and I." She absently ran a long, slender hand along the clay-caked tooth. He couldn't help watching her breasts swell against the cotton blouse under her outstretched arm. "We hid here from enemies— hordes of them."

She dropped her arm and turned, smiling, catching him staring. The smile faded. She said matter-of-factly, "You can make love to me if you want."

He swallowed, felt his face warm. He cleared his throat. "I'm nearly old enough to be your father."

"What are you doing here, then?"

He didn't say anything. He felt a pull in his groin so strong that it took the words away, thoughts . . . everything.

They walked outside in the brush along the river, their horses following. She quickly removed her clothes and lay in the soft grass, stretching her arms above her head. He removed his corduroy jacket, freshly laundered jeans, pinstriped shirt, and suspenders, and entangled himself in her arms and legs.

Afterward he rolled a cigarette and smoked as she lay with her head on his chest, her long, black hair falling across his belly and groin. She talked about books she'd read, her favorite cats, and about wanting to be a teacher, though her father wanted her to marry a rich cattleman like himself.

"Will you?" he asked.

She lifted her head and gave him an incredulous look. "No!"

Her horse, which had been cropping grass beside them, nibbled her ear. She giggled, stood, and offered him a handful of oats from her saddlebag. Stillman admired her naked beauty—her long, slender legs, boyish buttocks, and firm, upturned breasts.

He got up and stood behind her, caressing her shoulders and belly, nuzzling her neck. He'd never been so drawn to a woman. At twenty-two, she was little more than a girl, but a woman just the same. She turned and kissed him, long and deep. Then her eyes misted, and she knelt down.

Crows cawed in Stillman's aching head.

His eyes opened. He thought for a moment he was on the banks of the Yellowstone.

"Fay?"

The name came out as a rasp.

The birds' raucous laughter penetrated deep into his skull, making his ears ring. A squirrel joined them with a high-pitched chortle.

Stillman moved his head and felt the rough bark scratch his cheek. Where was he? He should know, but . . .

The war in the tree above him continued, sending lightning bolts through his brain.

Then his vision cleared. The tree he was leaning against swam into focus, as did the brown, bloodstained leaves at its base. He was colder than he'd ever been. His lips quivered; his muscles twitched. His back felt as though it were covered with hot tar.

He remembered the smell of mink and the sound of Delwyn Sleighbough's grunts and the whistle of the bullwhip cutting the air.

"Ah . . . god . . . *damn*!"

Anger filled him. He summoned all his strength to his arms and pushed himself back from the tree and onto his haunches. The cold air penetrated his back like knives, and he lifted his chin, his mouth drawn wide and his eyes squeezed shut against the pain.

"Bastard. Goddamn bastard."

He remembered hearing a pistol shot. Looking down for signs of a bullet, he discovered dried blood on his left side, just below his armpit. With his finger he traced a bloody groove and a long flap of skin. He looked at the tree.

Sure enough, the bark was torn bullet-fashion.

"Not much of a marksman, are you, Sleighbough?"

He sat with his butt on his heels, breathing and trying to orient himself, to remember where he'd come from and where he'd have to go to stay alive. He knelt there, blinking groggily, and looked vaguely around for his coat but didn't see it. He assumed it was gone.

The cold wind numbed the taut skin over his shoulders. He had to get off the butte or he'd die.

Spurred on by the image of Delwyn Sleighbough swinging the whip against his naked hide, he pushed himself to his feet and slid on his hip down the steepest part of the butte, cursing and yelling against the pain in his back.

He pulled himself to his feet by a pine branch, and moved carefully down the slope, switchbacking around molehills, feeling his knees giving out.

He stumbled over a talus scar, fell, cutting his hands and arms. He lay there for a minute, panting and cursing and looking around, wondering if he should look for a shelter of some sort—a line shack or a cave. Build a fire and wait for morning.

But how could he start a fire with no matches, no flint, and no energy to gather wood?

"Ah, shit," he said, squinting around at the cold, darkening hills. He pushed himself tenderly off the rocks and stepped carefully over the scar, the stones grinding under his boots, the cold night breeze penetrating his bones, his back feeling as though it had been doused with kerosene and set aflame.

Near the base of the butte his foot slipped out from under him and he fell on his butt, slid, and tumbled headfirst to the bottom. He lay there, working against the pain and exhaustion, a frozen wheel rut jabbing his side.

How easy to fall asleep! He need only close his eyes and the pain would be gone.

A few days ago that's what he would have done. Not even the desire for revenge would have driven him on. He would have relaxed his muscles, pressed his cheek to the soft grass, and closed his eyes and slept until the raw cold of night settled and carried him off for good.

But behind Sleighbough's image was Fay's.

He pushed himself unsteadily to his feet and walked with half-shut eyes, remembering that the deer trail would take him to the creek. Across the creek he should find the main trail and, hopefully, his horse.

Like a man in a dream, he pushed himself along the winding path, his feet heavy, his knees numb, mumbling the name of the only woman he'd ever loved.

The agonized screams of her father resounding in her head, Crystal spurred the black mare down the two-track wagon trail leading east from her sister's ranch. She was crying loudly and wiping the interminable tears away with her hands, watching through the tears for the windmill that marked a shortcut to the Harmon ranch.

Approaching it, she turned left into a shaggy ravine and followed a freshet to its source in a cleft of rocks and fir roots. She spurred the horse up the low ridge, past the rocks, and over the divide.

On the tableland above, she gave the mare its head, screaming as she rode at the image of her father and all he'd done to her, all he'd done to his family, all the beatings and degradations that had led to her riding away from him, screaming, with his blood on her hands.

"I *hate* you!" she yelled.

When she came to a familiar crease at the left edge of the grassy table, she reined the horse down through a juneberry swale, across a narrow creek, and onto a trail flecked with deer scat.

She rode for a long time between fir-crowned ridges, her eyes a veil of tears, her lips shivering, replaying the image of the bullet hitting her father's hand over and over in her mind.

"Why did you make me *do* that to you!"

Suddenly the mare lifted its ears and turned its head, pulling right. Crystal obeyed the horse's warning and looked around, spotting another horse about a hundred yards off the trail, in a meadow at the base of Shambeau Butte.

It was a saddled, harnessed bay with its reins dangling. It watched her as though it knew her.

"Sweets?" Crystal said to herself.

She reined the filly to a halt and looked around, cleared the phlegm from her throat. "Sweets? That you?"

The bay lowered its head to crop grass.

Crystal spurred the mare in its direction. "Sweets, what are you doing here?"

The bay blew and rippled its muscles as she approached and dismounted. Running her hand down the gelding's fine neck, she looked around for Stillman, but there was no sign of anyone.

Glancing around her cautiously, she tied Sweets's reins to her saddle, mounted her own horse, and rode back to the trail.

For a mile she scanned the distance and the nearby brush, calling Stillman's name at the top of her lungs, but was answered by only the echo and the occasional peeps of chickadees and the wind ruffling the reeds along the creek.

Finally she saw a figure ahead—a man in a red shirt walking away from her with his head down, his shoulders hunched. He walked as though his feet were made of lead.

She spurred toward him and saw that the red on his back was not a shirt but blood—deep horizontal gashes of torn skin and half-dried blood.

Then she saw the thick, gray-flecked, auburn hair blowing at his neck.

Her chest tightened. "Mr. Stillman," she whispered. She reined up next to him and got down. "Mr. Stillman?"

He stopped and regarded her curiously, like a stranger. His eyes were rheumy and red and distant, his mustache nearly gray, his cheeks ashen. His quivering lips were swollen and blue.

She said, her voice cracking, "My God, what happened?"

He regarded her with unseeing eyes, his hair blowing around his face.

"Fay," he said finally, his voice raspy and hoarse. The corners of his lips attempted a smile.

"Fay . . . that you?"

15

"Fay?"

Donovan Hobbs turned on his side and propped his head on an elbow. Firelight danced on the fir-paneled walls. His wife lay curled on the far side of the bed.

"Fay?"

He couldn't understand why a twenty-eight-year-old woman slept so bloody much. Probably all the riding. But then, when she wasn't riding she was reading the thick, leather-bound tomes she'd brought from home, hardly looking up to give him the time of day.

The Beaumonts were a petulant lot.

First light smeared the windows; birds chirped. Beyond the drawn drapes voices rose from the bunkhouse. The men were stirring, getting ready to ride. Hobbs smelled the bacon frying in the cookshack.

He sat up, inspected his underdeveloped biceps, and grabbed his doughy belly. Even ranch work couldn't erase a lifetime of leisure in three years. Soon, though, he'd be breaking broncs and wrestling steers, just like his men.

Fay sighed, muttered something in her sleep. Hobbs raised his free arm, lifting the goose-down comforter and peering underneath. He gave an appreciative frown, groaning, and felt a stirring in his loins. He slid closer.

Fay lifted her head and turned to him, then turned away. "Donovan," she complained.

"Just looking, my dear."

"It's rude." Her hair was a lush, black fan on her delicate shoulders. Sleep graveled her voice. "Sounds like the men are waiting."

"Let them wait. I was wondering if we might give a go at some offspring." He slid next to her and brushed her cheek with his mustache, stroked her thigh.

She stiffened and pulled away. "The men, Donovan . . ."

He reached out and fingered her hair, giving it a little more than a playful tug. "We *are* married, my dear. I have the papers on you. Don't you remember?"

How could I forget? she wanted to say. "I'm just a little tired this morning," she said, staring at the wall.

He slid his hand under her nightwrapper, walked his fingers up her long, smooth thigh, across her belly, and squeezed a breast. She closed her eyes and bit her lip.

Finally Hobbs removed his hand and grunted. Cold bitch. "Well, get your rest by the time I return. You're gonna need it."

He rolled away, swinging his legs to the floor and cursing under his breath. He stood, unbuttoning the long johns he'd taken to wearing after coming west, and stepped toward the bathroom, where a freshly filled tub awaited.

After his bath, Hobbs dressed in a wool shirt, jeans, fringed buckskin chaps, and the snakeskin tie he'd bought from a cardsharp in Mandan, completing the frontier look he donned so carefully.

"Tell Julia," he called to Fay, "that I'll have my bath a little hotter tomorrow. Nothing worse than a tepid bath."

Before the standing walnut mirror, he brushed his long, golden hair across his shoulders, combed and waxed his mustache, smoothed his goatee, then snugged his round-topped plainsman hat on his head with a strategic tip.

He paused, gazing into his own eyes. Somewhere in a London orphanage there was a four-year-old boy with the Hobbs family eyes and mouth and rich, golden hair—his son, though only he and the mother knew that.

What was her name? June. She served during bridge games at the Kensingtons. He'd been drawn to her sparkly blue eyes, hair the color of autumn stubble, breasts like turnips though she was all of seventeen. He wondered if she was still boiling sheets at Kensington Manor, floating around the big ballroom in her maid's skirts and dusting cap, offering cognac to the gamers.

He grinned. Fay might resist his charms, but that spry little tart from Kensington had all but mauled him.

Ernesto Bodio was tending a fire in the massive sitting-room hearth when Hobbs strolled down the staircase. Decked out like Buffalo Bill in Deadwood, Hobbs looked more like a goddamn fairy than a rancher, Bodio mused.

"Good morning, Mr. Hobbs," Bodio said with an Italian roll.

The Englishman nodded in the servant's general direction, producing a cigarette from a silver case lined with corrugated velvet. He bent to a lantern, lighting up, then strolled down the hallway of the main entrance, his white angora chaps buffeting and his Spanish spurs jingling like sleighbells.

The old servant looked at his wife, who was kneading bread in the kitchen doorway, and growled in Italian, "Dickless little worm."

In the Harmon kitchen, Crystal plucked a chicken carcass from the boiling water pot and set it aside while she spiced the broth, softly humming a song she'd learned in school.

She felt at home in this cabin, with its leather tack, mounted birds and elk heads, rough plank cupboards, mismatched cooking utensils, and flour-sack curtains.

There were always overalls, boots, and old yellowed magazines scattered about, and Jody was forever leaving his leather-tanning projects on the dinner table. Any femininity that Mrs. Harmon had brought to the place had long since vanished in the four years since her death.

Still, Crystal felt more at home here than she ever had in the ramshackle cabin she'd grown up in. There was love and tradition here, the clutter of wholesome industry. There was the prospect that she and Jody would carry on his parents' work and names here, too.

Crystal had covered the simmering broth and was tearing apart an old quilt for bandages when thumps and muffled curses carried from the bedroom. She moved to the door with worried eyes, and pushed it open.

"Mr. Stillman?"

He was on his side, grunting and cursing, trying to bounce himself out of bed. He stopped, looked at her, and sighed. His face was white, his hair disheveled. The blankets and quilts were twisted around his legs. "My jeans. Hand me my jeans," he said, catching his breath.

"Whatever for? You're sick."

"I'm feelin' better."

"You look like hell."

"How long I been here?"

"Just yesterday and today. I found you along the trail night before last. Don't you remember?"

He shook his head. "All I remember is Sleighbough and Cole. . . ." He sniffed and hacked up phlegm, weakly cast his arm toward the chair where his clothes hung. "Please hand me my jeans."

She folded her arms and stomped a boot. "I should say

I won't. I didn't dress those wounds just so you could break 'em open again.''

She pushed gently on his shoulders. Too weak to struggle, he gave in, slid back, and slowly dropped his face to the pillow, wincing.

He gave a ragged breath. "What's on my chest?"

"Jody's ma's concoction against pneumonia. One lung's teetering on the edge."

"It smells like hell."

"The sickness thinks so, too." She pulled up the covers and smoothed them across the large bandage on his back. "Are you hungry?"

He jerked his head sideways.

"You have to eat. I got chicken soup on. It'll be done soon."

After a moment he said, "I can't remember your name."

"Crystal. It's the concussion. You're at the Harmon ranch."

Stillman nodded, his chest wheezing. "I'm out of here tomorrow. I got scores to settle."

"We'll see."

The front door squeaked open, boots thumped, spurs jangled, and Jody stood in the doorway, flushed from riding.

"He awake?" There was a charcoal bruise around his left eye and a half-inch scab on his right cheek. He held a ten-gallon hat, buckskin coat, and pistol.

Crystal nodded.

His voice raspy and muffled, Stillman said, "Don't worry, young Harmon. I'll be back on the trail tomorrow."

Jody set the coat and pistol on the chair. "I was curious about where it all happened, so I checked it out. I found your stuff scattered in the trees."

Stillman's only reply was a long, belabored snore.

Jody looked down at him with pity. He turned without even glancing at Crystal and stomped out.

She followed, frowning, and gently latched the door behind her. Jody lifted his rifle from the rack by the door and walked out of the cabin.

"Where you goin'?" Crystal called.

He walked resolutely toward the barn, where his horse was tied to a hayrack.

"Where you goin'?" she called again.

His back to her, he leveled open the rifle breech, inspected it for shells, then slid the weapon into his saddle boot and grabbed the horse's reins. "I'm gonna go have me a talk with Donovan Hobbs and Weed Cole."

"Oh, that's smart."

"Smart or not, it's high time someone did somethin'. If Stillman's too damn broken-down to do it, maybe I can."

"And get yourself killed!"

He mounted his horse and looked at her angrily. "I have seventeen steers left, a handful of cow-calf pairs, and no bank or store credit. The deputy sheriff made burger out o' my face, and any day Hobbs and Cole are gonna come by and set my house on fire—unless I settle with them first."

He spurred his horse, and the gelding sprang off its hind legs.

In one fluid motion, Crystal slipped the rifle from its boot. "That's gonna be hard without your long gun."

Jody looked back at her, reining his horse around, his face bunching with annoyance. "Goddammit, Crystal Johnson, hand it over!"

She turned defiantly, walked into the barn, and poked the Winchester in a hayrack next to the oat bin. Jody stomped through the door as she was turning around. "Where is it?"

"I'm not telling you."

"I have another rifle in the house, Crystal."

She lifted her chin and wrinkled her nose. "Go get it, then."

He gave her a hard look, then turned and walked away.

"Jody . . . please don't," she said weakly, grabbing her arms, sobbing.

He stopped and looked at her. His expression softening, he sighed.

She choked and gave him her teary eyes. "Oh, Jody— you're all I have!" Her chest heaved, and she let out an anguished cry.

He wrapped her in his arms. "Crystal, what's wrong?"

"Pa, he . . . tried to kill me."

"What!" He pushed her back to look at her face, exasperated. "Why?"

"We were arguing about you and me again. He was drunk." She lifted her eyes to his. "I shot his hand . . . I—I was aiming for his gun and I shot his *hand*." She bit her lip, mouth drawn wide with sorrow.

He engulfed her again in his arms, rocking her gently as she sobbed against his chest. "Shhhh," he said. "It's all right now. Your pa ain't comin' near you ever again."

"I don't wanna lose you."

"You ain't gonna lose me. I lost my head there for a minute, that's all."

"You promise?"

Jody nodded. "I see us raising a family here, building on what my parents started."

He held her for a long time, rocking her gently. After a while they went back into a stall. He sat against the partition. She sat between his knees and leaned back against his chest.

He held her, lightly kissing her ears and neck and cheeks. They talked for a long time, hearing only the wind catching under the eaves and blackbirds flocking in the meadow.

Jody cleared his throat, gave a yawn. "Well, I reckon the horses'll be lookin' for their supper," he said, pulling away from her. "Not to mention, Mr. Stillman."

"No—wait," she said, turning to him. Her eyes were bright with urgency. "Let's stay here awhile longer. Please?"

"Crystal, honey—"

Her voice rose sharply, with mock anger. "If you don't want to make love to me, Jody Harmon, just say so."

He relaxed, looked at her blinking. "Mr. Stillman—"

"Is asleep. I'll check on him later."

She lifted her chin, laced her hands around his neck, and kissed him. Her mouth opened and she pushed her tongue against his, her breasts flattening against his belly.

Finally she sat up and looked at him seriously.

"Are you sure?" he said.

She bit her lip and nodded, blond hair falling in her eyes. She smiled.

Jody got up and took off his boots and watched as she unbuttoned her jeans and slid them down to her ankles, forgetting about her boots and having to work to get them off—wrestling there on the floor of the stall with her jeans around her feet.

She laughed, tossed a boot against the wall with a hollow bark, and went to work on the other, grunting, her hair in her eyes, her smooth neck flushed.

"Jesus," she said, tossing the second boot over her head. "Here we go."

She grunted again, kicking out of her jeans. She sighed, dropping her hands to her thighs, and looked at him sheepishly. "That wasn't very ladylike, I know. Your turn."

With a self-conscious grin, he removed his shirt, jeans, and socks. Finally he unbuttoned his long johns, peeled them down his arms and legs until they were piled around his ankles.

"The rest," he said.

She stood and unbuttoned her shirt and shrugged it off, then unbuttoned the undershirt and let it fall to her waist. A thin, knowledgeable smile crossed her mouth.

His knees weakening, his breath coming in short bursts through parted lips, he watched. Her round, pink breasts shone tender and firm in the dim light. He cupped them in his hands. She held him in hers, moving gently up and down until her silky fingers and warm palms brought him to a boil.

His breath caught in his throat. His chest heaved. "No . . . God!" He stumbled into her arms.

She gave a startled, "Oh!" and they fell together into the straw, laughing.

"Sorry about that," he said at length, panting and nuzzling her neck.

She was trembling uncontrollably now, as if a floodgate had opened. She snuggled against his chest and put both arms around him and squeezed him fiercely, sobbing, as if to quell the emotion washing over her.

He bent slightly and put his right hand behind her neck and his left behind her knees and moved her to the back of the stall where the straw was deeper.

Then he disappeared and returned with a blanket. She felt the warm, rough wool slide beneath her back and naked thighs. He knelt down, and his strong hands gently parted her knees. She sobbed quietly.

"Are you all right?" he asked.

She nodded.

"Should I stop?"

"Don't you dare."

He slumped down to her.

"Oh," she whispered.

"All right?"

"All right."

His hands were under her, his palms lifting. Her mouth closed over his shoulder. She shook and quivered beneath him, then responded to his tempo, her hips rising and falling with his.

Long after they'd fallen into a deep, afternoon sleep, Jody heard the door open and felt a draft.

"Hello, Jody. I see you're keepin' busy." It was Sophus Anderson, poking his long, hickory face over the stable partition.

Dazed, Jody looked around, saw Crystal curled at his side. "Oh, Christ!"

Crystal looked up, blinking, gave a scream, and pulled the blanket over her head.

The banker gave a bemused chuckle. "I'll wait outside," he said, and headed for the door.

16

When Fay heard the men leave, she rose and went out to the stables to saddle her favorite gelding for a morning ride. With all the ranch hands gone, there was an almost ethereal hush over the corrals and outbuildings.

Rosy light brushed the tips of the surrounding knobs, and the yard was a haze of blue shadows and misty edges. The cow ponies watched her quietly, their heads over the top corral slat, chewing their morning hay.

She loved these times alone. She could be herself now, without Hobbs, and forget the emotional mire her life had become.

"Hello, Banjo," she said, offering an apple. The tall, white-booted black dropped his head and sniffed the fruit, tickling her with his whiskers.

She ran an appreciative hand down the gelding's neck, then retrieved her gear from the tack room and coaxed the bit through the horse's teeth. He jerked his head.

"Oh, come on, Banj—none of your antics this morning, huh?"

Something rustled in the hay. Fay glanced toward the sound, then wrapped the bridle over the gelding's ears. "There. That wasn't so bad, was it?"

A stone bounced off the stall partition with a crack. The horse started, pressing Fay against the stall. She pushed the animal away with a grunt and looked around.

Blue morning light shone through the cracks in the chinking between the wall logs. Beyond the sashed windows the bunkhouse squatted near the corral, a ribbon of smoke thinning from its bent metal flue.

''Grubber?''

She stood between the stalls, listening.

The October wind sighed under the eaves and creaked the timbers. Horses blew and knocked their stalls. A distant heifer bawled for its calf.

''Who's there?''

Banjo stomped a hoof.

She turned to him. ''I'm coming. . . .''

A second stone arced before a window and hit the wooden oat bin with a hollow knock.

She turned and put her hands on her hips. ''Okay—very funny. Who's there?'' Her heart thumped and her stomach fell.

A horse nickered, stomped its hoof.

''You're frightening the horses.''

Scowling, she edged down the alley toward the far doors, looking from side to side. At the last stall, she held her breath and leaned forward to look behind the partition. A fly struggled in a web over the window. She felt a chill.

Angry, she turned and filled her lungs to speak, but before she could get the words out, she was flung sideways into the hay with an enormous weight on top of her.

The wind burst from her lungs in a clipped yell.

''Good morning, Mrs. Hobbs,'' the man said into her ear. He smelled like old leather and tobacco.

She struggled, filled her lungs again to scream. A hard-callused hand clamped over her mouth. A knife tip poked the soft flesh beneath her chin.

"You don't want your pretty throat cut, do you?"

He looked at her with raised eyebrows. "Don't scream."

She nodded almost imperceptibly, and the hand came away from her mouth.

She breathed.

He rolled to his side, looked her up and down, and grinned. "Lordy, you're a piece o' work!"

His windburned, unshaven face leaned close to hers, bathing her in hot, pungent breath. A tobacco-stained mustache horseshoed his mouth, greasy and wild.

"Who are you?" she asked, though she already knew. He was the gunman Ben had told her about, Weed Cole. The one who'd leered at her from Donovan's office the other night.

He pressed against her and whispered, "Secret admirer."

"Oh, God. Please let me go."

"Not until I see what was under that buffalo robe you was wearin' the other night." He laid the wide blade of the hunting knife against her buckskin coat and sliced off a bone button, then another, her arms pinned above her head with his other hand.

He opened the coat to her man's denim shirt, his eyes those of a man before a long-sought treasure. In one motion he stripped the shirt open. The buttons disappeared inside her coat.

"No," she whispered, the tears starting.

"Oh, Mrs. Hobbs. Don't cry."

"My husband will kill you for this."

He opened his mouth, widened his eyes in mock fright. "Oh, no. That big, nasty man!" He laughed derisively, unbuttoning his pants.

"Mrs. Hobbs?" a voice called from a distance.

Cole turned an ear to listen.

"Mrs. Hobbs?" It was the broken English of Ernesto Bodio.

Fay lifted her chin and yelled, "In here, Ernesto. In the stable." She hoped her voice, thin and spent, carried beyond the stable walls.

"Shit," Cole grunted.

Sheathing the knife, he gazed into Fay's eyes with the two spent embers of his own. "I just now staked a claim on you. Mr. Hobbs or no Mr. Hobbs—you're mine."

He fixed her with a wordless stare, then rolled aside, got to his feet, and threw open the two sliding doors.

As they knocked closed, the doors at the other end of the alley parted with a heavy rasp. Morning light poured around the short, stooped silhouette of Ernesto Bodio.

"Mrs. Hobbs?"

Fay's heart pounded. Feeling weak and sick to her stomach, she climbed to her feet and brushed the hay from her hair and clothes and pulled her jacket closed. She wanted to cry, but she got control of herself, cleared her throat.

"Yes, Ernesto."

"You have a visitor up at the house."

"Who is it?"

"Mr. Anderson from the bank." There was a pause. He squinted and shielded his eyes with his hand. "Something wrong, signora?"

What could Ernesto do? Any recourse would have to wait. She shook her head, moved toward the doors. "I'm coming."

Walking toward the house with the servant, holding her coat closed with both hands, she looked around for Cole, feeling her primal fear of the man in her stomach, in the sweat on her palms. She could tell Donovan, but what good

would that do? Ben had told her Cole was a gunman, a
cold-blooded killer.

She pegged her hat and scarf in the foyer. "Ernesto,"
she said, forcing a smile, "would you tell Mr. Anderson
I'll be a moment? I made a mess of myself out there."

She turned past the dining room and climbed the stairs.

In the bedroom, she changed her shirt and straightened
her hair, choking back tears. She sat on the bed, fists
clenched, composing herself. Then she washed her face,
touched perfume to her neck, and, chin up, went downstairs.

In the sitting room, overlooked by Donovan's game tro-
phies, Sophus Anderson sat on one end of an overstuffed
davenport angled before a sparking fire. A shaft of golden
light played across the buffalo-calf rug beneath his polished
shoes.

Donovan had had him out for dinner once or twice, but
she understood their relationship was only business. She
couldn't imagine what he was doing here at this hour.

"Mr. Anderson, what a nice surprise," she said with
forced cheer.

He set his coffee cup on its saucer and worked his way
out of the deep leather couch. "Good to see you, Mrs.
Hobbs."

His face flushed, betraying his embarrassment. She'd
long since grown accustomed to her effect on men, and had
assumed an informal air to set them at ease. But the affec-
tation was difficult now, and she found herself uneasy in
the presence of another male.

"Please sit down. I was just preparing my horse for his
morning ride. If I don't work him every day, he thinks he
owns the place. How is Mrs. Anderson?" she asked, keeping up appearances.

"Very well. I'll tell her you asked."

"More coffee?"

"Please."

She sent for Julia Bodio and sat in an armchair across from her guest. When Mrs. Bodio had come and gone, replenishing Anderson's cup and filling one for Fay, Mrs. Hobbs dropped a sugar cube in her coffee and smiled.

"So, tell me. To what do I owe the pleasure of such a distinguished guest? I take it Julia told you Donovan isn't here."

He smiled uneasily, adjusted his glasses. "Yes. I came to see you."

Her own smile in place, she studied him from head to foot with mistrust. He appeared older than she remembered. When he had struggled up from the couch, it was with the mechanical stiffness of the arthritic. His face was puffy and pink. He appeared harmless enough, but her suspicion was fueled by his business ties to Donovan.

Uncomfortably he set his coffee cup and saucer on the arm of the davenport, asked sheepishly, "Do you mind if I smoke?"

"Not at all."

He produced a cigarette from a gold, monogrammed case, tapped it, vaguely looked around for a match, then got up and strode to the fire. His large white eyebrows bunched in thought as he took a twig from the kindling box, set an end in the fire, then touched the flame to his cigarette.

Smoking nervously, he turned and pronounced in a high, strained voice, "I think it best if Donovan doesn't learn of my visit this morning."

"Why?"

"Because I'm here about Ben Stillman."

She stiffened. "I see."

"You and he are . . . friends, I take it?"

Looking for a sign of his intentions, she said, "How did you know?"

"I saw you outside his hotel-room door his first night in town. I was coming up the stairs for a private poker game."

He raised his hands. "It was a coincidence, I assure you. I have no intention of using the information against you in any way."

"Then why are you telling me this?"

"Two days ago he had the holy hell beat out of him and was left for dead."

She set her elbow on the arm of her chair, rested her head in her hand. "How bad?"

"Exposure, exhaustion, possible pneumonia in one of his lungs."

She stood and held her arms as if chilled. For years she'd managed to put him out of her mind while unconsciously taking comfort in knowing he was out there . . . somewhere.

"Where is he?"

"The Harmon ranch."

"Who did this? Was it Donovan's men? Was it Weed Cole?"

Anderson pinched his cigarette between his thumb and index finger and considered it. "Range disputes are like wildfire. They generate their own fuel. I don't know who's responsible for what anymore."

She smirked. "Mr. Anderson, you know and I know that my husband is behind this."

He said nothing, only studied the floor, smoking.

Her brown eyes lit by the dancing flames, she leaned toward the banker. "I have to see him."

He lifted his chin, meeting her gaze. He pursed his lips and nodded. "For your own safety, I have to advise against it." He lowered the cigarette and knocked ashes to the hearth. "But I figured you would."

17

"Take the steers down to Goodnight on the river," Donovan Hobbs ordered. "Count them before he does. If I find out he's number fudging, I'm going to feed him to my hunting dogs. Tell him that."

Delwyn Sleighbough nodded, the enormous hawk feathers in his hatband bending in the breeze. "Yes, sir, Mr. Hobbs."

"I'll expect you men back at the ranch tomorrow night before sundown."

"Yes, sir."

Hobbs watched the rider gallop toward a herd of longhorns at the bottom of a long, grassy mesa.

They were culling the herds in the southern Two Bears, at the western crook of White-Tail Creek. It was Indian-summer warm and the black flies were biting. The rising dust irritated his sinuses.

One of the cowboys yelled, indicating a rider making his way through a notch in the ridge behind Hobbs. The Englishman turned to watch Weed Cole approach.

A mischievous smile straightened the gunman's mustache. Smug bastard. "Just where in the hell have you been? I've been looking for you for the past two hours."

142   *Peter Brandvold*

"My horse turned up lame. Had to stop and doctor a crack in his hoof."

"That's funny—it looks fine now."

"Well, I'm a good doctor." Cole smiled.

Hobbs regarded him skeptically. He hated the man's casual insubordination but had found the other hands were more respectful when the gunman was around. Business transactions flowed more smoothly as well.

Another rider approached at a gallop, batwing chaps flapping. "Mr. Hobbs, that crazy Dutchman in Hungry Hollow said he wouldn't leave and we could all go to hell."

Hobbs sighed and rolled his eyes, his sallow cheeks reddening. "These people are one headache after another. Where is he?"

"He and his hired man are holed up in their cabin."

"Lead the way, Mr. Duffy."

Hobbs and Cole followed the cowboy up a switchbacking game trail and over a grassy ridge. Halfway down the other side they heard sporadic bursts of rifle fire.

"I offered that man good money for range he has no legal claim to, and this is the thanks I get!" Hobbs yelled.

Weed Cole rode behind him, grinning.

Dug into a low hill and fronted by a small corral and pole barn, the cabin sat in a hollow filled with ash and tangled box elders. A creek trickled over a wide, stony bed. A handful of scrub cows stood in the water, which barely covered their hooves, chewing and dully watching the three riders approach.

Four of Hobbs's men, armed with Winchesters, had taken cover behind trees. Two sat on the hill above the cabin, pointing their carbines at the sod roof from which a tin, bullet-riddled chimney tilted.

Hobbs, Cole, and Duffy halted their horses behind a

sprawling, fork-trunked box elder about seventy yards from the cabin door.

Regarding the structure, Weed Cole said, "Shit, they could hole up in there till the cows come home. Who knows how far they're dug into that hill!"

A figure appeared in the cabin window. "Leave us be! Git! We ain't comin' out!" The man's voice was shrill with fear. He poked a rifle through the broken glass, fired, and ducked away.

Two riders returned fire.

Hobbs waved them off. "Hold your fire! Hold your fire!" Turning to the cowboy, he said, "Burn 'em out."

"We done tried that, Mr. Hobbs," Duffy said. "The grass won't take. It's still wet from last night's rain."

Hobbs eyed the cabin and considered the information. "Well," he said at length, giving Cole a cool, self-confident look. "I think it's time for a little British ingenuity."

"With all due respect, that British ingenuity might just get your ass greased," Cole drawled in his Missouri twang.

Ignoring the remark, Hobbs pulled a thick leather wallet, pen, and traveler's ink vial from his inside coat pocket. He gave the vial to Duffy, who held it while Hobbs inked the steel-tipped pen and scribbled a check, tilting his head sideways and pressing his tongue to his lower lip.

"That should do it," he said self-importantly, returning the wallet, pen, and ink to his pocket.

"What are you gonna do?" Cole said.

"You'll see, Mr. Cole. You'll see."

The Englishman dismounted, gave his reins to Cole, and stepped out in front of the tree.

"Mr. Hobbs," Duffy warned, cutting his eyes at Cole.

"He's just showin' off," the gunman growled.

Hobbs removed his cartridge belt and holster, held them

above his head in one hand, the check in the other. He
yelled at the cabin in his high, screeching accent: "Mr. Van
Orsdel. I have a check here for your land. I'm going to
bring it to you. I'm unarmed. No tricks. Then my men and
I are going to leave."

"Crazy bastard," Cole said under his breath.

Hobbs dropped the gunbelt and, head erect, started across
the barren, deep-rutted ground before the cabin. The check
ruffled in the outstretched hand above his head.

"Mr. Hobbs!" someone yelled.

Hobbs raised his other hand and continued walking, not
stopping or looking back.

"He's even dumber than I thought," Cole said to Duffy.

"He is—he's just showin' off, ain't he?" Duffy said.

Hobbs was halfway across the meadow, the small, gray
cabin growing before him. The window frames were dark,
edged in torn newspaper curtains and broken glass. Several
badger and beaver hides stretched on the log wall. He
watched the bullet-splintered door, the check ruffling in his
left hand, the other swinging freely.

He figured Van Orsdel and his hired man were covering
him, letting him get as close as he wanted. "As you can
see, I'm alone and unarmed, Mr. Van Orsdel. Please don't
shoot."

He walked up to the door and knocked.

"Mr. Van Orsdel, this is Mr. Hobbs," he announced. "I
think it's time to discuss this situation like civilized human
beings."

Several seconds passed.

Then the latch rattled, the door opened a crack. A nose
poked out. Two eyes stared.

"Mr. Van Orsdel, I am a businessman, not a killer.
Please open the door and let me say my piece."

The eyes blinked, amazed. Van Orsdel fell back, pointing

the rifle from his shoulder. He was tall and thin with a long, hooked nose, clean, hairless face, and two sets of brown curls parted by a bald swath. His hawklike eyes were bright with fear.

Hobbs stepped in. "Here is a check for your land," he said.

The man looked at the paper. He licked his lips. "How much?"

"Five percent above the going price."

The man studied him suspiciously. He cut his eyes to another man sitting against the wall, the man's elbow on his knee, resting his cheek in his hand. He could have been reposing there after a hard day's work. Blood oozed between his fingers. He seemed too tired and in too much pain to meet the other's gaze.

"No," he said weakly, shaking his head. "It's a trap."

Van Orsdel looked at Hobbs. "How do we know it ain't?"

"You have my word as a gentleman and a subject of the Crown. I am a businessman, not a killer."

"Horseshit. It's horseshit, Gunther," the wounded man said.

"What if we don't accept?"

"Then we burn you out and steal your cows," Hobbs said matter-of-factly.

Van Orsdel gritted his teeth, raised the rifle. "You snakey bastard—where do you get—"

Hobbs raised his voice, his long hair brushing his shoulders with each syllable. "If you shoot me, sir, you will get nothing!"

He stared into Van Orsdel's enraged eyes. It was one thing to shoot a man from a distance, when you couldn't see his eyes. It was another to shoot him from only a few feet away.

The man reached out his hand and grabbed the check.

"Don't do it, Gunther," the wounded man pleaded.

Van Orsdel looked at the paper, then at Hobbs.

Hobbs held the double-barrel derringer he'd just shaken from his sleeve. He fired before the man could tighten his trigger finger. His forehead exploded, blood and bone spraying the wall behind him. He jerked back, fell to his knees, slumped down, and fell on his face.

The other man held his head in his hands, sobbing. "I told ya . . . I told you not to do it," he said.

Hobbs held the pistol to the man's thin, sweat-matted hair. "Tsk, tsk, tsk. What a pity he wouldn't listen," he said, and pulled the trigger.

He turned and walked back to his horse, basking in the stares of the men coming out of the trees.

"Thought you said you didn't want anymore killin'," Cole said.

Hobbs climbed haughtily into his saddle. "Those men were . . . *filthy*."

Fay led the gelding from the stables, one of Hobbs's pistols in her hand, looking around for Weed Cole, not wanting another encounter but wanting one, just the same. She'd never shot anyone, but she could put a bullet between those dull eyes of Cole's, and she would if she got the chance.

She wrapped the reins around the saddle horn, pushed a boot through the stirrup, bounced on her right foot, and propelled herself into the leather.

Following Sophus Anderson's directions to the Harmon ranch, she rode as the crow flies—cross-country, avoiding roads and popular trails, not wanting to be seen. She knew Donovan's malevolent mind well enough to realize that if he ever grew suspicious of her . . .

Several creek fordings and ridge climbs behind her, she

rode into a wide ravine in the shadow of Long John Butte. A dense conifer forest rolled down the southern slope. The northern slope was gentler and covered with long, rusty grass, with here and there a wind-gnarled fir and scads of mule deer shaded in the pines along the rim.

The intermittent cracks of a distant rifle invaded the dense silence.

They came from a mile ahead and grew louder as she rode. She reached into her saddlebag for her pistol and held it in her lap, calming Banjo with occasional words of encouragement, stroking his neck.

The trail rose and descended for another mile, the shots growing louder, until a log cabin, barn, and corrals spread out below. She followed the trail down the rise, which leveled out at a Texas gate on which the Harmon name had been burned.

Passing through the gate, she looked around.

No one appeared on the cabin steps to greet her. The windows were dark. Across the hard-packed yard, the barn doors yawned wide. Before them, a dog hunkered under a hay wagon, yipping at each rifle report echoing off the ridges.

She spurred the horse across the ranchstead, following a stock trail through the meadow behind the barn until she neared the willows along the creek. A long-haired girl in a sheepskin vest and jeans stood in the meadow. Beyond her, a man lay against the creek bank, where the willows opened.

He wore a red-and-blue-striped blanket coat—the kind she'd seen Indians wear—and a ten-gallon hat. With a carbine propped on the bank, the stock snugged against his cheek, he was shooting at rocks in the eroded clay bank across from him.

The gun flashed and boomed. His shoulder jerked.

As Fay approached, recognition grew in the girl's eyes. She answered the woman's inquiring glance with a shake of her head and a shrug, turning again to the man with the gun.

Fay approached him with hesitation, unsure of herself, frowning, tilting her head to catch a glimpse of his face.

He raised the gun, resting the barrel on the bank, took aim, and fired. The boom was like a cupped hand hitting her ears. The gelding whinnied.

The man's back stiffened. He turned awkwardly, swinging the rifle around, his eyes wild. She stopped, flinched, certain he was going to shoot her.

He squinted, the gun held before him, a cigarette in his teeth. "Fay," came the gravely baritone.

With his haggard face and slumped shoulders, he could have been Ben Stillman's older brother. Even so, her heart lifted.

"You shouldn't have come here," he said. But his eyes betrayed him.

Suddenly she was choking on tears and jumping from her horse.

He pulled himself slowly to his feet, holding his back straight, the big coat hanging awkwardly from his shoulders. She ran to him, and he opened his arms.

"Fay," he said, smiling wanly and dropping his cigarette.

She kissed him deeply, savoring the taste of him, and thrust her face against his chest. Through the coat, she felt the heavy bandages on his back, heard the phlegmy rattle in his lungs. . . . But he was alive. He hadn't left her.

He held her there, smoothing her hair, rocking her gently, and calling her name. She cried as freely as a child, safe at last in his arms.

18

Under a golden canopy, Stillman and Fay sat beside a spring creek, on a wool blanket, in a high-walled ravine deep in the Two Bear Mountains. It was cool and bright. Nearby, freeze-dried chokecherries clung to branches with only a few remaining leaves, crimson now with the early mountain fall.

They'd managed to meet secretly three times since she'd first come to him a week ago. Stillman was recuperating from his wounds, which Crystal Johnson had doctored after consulting her *Home Medical Advisor*. Fay was reading aloud to him from a leather-bound book as worn as old saddle leather.

"The immortals will send you to the Elysian plain, at the ends of the earth," she read slowly, carefully enunciating every word, "where fair-haired Rhadamanthys is. There life is supremely easy for men. No snow is there, nor ever heavy winter storm, nor rain, and Ocean is ever sending gusts of the clear-blowing west wind to bring coolness to men."

"Not bad," Stillman said. "Who wrote it?"

"Homer."

"I'd forgot you liked poetry. Does your husband know you come here and read Homer?"

She laughed. "He'd think it very suspicious. He's a businessman. He looks at the world in terms of pluses and minuses."

" 'Many evil men are rich, and good men poor, but we shall not exchange with them our excellence for riches.' "

She frowned. "Who's that?"

"Don't recall."

She closed the leather-bound volume and held it in her lap. "You're an educated man, Mr. Stillman."

"Montana winters get long even for lawmen."

"Yes, I remember. You liked Mr. Emerson."

"Still do."

She had brought them lunch in a picnic basket. Fried chicken, potato salad, sourdough biscuits, and rhubarb pie.

"Open this?" she said, handing him a corkscrew and a bottle of wine.

"Whoo-eee." He chortled, reading the label. "Chato dee bla—"

"God, forget what I said about the education." She laughed.

"Raiding the master's cellar again, Mrs. Hobbs?"

"You know how much that cost?"

"More than I made in a year protecting the public, no doubt."

"Considerably."

He filled their glasses, counting on her presence to keep him from bingeing. Besides, he'd never been a wine drunk. "Cheers," he said, nudging her glass with his.

They sat together under the balm of Gileads and drank the wine and ate the chicken and potato salad and bread and followed it with rhubarb pie.

The breeze was cool and rife with the mossy smell of the creek and the cinnamon smell of turning leaves. Stillman felt at ease for the first time in days.

Fay laughed as they talked, threw her hair out from her neck, and leaned back on her elbows, closing her eyes and lifting her chin to the speck of sun filtering through the leaves. He rolled a cigarette.

"Roll me one?"

"Why, Mrs. Hobbs . . ."

"Stop calling me that."

He gave her a cigarette and she took it delicately between thumb and index finger and drew on it. Exhaling smoke, she studied the burning ember.

"Not bad, huh?" he said.

"Not bad. I wouldn't make a habit of it, but not bad."

"It doesn't burn your lungs?"

"I'm not a sissy," she said, drawing on the cigarette again. She lifted her chin to exhale. "I can shoot straighter than my husband, ride better, and I'm sure I could drink him under the table if I ever got the chance." Her cool eyes settled on Stillman, and she smiled defiantly.

"Do you love him?" he asked. His jealousy chafed, but he couldn't help himself.

She leaned back and the pale sunlight rested again on her face. The smile had disappeared without a trace. "How like a man to ask such a question on such a lovely day."

"I'm sorry."

She didn't say anything for a long time. Then: "He doesn't love me, either."

"Did you ever?"

"I thought I did . . . once. I wanted to because Father wanted me to. I had nothing else and he offered so much. He even seemed—you know—exotic, with the accent and all. I was young, and you can make yourself believe anything, you know."

"I do believe life has jaded you, Fay."

"I was born jaded. I was just happy when we were to-gether."

"Me, too."

Stillman finished his wine, got up, and gingerly moved his shoulders to loosen his back. The wounds had scabbed, and most of the pain was gone, but he had to be careful not to stretch the tender skin and open the sores.

"How 'bout some water to chase the wine?"

She shook her head.

He'd offended her, he knew, and he wasn't sure how to undo the damage. I'm too damn stupid for the likes of her, he thought. Feeling like a fool, he turned and followed a deer path to the creek, filled his glass with water, and re-turned to the blanket.

"My turn to ask a tough question," she said.

"Uh-oh."

"Why did you leave?"

Stillman sighed and looked off, as if the answer lay in the willows screening the creek. "Not to place blame—it was my own damn fault—but your father asked me to."

Fay looked at him sharply, her eyes growing cool. Her thick black hair fell over her face when she lowered her head to study the glass in her hands.

There I go again, Stillman thought. He shoved a curl back from her cheek. "Hey, I didn't tell you that to turn you against your pa. He was a good man."

"A nosy man, prying where he didn't belong."

"He was a father," Stillman said forcefully. He shrugged. "It made sense. He wanted you to marry a good man who could give you the kind of things you were raised with. That man certainly wasn't me."

"No, it was Donovan Hobbs," she said sardonically.

"Speaking of him, we can't meet again for a while," Stillman said, changing the subject.

She lifted her chin, shook the hair from her eyes. "What are you talking about?"

"I'm going after him."

"Alone? That's crazy."

He scratched his forehead. "I'm gonna track the rustled herds. I'm guessing he's keeping them separate from his own. He'll move them all at once instead of risking several trips. Where and when I don't know, but when I find out, I'll wire the territorial marshal in Helena."

She gazed at him. "Then what?"

"He'll send deputies."

"No. I mean you and me."

"That's up to you."

Her gaze shifted to the grass beneath her knees, and she got a troubled, faraway look. "Ben . . ." she said at length, furling her eyebrows. She wanted to tell him about Weed Cole and how afraid she'd become. Fearing even more the danger Ben's anger could drive him to, she changed her mind.

"What is it?"

She shook her head, reached for her glass. "Nothing."

Not wanting to put his foot in his mouth anymore today, he stood and snugged his hat on. "I reckon we best head back."

She looked at him, frowning. "Really? What time is it?"

He glanced at the sun. "Pret' near four, I'd say. Hobbs will be wonderin' where you are."

"I beg your pardon, Mr. Stillman, but I can take care of myself."

"Fay, don't you think it's best if we—"

She stopped him with a poignant look. "You can make love to me if you want."

Suddenly bashful, he dropped his gaze and stammered. "Why . . . I figured you were mad at me."

Her eyes glistened. "How could I be mad at you? You're my knight in shining armor."

His ears turned red.

"Come here," she said.

He knelt next to her on the blanket, and she put her arms around him. She looked into his eyes and smiled. He kissed her, long and deep. Her lips were full and sweet tasting. She pulled away, smiled again, then rose to her feet. She undressed before him, removing her blouse last. A breeze stirred, and the goose bumps rose on her full, round breasts.

He stood, and she helped him with his shirt and jeans, both of them breathing heavily, laughing nervously. She lay back on the blanket, and he positioned himself between her fine legs, lowered his head to her breasts, and felt her whole body quiver. She moaned softly and called his name.

"It's been so long, Ben," she said softly. "So, so long."

"Fay . . . you don't know how much I regret—"

"Shhh . . ."

If they'd possessed the acute hearing of a predator—a wolf, say, or a mountain lion—they might have heard Weed Cole on the ridge above them. Perched on a rocky escarpment and tilting his head to see through the trees, he focused his spyglass on the coupling lovers below.

"Either I'm seein' a ghost or I gotta stop leavin' a man's work up to the likes of Delwyn Sleighbough," he drawled.

He ground his teeth and shook his head at Stillman's hands on Fay's naked back as she worked away on top of him. "Tsk, tsk, tsk. Naughty, Mrs. Hobbs. Very naughty."

The next morning, the screech of a golden eagle followed Stillman along the ravine bottom like fingernails on slate, and his laudanum hangover fuzzed the world like the morning mist that crept up between the pines and scrub cedars around him.

Having turned cold during the night, it was misting, and if the mercury kept falling, it would soon be snowing.

"Friggin' mountain weather," he said to no one.

The trail was pocked from cattle and horses and littered with deadfall. He coaxed the horse with gentle commands. The brush rustled and hooves thumped in the woods to his right. He slipped his pistol from its holster in one quick motion, thumbing back the hammer.

The horse stopped abruptly, jerking its head and twitching its ears. The deer arced across the trail in a brown-and-white blur. Flag waving, it disappeared in the woods at Stillman's left.

He lifted the pistol barrel and released the trigger, shaking his head and emptying his lungs with a sigh. "It's okay, Sweets," he said. "Just a little spooky is all."

He came to a bowl in the ravine where a stock pond sank, its two or three inches of glassy black water rippling fallen leaves, twigs, and cottonwood seed. A few yards up the ravine sat the windmill tower Jody and his father had been building before Bill was slain.

Stillman crawled out of the leather, wincing against the pain in his injured back, and tied the bay to a tree. Sweets chomped his bit and dipped his head, agitated. Could the smell of his old rider linger here?

The ex-lawman walked around the tower, frowning. Just north of the structure the grass was splashed with brown blood. There were several sets of horse tracks, but all distinguishing marks had been weathered away.

Near the tower, where the wind and rain had left it alone, one impression of a split rear hoof remained clear. Stillman had checked the feet of the Harmon horses present that day. None had a split hoof. He stared at the track, bit his upper lip. He'd bet good rib steak against army biscuits that this print belonged to the killer's mount.

Nodding, he observed it more closely. From its depth, he judged the rider had been mounted when the print was made. The way it and the faded other three were angled, he judged it was an old animal, probably on its last legs or that had been ridden a long ways with little rest.

He backed up and turned, for several minutes appraising the grass in a fifteen-yard radius as though he'd lost something. He stopped, squinted, and leaned down.

He straightened slowly, studying a shard of glass from a pint jar. Bringing it to his nose he sniffed. Nothing. But what besides whiskey would find its way here in a pint jar? He had to remember to ask Jody if his father had taken to drinking on the job.

He dropped the glass when something else caught his eye in a clump of buffalo grass. He picked it up and studied the brass rifle casing between his thumb and index finger. It was from a .45/70 favored by old hunters and soldiers. The day he was killed, Harmon had been packing a .56 Sharps.

Stillman pocketed the casing and, after finding no more, mounted the bay and rode up the canyon, through the crease between two mountain slopes carpeted in knee-high buffalo grass. He followed the winding ravine for five miles, until he topped out on a saddle overlooking the Clear Creek Valley.

He halted Sweets, grabbed the cantle, and stretched his tender back, wondering why the person who'd killed Bill hadn't taken his cattle or cut his fence. Maybe, as Jody had speculated, Bill had foiled their attempt. Or maybe they hadn't come for his cows. . . . Stillman chuffed. Craziest damn country he ever saw.

From where he sat his mount under breaking clouds and in a warming wind, he watched the taut strands of Glidden wire. Stumbling southward over tawny benches to the long coulees beyond, they vanished finally in the rising mass of the southern Two Bears.

Stillman shook his head. There were eighteen miles of fence along this western boundary of the Hobbs ranch, and another twenty-five on the eastern edge. Hobbs's range pushed south into the Missouri River breaks. It had to have taken an army to cut that many posts and haul them down the mountains, then to dig the holes and stretch the wire.

The Brit was a determined little bastard, he'd give him that.

Stillman wandered his gaze across the valley to the brushy creek bottoms peppered with red shorthorn Durhams, the Over H brand scorched on their flanks. He wondered how many other brands grazed that grass. But if Hobbs was smart—as Stillman had told Fay—he'd keep the rustled stock separate and hidden, moving them quietly all at once. He no doubt had a separate buyer for the stolen beef, and separate books and figures.

Unconsciously, Stillman's eyes turned southward, where one ridge shouldered behind another all the way to the vast, empty breaks of the Missouri River.

"If I was him, that's where I'd take 'em," he muttered, reining his mount in that direction.

It wasn't long before he came to a ramshackle ranchstead nestled in a shallow ravine. He stopped on the rise above it and consulted the map he'd drawn with the help of Jody and Amiel Mundt. If he had it right, this would be Warren Johnson's claim.

Stillman refolded the map, tucked it back in his shirt, and with both hands on the saddle horn, studied the small gray shack fronting a lean-to woodshed, two burn barrels, and a trash pile.

Feeling uneasy without knowing why, he clucked to the horse and rode down.

19

Stillman halted his horse before the cabin. An eerie hush hung over the place, the only sound that of an empty birdcage knocking under the eaves.

"Anybody home?"

"Looks like I got company."

He turned. Johnson was sitting in the back of a buckboard parked between the two open barn doors. A dead hog hung by one rear hoof from a tree branch a few feet away. Stillman dismounted and walked over.

"Johnson." He nodded. "Ben Stillman. We met at Mundt's."

The rancher scrutinized him with one eye closed against the washed-out sun. He was wearing a long buffalo coat and a beaver cap with earflaps. A pint jar rested next to his thigh. "Figured you would've hightailed it back to Great Falls by now."

"Almost. Where's your Missus. and your kids?"

"Hell if I know. I sold to Hobbs and they done moved out. Fuck 'em."

"If you can't beat 'em, join 'em. That it?"

"Somethin' like that." Johnson held out the jar. "Snort?"

Stillman tied his reins to a corral post, hiked up next to Johnson on the buckboard's bed, and lifted the jar to his nose. The fumes made his eyes burn.

"Jesus Christ."

"That's my son-in-law's concoction. If you can get past the first few sips, it grows right sweet." Johnson smiled and tipped back the jar for at least two seconds. Stillman's stomach turned.

"Well, I was just stopping by to see if you lost any more beef to rustlers, but I guess I got my answer. Good Lord, what did you do to your hand?"

Johnson held up his left hand, wrapped with rags, stained with dried blood and pus. "My daughter Crystal. She was my sweetheart once, too."

"What got into her?"

"She turned loco when she took up with Harmon's Injun boy."

"He's a good kid."

"He's Injun."

"The wars are over."

Johnson grunted. "That's what his—"

Stillman looked at him.

"Nothin'." Johnson held out the jar and Stillman waved it off.

They sat in silence, hearing blood dribble from the hog's slit throat into a lard tin and looking across the barnyard. Stillman was watching the old gray mule in the corral, wishing he could inspect its hooves.

"Nice mule you got there."

Johnson laughed.

"No, I bet he was a fine mount in his day. Mind if I take a look?"

"He's ornery. Just run from you."

Stillman nodded. He tried to keep his tone conversational and offhand. "Damn shame what happened to the Mundts after we left."

"Ain't it?"

"You were lucky you left when you did." He turned his chin to the rancher as though the question had just dawned on him. "When was that, anyway?"

Johnson cut his eyes around. "Right after you. Why?"

Stillman shrugged. "You must have just missed the gunmen."

Johnson had no reply.

Stillman let time yawn before he said, "I was just over to where Bill Harmon was killed. I found a broken pint jar just like that one."

"So what?"

"I was just wonderin' if maybe you and Bill shared a lick that day."

Stillman didn't look at the rancher, but he could sense him trying to clear the alcohol fog from his brain. "Oh, yeah. I think we did."

"When?"

Johnson shrugged. "Don't recall. Noon maybe. Me and Bill was buds. I didn't want Crystal takin' up with his son, but Bill, he was all right."

Johnson pulled off the left shoulder of the buffalo coat and rolled up his shirtsleeve to a lumpy white scar the size of a quarter and shaped like a triangle. "I got that at Beecher Island, and I got two more in my leg just like it."

Stillman wagged his head. "That's awful, but the wars are over, Johnson."

The rancher took another drink and belched. "That's what they tell me." He took a handkerchief out of his back pocket. He blew his nose and dabbed at it thoughtfully.

"They held us there in the rifle pits for more'n a week.

Old Roman Nose made one charge after another. The guy shootin' next to me finally got the old bastard. That saved us. Took the pluck out of the others. My tunic was all covered with brains and horse blood. The surgeon was dead, so I had to dig the rifle balls out of my ownself.''

His eyes narrowed and his jaws tightened with remembered pain. ''I can still hear those Injuns howlin' and those horses and men screamin', and the lead balls plunkin' into flesh just like it was yesterday.'' He shook his head, drank from the jar, and turned to Stillman. ''You fight?''

''Nothin' like you're talking about.''

Johnson regarded him with one eye closed. ''So who are you after? Rustlers or the man who killed Bill?''

Stillman lifted his hat and scratched his head. ''Well, I thought they were one and the same, but now I'm beginning to wonder. I'm starting to think Bill didn't realize what he was up against until the last minute, which kind of cancels out rustlers, don't it?''

''Then why are you chasin' rustlers?''

Stillman laughed sardonically. ''Hell if I know. This is the craziest damn place I ever been.'' He got down, stretched his back, and headed for his horse. He untethered the reins and held them, pensive.

Squinting at Johnson, he said, ''You have any idea who'd want to see Bill Harmon dead—aside from rustlers?''

''Can't imagine.''

''Well, that's what I figured,'' Stillman said with fake resignation, and mounted up. Sweets jerked around, ready to go. Stillman held the reins under his chin.

Looking around at the lonely ranchstead, he said, ''Where you gonna go, Johnson? What are ya gonna do?''

Johnson raised his jar. His dull eyes tried a smile. ''I live for the moment.''

• • •

The southern Two Bears was a vast, haunted place, with every quiet canyon, eagle cry, and wind-brushed ridgetop lifting the hair on the back of the ex-lawman's neck.

He rode up one draw and down the next, looking for signs of moving beef but finding mostly twisting game trails littered with elk and deer scat, blow-down, wolf tracks, and bleached bones.

Riding through an arroyo, he came upon a cottonwood scarred by grizzly tines. Shredded bark littered the ground. His wounds ached at the sight. He slipped his Henry from the saddle boot, glanced around, and rode on.

When the draws purpled and salmon clouds swirled, he picketed and unsaddled his horse along a creek, gathered bark and wood, kindled a fire, and set coffee to boil. Sweets rolled in the dust and pine needles, blowing and nickering in leatherless joy.

A coyote yipped and squealed as though in misery. Following it by only a second or two, another tuned up with its own variation on the same theme. Then another and another, until the dissonance grew into one great cacophony.

He paused while eating his beans and bacon, his breath clouding in the crisp night air, and listened. How did the old Zuni legend go? When a hunter coming home late hears a coyote howl, he thinks of the time when he'll say farewell to the living, and make his way to the Lake of the Dead.

He banked the fire and snuggled into his bedroll, falling almost instantly into a long, dreamless sleep. At dawn he rose feeling vigorous.

''Nothing like a cold morning to clear the brain, eh, Sweets?'' he said as he swung the saddle over the horse's back.

He wandered southeast, cradling his rifle, his eyes on the

ground, his hat pulled low against the wind. Around noon he found a deep-rutted wagon trail and followed it south through rocky buttes and timbered benches.

An hour later he came upon an L-shaped cabin nearly hidden behind neatly stacked stove wood. A canvas-covered freight wagon attached to four swarthy mules stood outside, and three horses roamed the corral sitting kitty-corner in front. Conversation and laughter pushed through the buffalo-skin curtain in the cabin's doorway.

"Anybody home?"

The corral gate knocked and squeaked in its leather latch. The wind tore smoke from the cabin's tin chimney. A lanky black man in a calfskin vest appeared in the door and walked out, frowning.

"This a roadhouse?" Stillman asked.

"Yes, suh."

"How's your coffee?"

"As black as the hair on my ass." The man offered a smile.

Stillman returned it. "Say, that's how I like it."

The man led Sweets to the corral while Stillman ducked through the cabin door, took a seat at a crude pine table, and looked around.

Three freighters conversed in Scandinavian, and a long-faced man warmed himself by the potbelly stove. The man wore a cheap suit and a string tie, and his hair was long, thin, and sandy. Round, blue spectacles hid his eyes. He scribbled in a gray book, concentration creasing his thin nose and hollow cheeks.

The black man came through the door and disappeared in the kitchen. A moment later a frail Indian girl of about sixteen came out carrying a cup of coffee in both hands. Wearing a gaudy pink dress, undershot boots, and a queer smile, she set the cup carefully before Stillman, then gave a festive giggle and ran back to the kitchen, scuffing her boots across the floor.

A minute later she returned and, moving her lips as if to speak, set a steaming plate on the table, then disappeared.

The black man had followed her out. "Don't mind her—she's daffy," he said. "Where you headed?"

Stillman forked some Swiss steak in his mouth and chewed. "I'm not sure yet. I'm lookin' for a herd of rustled steers."

"Lawman, are you?"

"You could say that." He held out his hand. "Ben Stillman, deputy U.S. marshal, retired."

The man looked at him askance, buried his eyes under kinky black brows. "Nah! . . . I thought you was dead."

"Popular misconception."

"Well, pleased to meet you." The black man gave Stillman's hand a brisk shake, pumping his arm. "I heard o' lot about you. My name is Leon McMannigle. Corporal, Tenth Cavalry. Retired."

"Just you and the girl run this outfit?"

The black man nodded. "Two years back an old miner left her, said he'd be back in the spring. He never showed, so here she is. Daffy as all to-do, but she sure can split the wood!"

Stillman was half finished with his meal when the freighters walked out in a roar of broken English, snugging their hats on their grizzled heads and fowling the air with cheap tobacco.

A few minutes later the tall, thin man in the corner got up and slipped the book in his coat, flipped his tangled hair out from his collar. Studying his reflection in the window, he carefully adjusted his black, flat-brimmed hat, then dropped some coins on the table and took long strides toward the door, stiffly swinging his arms. The queer blue spectacles did not turn toward Stillman.

As the man's hoofbeats diminished in the distance Stillman pushed his plate away and finished his coffee.

McMannigle appeared in the kitchen doorway, toweling a cup.

"That man's name is Goodnight," he said evenly. "You'll want to follow him."

Stillman sized up the man's serious demeanor, then nodded, dropped a coin on the table, and tipped his hat.

"Much obliged."

Solemnly the man said, "Luck to you, suh."

Goodnight's dust trail led through buttes and ravines. Clouds swirled and a brisk wind scurried. Stillman followed at a distance, rifle ready, wary of an ambush. Soon the trees thinned and the hills lowered, offering little cover.

He gave the rider a half-mile lead and followed his tracks. In a crease between hills he heard the rising intonations of bawling cattle. Manure wafted on the wind. He rode halfway up a round-topped butte, dismounted, and ascended the ridge, keeping his head low.

He lay down, removed his hat, and inched his eyes over a hummock of bluestem.

About a hundred yards down the gentle grade, the wide Missouri River curved between cutbanks, and a riverboat with two steam stacks and a long white cabin flanked by a paddle wheel was roped to shore posts. Shacks, tents, and two corrals filled with cattle spread along the bank. In a third corral where two horses stood nose to rump, Goodnight dismounted his black, removed the leather, then headed for a plank-walled cabin in which tin plates clanked and a voice rose.

"Ouch—that's hot, goddammit!"

A man laughed. Goodnight went inside. After the door

had closed behind him, Stillman hobbled Sweets and loosened his cinch, looped a feedbag over his head. Back on the butte, he lay on his side, rested his rifle barrel in the buffalo grass, and peered down at the encampment.

Son of a bitch, he thought. Hobbs is running the rustled stock down here and shipping them out by riverboat. But where to? And who in hell is Goodnight?

He lay there until twilight, weighing his options. Two men walked out of the cabin and moved drunkenly toward the corrals, their voices loud and contentious.

"You were lookin' at my cards, dammit. I seen you."

"Go to hell."

They drifted from one corral to another, arguing and giving the stock a cursory inspection. Spooked, the animals bawled, thumped their hooves, and knocked against the slats. A horse whinnied.

A voice yelled from the cabin, "I told you to check the stock, not start a stampede!"

"Fuck you, Goodnight!"

The men laughed and drifted back to the cabin.

Keeping an eye on the firelit windows where occasional shadows passed and heated voices rose, Stillman crept down the butte. It was a cool, quiet night, and he could hear the Missouri rippling over snags and the riverboat complaining against its ropes.

Under the cover of the stock's agitated moans and thumps, he ran softly to one of the empty shacks, peered around the corner at the cabin, then stepped toward the nearest corral.

The cabin door squeaked open and boots scraped on the stoop. Stillman hit the ground and lay with his cheek in the grass. A man stood silhouetted in the doorway, unmoving. Stillman winced. He'd started inching his rifle up to lever a shell when he heard hissing and the dull sound of water puddling on the ground.

He relaxed. After a while the sound subsided. The man's shoulders hunched, his head bobbed, and his knees bent. A moment later he turned and reentered the cabin, closing the door behind him.

Stillman pushed himself up and trotted to the corral. The cows spooked, eyeing him cautiously.

"Shhhh. Easy," he whispered.

Squinting his eyes in the dim light, he stared at the rump of a year-old steer until his eyes adjusted and Amiel Mundt's Circle-M brand swam into focus. He appraised several more he didn't recognize until he found Bill Harmon's Bar H.

He hooked his hands over the top corral slat and considered. Must be two hundred head here, and every brand in the Clear Creek Valley. Except Hobbs's.

It was all the proof he needed to wire the territorial marshal. But the cows could be long gone by the time Dale True arrived from Helena.

Mulling ways to obtain more proof—besides confronting the three drunks in the cabin and driving the stock to Helena solo—Stillman made his way back to his perch on the butte and trained his gaze on the starlit encampment below.

Lumbering shadows jostled the corrals. An owl hooted. A wolf howled in the velvet buttes across the river. The light in the cabin windows softened, and the drunken voices were losing their heat.

Stillman bit his lip, fidgeted a finger along the cold steel of his rifle, and decided.

One way or another, he had to get into that cabin.

20

Muffled voices rose. Stillman opened his eyes. His mustache prickled with hoarfrost. Gray smudged the eastern sky, limning the buttes, mesas, and bald ridges along the river.

He'd spent the night on the butte's brow, reclining on his bedroll, rifle in his arms. He'd slept lightly but dreamed little, awakening now and then when Sweets shook his bridle or nickered in his sleep, to glance at the encampment and regard the broad swaths of stars dusting the velvet sky.

Too stiff yet to rise, he shouldered a look over the butte. Firelight flickered in the cabin's windows. Solid knocks and thumps rose. Men hacked phlegm from their throats. Pans clattered. The smell of bacon carried from the chimney.

Stillman's belly growled.

He got up slowly, flexing his muscles, and walked softly down the butte toward his horse. Whispering, he stroked Sweets's neck; the gelding blinked sleepily and lowered his head to crop grass.

After tightening the horse's cinch and relieving his bladder, he hacked up phlegm, retrieved a tin from his saddlebags, opened his shirt, and rubbed Crystal's lung concoction on his chest. The stench burned his nose. Sweets spooked, shaking his mane.

"My sentiments exactly, boy," Stillman told the horse, "but if I don't use up this whole tin, I'm liable to get a tongue-lashin'."

When dawn had gilded the purple horizon, two men walked out of the cabin with their saddles on their shoulders. Neither had Goodnight's long, stiff strides. Silently smoking, they rigged two horses in the corral, mounted, and rode west. From the butte top, Stillman watched them disappear between the hills.

The ex-lawman bit an apple, chewed. That leaves Goodnight alone, he thought. The odds don't get better than that.

He finished the apple, core and all, then walked down the butte past Sweets, who watched him curiously and nickered.

"Easy, boy. I'll be back."

Rifle in his hand, he crept east around the base of the butte until the cabin lay a hundred yards before him, end to end. The four dark squares of a sashed window glared. He made his way farther north through knobs and low hills until he lay amid cattails at the bottom of a spring wash, facing the cabin's windowless backside. The wind was picking up as the gray dawn deepened into morning. He hoped it would cover his footfalls.

Keeping his head low, he ran lightly, watching for gopher holes and sage clumps. He made the cabin wall and bit his tongue, suppressing his weak-lunged rasps and wheezes. He pressed an ear against the rough, weathered wood. Someone was snoring softly into a pillow. He moved around the cabin to the front door. He took a breath, held it, levered a shell into the chamber, and kicked the door.

He stepped inside before the door bounced back, and looked around the dim haze. A cot creaked. An angry, muffled voice rose. "What the hell . . . who is it?"

Goodnight lay on the cot in faded red long johns. He

twisted back from the wall to give Stillman his creased forehead and furled eyebrows. Long, tangled hair framed his beleaguered face.

"Keep your hands where I can see 'em!" Stillman roared.

"Who the hell are you?"

"The law. I'm taking you in."

"What for?"

"Stealin' cattle."

"Oh, bullshit!"

With a glance Stillman took in the mess of newspapers and chairs and mussed cots, and the small round table next to the potbelly stove buried under dirty tin plates, playing cards, and coffee cups. The air was rank with sweat, tobacco, and mouse turds. He kicked a bottle across the warped wood floor and it rattled to a halt against the wall.

Stillman grabbed the frock coat hung over the chair next to Goodnight.

"Hey, give me that."

Stillman butted the man with his rifle. "Oh, my head!" Goodnight fell back on the cot and grabbed his forehead, a silver pinkie ring catching the gray window light.

Stillman went through the coat pockets and produced a small, gray ledger book with blue and red lines and columns of inked figures and brands. He turned the pages, chewing his lower lip, his heart quickening. Finally he closed the book and slapped it against his palm.

"Pleased to meet you, Mr. Edward Goodnight, Indian agent, Fort Peck Reservation."

"Fuck you."

"Get dressed."

"I don't know who you are or who sent you, but when Donovan Hobbs finds out about this—"

Stillman grabbed the man and flung him to the floor. "Get dressed!"

Goodnight gathered his clothes and dressed, mumbling and cursing, then donned his blue spectacles, grabbed a bottle from the table, and tipped it back.

Stillman watched the air bubbles roll back from the lip and imagined the honey liquid bubbling down his throat and swaddling him in gauze. His mouth watered.

The Indian agent pulled the bottle from his wet lips with an evil grin. He held the bottle out to Stillman. The amber rye slid back and forth against the glass.

"Drinkin' man, are ya?" Goodnight sneered.

Stillman grabbed the bottle and smashed it against the wall. "Grab your saddle, let's go."

"Where we goin'?"

"Grab your saddle."

The man shook his head and bent down for his saddle and blanket by the door. "You're a fool."

"You're buyin' stolen beef with government money, and I'm the fool?"

Stillman pushed the man out the door and steered him across the compound to the corral. "Saddle up."

Reluctantly Goodnight laid the blanket over the back of his gelding, then hefted the leather over the blanket with an angry grunt. "When Donovan Hobbs finds out about this, you're a dead man."

"You'll be swingin' from the same branch as him when Uncle Sam finds he's been buying stolen beef for the Indians at Fort Peck."

Tightening the latigo, the man gave a shrill, mirthless laugh, jerking his queer blue spectacles toward Stillman. "You think the government's gonna squawk at buying cheap beef? What do the taxpayers care? What do the Indians care?"

"What do the poor, dead cattlemen care, huh? Mount up." Stillman glanced around, found rope on a gatepost, and tied the man's hands under the horse's neck, his ankles under the belly. "Oh, for chrissakes," the Indian agent said. "This is ridiculous!"

Stillman took the black's reins and led it toward the butte where Sweets was hobbled, Goodnight cursing and berating him with every step. "I can't ride like this, you fool! Free my hands."

"I suggest you take a mouthful of mane there, or you'll end up hanging from the belly."

"Goddamn you to hell!"

Halfway to the butte, Stillman heard hooves thumping. He started running, but the black spooked and fought him, pulling at the reins. He turned. Seven riders pounded down from the hills east of the cabin.

Goodnight hooted. "Now you'll get what you paid for, you old fool!"

Trying to calm the black, Stillman eyed the riders, his heart drumming in his ears. One man broke from the group and trotted toward him, his head cocked curiously, one eye closed. "What's goin' on?"

"Stop this man, you idiots!" Goodnight bawled.

Stillman leveled his rifle and fired. The man's horse bucked and turned. "Come on," he yelled to the others.

Stillman scrambled to mount the horse behind Goodnight as the riders came at a gallop, firing their pistols and yelling. Goodnight's black buck-kicked. Stillman slid down its side and fell, grabbing the reins. He regained his feet, dropped to a knee, and levered his Henry at the approaching riders, dropping two. Then he mounted behind Goodnight and galloped up the butte.

Smoke puffed on the ridge before him, and a rifle

cracked. He was surrounded. He reined the horse to a halt
and drew his pistol, aiming toward the rifleman, but just
before he squeezed the trigger, a black hand waved a rifle
and a familiar voice yelled, "It's Leon. Get your horse. I'll
hold them off as long as I can."

Stillman reholstered his pistol and spurred on over the
ridge past Leon McMannigle, who lay on the ridgetop in a
floppy brown hat, scarf, and deerskin tunic, gripping a
Sharps rifle, his cheek snugged against the stock.

Stillman jumped off Goodnight's black and wasted no
time unhobbling his own horse. He took the black's reins
in his teeth, mounted Sweets, and tied the reins to his saddle. Then he spurred westward through the crease between
the buttes, Goodnight whooping and hollering behind him.

Five minutes after the reports of McMannigle's rifle
ceased, Stillman heard hoofbeats and turned to see the black
man spurring toward him, grimacing and shaking his head.
"They're a-comin'. Follow me!"

A mile and a half up the trail, McMannigle slowed his
horse to a trot and studied the scrub cedars in the ravine to
his right and yelled, "This way!"

Hooves catching on roots and sliding in gravel, the
horses picked their way down the steep grade through thick
brush. The trail leveled out at a creek bubbling in a boulder-
lined cutbank studded with ponderosa pines. They followed
the creek for a mile, switchbacking around rock walls and
butte shoulders, and wading to cover their trail.

McMannigle stopped his horse in the creek and cocked
his head to listen. Behind him, Stillman reined Sweets and
Goodnight's black to a halt. Hatless, Goodnight lay against
the black's neck, his face flushed, his hair wild, gripping
the black's mane with his teeth.

"I think we lost 'em," McMannigle said.

"There's seven of 'em, though. They can cover a lot of ground."

"Better wait here till dark, then."

Goodnight spit the mane from his mouth, raised his chin, and yelled hoarsely, "We're here! We're here, you idiots!"

Stillman gave McMannigle an apologetic look. "I'd shoot him, but I'm gonna need him and his ledger." He spurred the bay up the bank, dismounted, and walked back to Goodnight. He pulled a handkerchief from the agent's back pocket, and stuffed it in his mouth.

Then he and Leon McMannigle picketed the horses in the pines, leaving Goodnight tied to the black. Sitting on a blow-down log, they passed a canteen. McMannigle opened a can of peaches and fished one out with his fingers.

"Why are you risking your neck for me, McMannigle?"

"Leon."

"Okay, Leon."

The black man sucked a peach in his mouth, chewed, and offered the can to Stillman, who waved it off. "You're my angel o' vengeance. Several o' those riders savaged Mary Beth when she was down to the creek for water."

"Mary Beth?"

"My Injun girl."

"That what's wrong with her?"

"Nah, she was daffy before that. Hell, I don't even know if she knew what they done to her. When I found her, she had that fool smile and her clothes all torn. Later I found a miscarried baby in her bed. I don't think she knew about that, neither. But I know one thing. When I find those cow-pokes, I'm gonna kill them—sure as shit."

Ten minutes later Stillman heard leather creaking and hooves clomping on the rim above. He raised his hand to McMannigle, who was filling his canteen in the creek. He pointed and they looked up through the trees and saw the shadows of two riders.

Stillman grabbed his rifle and stepped into a crack among the rocks that gave him a view of the rim. A horse whinnied behind him and Goodnight fell under the black with a heavy thump, spraying gravel. He stood and ran, spitting the gag from his mouth and priming his voice for a yell, but the frayed rope at his ankle caught the other and tripped him. He fell on his hands, lifted his chin, and yelled in a thin, quaking voice, "Here—"

McMannigle caught him, grabbed him by the hair, pulled his head back, and ran the wide blade of his bowie knife along his neck. Goodnight fell face-first, clutching his throat and gurgling as though drowning. In a few seconds he was still. The dirt quickly reddened beneath his neck.

McMannigle tossed Stillman a worried look. Stillman returned it. Both men stood where they were, looking up the slope. It was quiet, with only the wind and the creek murmuring and a woodpecker tattooing a tree trunk. Blood sheeted along Leon's knife and dripped onto the pine needles.

Stillman stepped out from the rocks, keeping the carbine in the hollow of his arm. "With the wind, it's noisier up there than down here. They may not have heard."

"If they did hear, they might be bringin' more. They could pin us in here till hell freezes over and the devil has icicles in his beard."

"Stay with the horses."

"Where you goin'?"

Stillman retrieved ammo from his saddlebag and loaded his rifle. "Up on the rim."

21

He crept up the slope under cover of the trees and made the rim with his breath coming hard. The lip fanned out on both sides to grassy saddles. Ahead, another ravine fell southward, filled with pines and boulders.

He bit his lip, wondering if they'd heard Goodnight and were setting a trap, or hadn't heard and were gone.

He turned to head back down the canyon when a man on a brown horse rode out of an aspen grove down the saddle to Stillman's right.

Stillman ducked, removed his hat, and watched the man rein his horse across the saddle. He was a big man in a cream duster, with hawk feathers buffeting in his hatband, and a curly red beard. Delwyn Sleighbough.

Another rider wandered out from woods to meet him. He cradled a rifle in his arms. They sat talking, their horses' tails blowing in the wind, then ambled away.

Stillman made his way back down the slope and found McMannigle concealing Goodnight's body in a raspberry thicket.

"I don't think they're up to anything," Stillman said. "They're riding northwest along the saddle. One of 'em is Delwyn Sleighbough. You know him?"

McMannigle looked at him darkly. "He's one that savaged Mary Beth. That saddle crosses the mountain behind my roadhouse. Mary Beth's there alone."

"Let's ride," Stillman said.

They made the ridge behind the roadhouse an hour later, concealing themselves in the chalky, hollowed-out shoulder of a butte. Below, smoke curled from the chimney. The windows paled with the westering sun. Three horses stood like statues in the corral, a chill wind ruffling their manes.

"Those yours?" Stillman asked.

McMannigle nodded. "Doesn't look like anyone's here except Mary Beth."

Stillman inhaled and released it slowly through his nose. "I don't like it. They probably saw you back there. No offense, but a black man stands out in this country."

"They'll come, sure enough."

"I believe I've caused you trouble, Leon."

"No more'n I caused myself, Marshal."

"Ben."

McMannigle smiled almost imperceptibly, a red bandanna fluttering at his neck, his battered hat creased by the wind. "Okay, Ben."

"I'm going down to check it out. Cover me."

Stillman crept down the butte and, zigzagging between boulders and trees, made the woodpile behind the roadhouse. Looking around, he stepped to a window and looked in.

The room was empty. Flames flickered around the stove's door. He stepped lightly around the cabin and pushed through the buffalo hide. The fire's warmth and the smell of onions and burning cedar engulfed him.

"Mary Beth," he called.

Nothing.

He jacked a shell into the Henry's breech, bent down to

glance under the tables, then opened the kitchen door and stepped in.

A big cast-iron stove stood against the far wall, covered with dirty plates, eating utensils, and muffin tins. A low fire ticked inside. A fat-marbled roast sat on the chopping block under shelves of canned goods. A half-chopped onion and a carving knife lay beside it.

"Mary Beth."

He smelled mink just as he heard the boot squeak the floorboard behind him and the metallic rasp of a lever jerking a shell home.

"We meet again, chicken farmer."

Stillman froze.

"Drop your rifle and turn around," Sleighbough said. "I want you to see this."

Before Stillman could do anything, something squeaked and thundered behind them, making the floor jump. He turned to see the Indian girl bound up through a trapdoor in the floor and, with a hideous shriek, sink a woodsplitter into Delwyn Sleighbough's shoulder with a sickening crunch of breaking bone.

Sleighbough screamed and fired as Stillman nudged his rifle, sending the lead into the rafters. The girl's shrieks, Sleighbough's screams, and the echoing rifle boom rang in Stillman's head, the smell of gunpowder filling his nostrils.

Sleighbough sank to his knees, his mouth and eyes drawn wide with pain. The woodsplitter fell from the splintered bones in his shoulder. Weakly, he lifted his blood-splattered rifle, face bunched in pain and rage, and levered another shell. Before he could lift the barrel, Stillman lowered his carbine and finished him.

Behind Mary Beth, another gunman jumped through the door, shooting wildly. Stillman grabbed the girl and hit the floor, rolling under a cupboard. Raising his pistol, he emptied all six chambers. The rider danced backward as the bullets punched through his duster and hit the floor with a groan.

"It's all right now," he told the girl, but she lay curled at his side, unmoving.

He pulled his left arm out from under her, turned her onto her back, and saw the blood staining her gaudy pink dress. McMannigle came in with his pistol drawn. "Ben? Mary Beth?"

"In here," Stillman said.

The black man turned and stepped through the kitchen doorway. When he saw Mary Beth lying curled at Stillman's side, he stopped. His pistol fell. His eyes widened.

"Mary Beth?"

Stillman shook his head.

Leon stood there for a long time, his face a mask of disbelief. Then he moved slowly forward, stepping over Sleighbough. He fell to his knees, held the girl's right hand for several seconds, his eyes squeezed shut. Then he lifted her in his arms, her thin limbs falling at his sides, the scuffed cowboy boots bobbing as he turned and moved through the door.

When he was gone, Stillman got slowly to his feet and holstered his pistol. He found a coffeepot and a cup, went into the other room, and sat down at a table in front of the stove.

After a while he heard a long, plaintive wail rising from the shed by the corrals. He sat listening, one elbow on the table, his coffee in one hand, his face in the other.

At the Hobbs ranch, Fay sat at the writing table in her bedroom, pen in hand, trying to compose a letter to her cousin Gwen in St. Louis. Donovan, whistling as he bathed in the next room, was an irritating distraction. Frowning, she got up, closed the door, and returned to her chair.

Dipping her pen, she heard a man's muffled, singsong voice outside. She placed the pen in the ink jar, stood, and parted the curtains. A man in a Stetson hat and duster sat in the tree swing below, swinging with the casual industry of a boy playing hooky from school.

He pulled back on the ropes and swung forward, boots straight out in front of him, duster blowing out behind. He lifted his head, revealing the dark, bristled cheeks, scarred nose, and lewd leer of Weed Cole.

"I . . . gotta . . . seeecret. . . . I . . . gotta . . . seeecret . . ."

Fay fell back, startled, stifling a scream. Enraged, she looked around and found her pistol and a box of shells in the chest at the foot of the bed. She loaded the gun and rushed downstairs. Julia Bodio was standing in the kitchen window facing the backyard, hand pressed to her bosom, a distressed look on her face.

"Go back inside, Julia," Fay ordered.

She marched off the porch and approached the tree where Cole was swinging. Raising the pistol with both hands, she stopped. Cole's boots scraped the ground.

"Hey, hey, hey!" he said, raising his hands in mock fear, a grin raising his mustache and revealing a jagged line of chipped, yellow teeth. "I surrender."

"I'm going to blow your brains out, you filthy bastard." She pulled back the hammer.

"Easy now—that thing's loaded."

"You're damn right it's loaded."

Cole laughed. "You're not gonna shoot me."

She closed one eye and put the front sight on the gunman's forehead. Try as she might, she could not pull the trigger.

"See, I told ya," Cole said smugly.

"How dare you come into the yard!"

"I came to tell your husband about his little kitten and Ben Stillman."

"What are you talking about?"

Cole laughed, kicked his feet out, and swung. "I seen you gruntin' around like a coupla spring pigs the other day."

Her stomach took a dive. Her head swirled.

"No use denyin' it. I seen ya with my very own eyes, and I gotta tell ya, you make an even pertier picture with your clothes off than on. Some women, they look all right dressed, but then when they take their clothes off, well . . . ."

"What do you want?"

"You."

Fay turned sharply and started back to the house.

Cole stood abruptly, raised his voice. "Don't think he'll believe me, do ya? Why would I make up a story about you and Ben Stillman? No, he'd look into it, no doubt find the same coupla cowpunchers I found who worked for your father about the time you and Stillman were, uh . . . an item."

She turned back to him, her face flushed with rage. "You can't have me, you animal."

Cole looked off speculatively. "I wonder what he'd do if he found out. Mighty jealous man. Violent temper. Unbalanced."

"I don't care."

"Wonder what he'd do to Stillman and the kids he's shackin' up with over at the Harmon ranch."

Feeling cornered, she studied him, thinking. She squeezed the gun at her side. She wanted to bring it back up. She could shoot him now.

"How could I be with you?" she said angrily.

"I ain't sayin' like it's forever. A few laughs, a few

horseback rides, a few bottles of your husband's wine . . .
that's all.'' He grinned mischievously.

She didn't say anything.

"Meet me one week from today," Cole said seriously.
"Same place you and Stillman met the other day. Just you.
Not Stillman or anyone else. You understand? Or I'll give
away our little secret."

He looked at her for a long time. Then he stepped out
from the swing, tipped his hat, and walked away.

Donovan Hobbs met his wife on the stairs but did not
see the pale, vacant look on her face, or the gun only partly
concealed in a fold of her dress. He had business on his
mind. In passing, he pecked her cheek.

"I'm off, my pet. Stay in today, please. It's turned
colder, and I don't want you catching a chill."

He lit a cigarette on his way out the door, fretting over
the news last night's riders had delivered. A black man and
the ex-lawman Hobbs had met in town a few weeks back
had nabbed Goodnight.

For crying out loud. Hobbs hadn't given the man a second thought. Who'd have figured he'd have the gall . . . !

In front of the corrals, the men were saddled up and
ready to go, hunkered down in their winter coats. Cigarette
smoke and steam puffed around their heads. Cole sat his
copper-bottom stud, resting an elbow on the horn of his
Mexican saddle horn and biting chew from a plug.

Next to Cole, Warren Johnson sat one of Hobbs's pintos
in a buffalo coat. He'd wrapped a wool scarf over his head,
tied it under his chin, and snugged his hat over it. He
looked in such bad need of a drink, Hobbs had to laugh.

"Good Lord, Warren, you're sober!"

Johnson's nostrils flared.

Hobbs laughed again, good-naturedly. "So this Stillman
is staying at the Harmon ranch, you say?"

"That's right."

"Shackin' up with Harmon's son and your daughter."

Hobbs cut his eyes around the group, igniting laughter.

"She ain't my daughter no more. I disowned her."

"Her loss, I'm sure," Hobbs said dryly, taking his gelding's reins from Grubber Early and mounting. "All right, men. The Harmon ranch it is!"

22

They buried the Indian girl in the woods above the road-house. It was a cold, gray morning, and the clouds caught and tore on the mountaintops. A thin mist blew.

Leon knelt down to straighten the rough wooden cross in the rocks he'd mounded against coyotes and wolves. He'd spoken little since yesterday, and Stillman didn't oblige him to, allowing his new friend all the grieving room he needed.

"She didn't deserve half o' what she got," Leon said now.

Stillman stood behind him, holding their horses' reins, hat tipped into the wind. He stared at the grave in silence.

"You wouldn't think a little girl like that could split wood, but she'd have a whole cord split before I even got my sorry ass out o' bed!" He turned his dark eyes to Stillman, half smiling, half crying. "I loved her."

Stillman nodded.

Leon stared at the grave, absently pulling up grass, the knitted gray scarf blowing at his back.

" 'Think not disdainfully of death,' " Stillman recited from the *Meditations* of Marcus Aurelius, clearing his throat, " 'but look on it with favor; for even death is one of the things that Nature wills.' "

Leon nodded and wiped his nose.

Stillman gave him his reins then climbed into his saddle. "Well, I'm heading out. Take care of yourself, Leon."

McMannigle looked at him, exasperated. "I'm goin' with you!"

Stillman shook his head, holding the reins as Sweets shuffled his hooves, eager to get started. "I've done enough damage to your life, my friend."

"The hell you say!" Leon grabbed his saddle horn and thrust his left foot through the stirrup. "I'm goin' after Hobbs same as you. Now we can ride together or separate, but to my way o' thinkin', two together's got a better chance than two separate." He jerked a nod at Stillman, raising his eyebrows. "You with me?"

Stillman shrugged, sidled alongside McMannigle's horse, and stuck out his hand. "If you can't beat 'em, I guess you gotta join 'em," he said resignedly.

They picked their way down the mountain, then rode northeast, keeping to the draws and gullies, knowing that Hobbs's riders were on their trail. Mid-afternoon, they pulled up to a creek with a boulder-strewn cliff behind it. Stillman dismounted and gave his reins to his partner.

"I'm gonna scout our backtrail."

"From where?"

"That shoulder there."

McMannigle studied the rocks rising nearly straight above the creek. "You gonna climb that? How old are you?" he asked, his mood lightening.

"Forty-four."

McMannigle sighed and chuckled. "Forty-four's too old to be rock climbin'. I'll go."

"How old are you?"

"Twenty-eight."

Stillman scowled with mock disgust. "Well, then you're damn right you'll go! I'll hold your horse."

He opened a can of Leon's peaches and rolled a cigarette, then sat on a rock. He watched McMannigle crawl up the brushy, terraced side of the shoulder, slipping and cursing and unloosing an avalanche of stones behind him.

When he'd made the ridge, he hiked the grassy mountain above it, keeping to the chokecherry shrubs for cover. Above the tree line, he crouched behind a dike, got out his spyglass, and scouted their backtrail—a mosaic of forested slopes, canyons, and watersheds unrolling beneath a bright, cold sky.

The sun was at a good angle, the dun-green distance clear as crystal. He could see three riders picking their way down the next saddle south, the lead man leaning out from his horse, looking for sign.

Leon put away the glass and made his way back down the shoulder, sliding on his butt the last several feet and landing in the creek with a splash.

"Three men about three miles south," he said, taking long strides to the creek bank.

"Christ." Stillman got up and handed Leon the half-empty peach tin. "They must have stopped at your place and found the bodies, picked our trail up there."

"Let's just wait here and pick 'em off."

Stillman shook his head. "Hobbs probably has others coming from the north. By the time we take care of those three, he could have us surrounded."

McMannigle gulped the last of the peaches and took his reins back from Stillman. "You're the marshal."

They kept an eye out each time the trackers appeared atop a hogback or came out on a level plateau behind them. They forded White-Tail Creek in the late afternoon and climbed the sloping buttes above it, topping out on a grassy park.

Hooves drummed in the distance. Stillman turned, eyes wide. A half dozen or so riders galloped along a grassy ridge a half mile east, heading south and led by Donovan Hobbs—Custer locks winging out behind him.

"Shit!"

They spurred their horses into a gully and hid amid woods, watching the riders disappear among the ridges and hogbacks, angling southeast.

"They overran us," Stillman said. "Maybe we got lucky."

But he knew there'd been no luck when they descended a ridge and saw two fallen riders on opposite banks of a dry wash.

Stillman dismounted, turned the first man over, and saw the firm young face of Bud Harrington, dead blue eyes dully reflecting the afternoon light. A penny-sized bullet hole defiled his forehead.

Stillman heard a yell and turned the boy back over as he'd fallen. He looked toward the sound. The other rider was moving. Stillman recognized the grimace of Smoke Harrington.

Riding over, Stillman and McMannigle found Harrington's left leg pinned under his horse. The horse was dead, its tongue hanging like a dead snake from its mouth. Harrington's face was creased with pain, his eyes wide, his teeth bared.

His leg was buried to the hip, a splintered, blood-darkened thighbone poking through his bloodied jeans. He pushed his free foot against the saddle and gave up, exhausted from the pain.

"We'll get you out," Stillman told him.

Harrington grunted and rolled his eyes. It was cold, but

his hair was matted to his head, his face beaded with sweat. "No—I want my gun!" The rancher was reaching for his pistol several feet beyond his outstretched hand.

"What for?"

"Give it to me." He breathed in short rasps.

"Just wait, mister," Leon said. "We're gonna get you out of here."

Harrington groaned. "My boy . . . he dead?"

"Yes, he's dead," Stillman said as he and Leon heaved against the horse. The animal wouldn't budge.

"My leg—it's all twisted in there. Oh, *Jesus*!"

"We'll have to dig you out."

"You don't have time."

"What?"

Stillman lifted his eyes, following along Harrington's outstretched arm. Dust rose along the horizon.

Leon said, "They've picked up our trail. They're heading back."

Harrington moaned with agony. "Shoot me," he pleaded.

"I can't shoot you," Stillman said.

"Then give me my gun and let me do it!"

Stillman cut his eyes at McMannigle, who looked down. "Oh, Jesus." Leon sighed.

Stillman looked at the line of riders growing on the horizon. Then he looked at Harrington. "Lord, forgive me," he said, giving the man his pistol.

They were only fifty yards away when Harrington's gun cracked. Neither looked back.

They galloped, leaning forward in their saddles and keeping their heads down. Not wanting to lead Hobbs to the Harmon ranch, Stillman and McMannigle turned sharply west, splashed across a creek, and followed a crease up a wooded mountainside, ducking under branches and avoiding deadfall and blowdown.

They topped out on the ridge and, without stopping, spurred into the heavy pine forest below.

Their horses winded and sweat-lathered, they pulled into a small canyon lined with boulders and small cedars. A spring bubbled at the bottom. Dismounting, they led the horses down for a drink, keeping an eye on the forested slope behind them. They waited there watching until they were certain they'd lost their pursuers.

Then they walked their horses up another steep, brambly grade, mounted, and followed several ridges north. It was shading toward dusk and the low-gray sky was dropping snow pellets when they topped the hill overlooking White-Tail Creek and the Harmon ranch.

Stillman paused there, looking for a good way down to the creek, when he realized the cabin and barn weren't there.

"Oh, my," Leon crooned.

For what must have been several minutes Stillman sat his saddle, staring down into the greensward where the Harmon cabin once stood. Must have made a mistake, he thought. I deadheaded on the wrong ridge.

But there was the creek and Bill Harmon's grave mounding up near a bend. In the meadow over west, where the ranch buildings should have been, ruined timbers smoked, and occasional flames guttered under charred logs. Resin sizzled and sparks flew.

Nausea bubbling in his throat and his heart tattooing his breastbone, he spurred down the ridge. When he'd crossed the creek and rode into the clearing, he could smell the smoke and see the virtually consumed cabin and barn logs scattered amid mounds of blue-white ash and glowing coals. All that stood were the stone hearth and chimney and the coal-black kitchen range, pots and pans scattered in ashes.

"Jody . . . Crystal," he mumbled as he drifted around the ruins.

Turning to look across the yard, he saw that the rope used to pull down the corral was still tied to a post. The yellow dog, Duff, lay dead by the corral, his hind legs stretched out, a hole in his head. "Even killed the poor dog," Stillman said to himself.

Leon was poking around the smoking barn rubble.

"Any sign?" Stillman called.

McMannigle shook his head.

Stillman poked here and there in the charred ruins with a half-burned plank, then walked out along the meadow where the two might have run and been gunned down. Mounted, Leon searched along the creek.

Stillman was east of the corral when Sweets whinnied, tethered in the yard.

Spread apart and toting carbines, two riders descended the eroded ridge, their horses slipping in the wet clay, the tails of their buttoned dusters blowing out behind them. Stillman went to Sweets, shucked his Henry, and mounted up. He looked around but saw no sign of Leon.

The snow, falling faster now, blurred the air between Stillman and the oncoming riders. Fueled by rage, Stillman stood his ground. The saddle creaked beneath him as Sweets shifted nervously.

He studied the approaching men. One he didn't recognize. The other was Weed Cole, who rode up lazily on his copper-bottom stud, eyes laughing.

"Home sweet home, eh, Stillman?"

Stillman's jaw tightened. "Nice work, Cole. Where's Jody?"

"Shot 'im and left 'im to the wolves." Cole cut a grin

at the snaggletoothed cowboy in a patched suitcoat beside him. "Him an' that white whore o' his."

Stillman watched him, stony-faced.

Cole leaned forward, his face bunched demonically. His voice rose hoarsely. "You're all mine—all mine—old man! Now hand over what you took from Goodnight."

"What are you talkin' about?"

"What am I talkin' about?" Cole mocked.

The other man cut his dull eyes uncertainly between them. Cole jerked. In a blur, his Colt Navy was aimed at Stillman, who flinched.

"I'm talkin' about the ledger. We found the son of a bitch where you tried to hide him. Now, you can either hand it over or I can shoot you and take it. It's up to you."

Stillman spread his hands and smiled thinly. "I hid it."

Cole rose up in his saddle and extended the pistol. Grinning, he grabbed his crotch with his other hand. "I'll say good-bye to Mrs. Hobbs for you."

As he pulled back the hammer smoke puffed on the ridge behind the gunmen, a rifle cracked, and Stillman knew that Leon had gotten off the first shot. Blood spat from Cole's partner's chest. The man yelled and pitched forward.

Cole glanced at the snaggletoothed cowboy, who hit the ground with a sharp grunt and a whimper, then lay still. Stillman lowered his carbine and fired, but Sweets jumped and fouled his aim.

Fighting with the reins of his agitated horse, Cole brought his gun to bear. Stillman dismounted and ran toward the chimney. Cole took several errant shots before he spurred his black up the meadow, zigzagging.

Leon squeezed off three more shots. Head down and chaps winging, Cole galloped up the northern grade through the blowing snow and disappeared over the butte.

A few minutes later Leon rode out from the willows on

the other side of the creek and galloped across the meadow. "I seen 'em comin' and hid up in the brush," he said, half yelling.

Stillman resheathed his rifle and shook his head. "That's twice you had to save my ass."

McMannigle tightened his scarf. "You find out anything about them kids?"

"No, but I think they got away. Cole would have celebrated more if they were dead."

"I think so, too. But I don't know what kind of shape they're in."

"Say what?"

Leon reined his horse around toward the meadow behind the smoldering ruins of the barn. Stillman followed, concern tightening his face. Leon reined up a few yards before the creek at a rock he'd tied with a red bandanna. He pointed out several drops of blood beside a boot print.

Stillman lifted his hat and ran a hand through his hair with a sigh. "Find any more?"

"In the reeds there. They're heading east, prob'ly keeping to the creek for cover."

"Goddammit—it's getting cold," Stillman snapped. "Without shelter, they could freeze tonight."

"Why don't you head to town with the ledger and wire that marshal? I'll try to track 'em."

Stillman squinted off, puzzling it over, anxious to make the right move. "I think we best stick together. There's a storm coming on. Besides that, I think I know where they might have headed."

They rode out along the creek, Stillman glancing back at the burned-out ranchstead, where smoke tore on the wind and occasional coals glowed and died. All the animals were gone, probably shunted off toward Hobbs's range, appropriated without thought.

Jody and Crystal had made it away on foot, but how far and in what condition?

Stillman lifted his collar against the wind and led the way along the winding game trails hugging the creek. Several times they drew up to study their backtrail and work the cold from their legs.

It was dark by the time the creek angled back to the road. The wind stiffened Stillman's face, pelting him with snow. His toes were numb. Turning, he saw McMannigle hunkered down in his coat, his hat tied to his head with a scarf—a vague outline in the growing dark. If they didn't find Jody and Crystal soon, they'd have to hole up in the brush and resume their search in the morning.

But before they were ready to give up, the road angled through wooded hills, giving them a break from the wind. They entered the canyon where Olson's Roadhouse hunched, snow swirling before its lamplit windows. There were tracks in the light snow around the stoop and leading off to the woodshed flanking the house.

Leon took their horses, and Stillman rapped on the door.

Iver Olson opened it a crack and peered out suspiciously, said, "What can I do for ya?"

"Is Jody here? I'm Stillman. I stopped here with Crystal a few weeks back."

Olson nodded and drew the door wide. "She's been waiting for ya."

At the back of the room a door opened and Crystal appeared, holding a pistol at her side. "Mr. Stillman?" she said thinly.

She met him halfway across the room, threw her arms around him, and buried her face in his coat, sobbing. "Did you see what they did to the ranch?"

"I saw. Are you hurt?"

She shook her head. "We were going to raise a family

there.'' She pulled away and lifted her damp eyes. ''They shot Jody. We were trying to get away—''

''I saw the blood. How bad?''

''Bad.'' She turned, and he followed her into the room where Jody lay on a cot against the wall, buried in wool blankets.

His hair and face were damp with sweat. He was shaking. A gas lamp burned on a table, but Stillman couldn't tell if the boy was awake until he said, ''Hello . . . Mr. Stillman,'' his voice tight with pain.

''Hello, son. Rest easy. You're gonna be all right.''

''We were makin' a break for it across the pasture, and—''

''Shush now, easy.'' Stillman pulled the blankets back to a red-stained bandage taped to his chest and tied around his shoulder.

''Did you see what they did to the ranch?'' Jody said, wincing against the pain.

''Don't worry about the ranch. We got to get you mended.'' Stillman turned to Crystal. ''Anybody do any doctorin' around here?''

Iver Olson appeared in the door with a basin of water and fresh rags. His towheaded grandson stood behind him, gripping his elbow and staring wide-eyed at Jody.

''No more'n me, and that ain't much.'' Olson gave Crystal the basin and rags. ''We gotta get that fever down and get him to town as soon as we can, give Doc Nelson a look at him.''

Crystal shook her head, biting her lip. ''He's lost a lot of blood.''

Stillman sighed, squeezed Jody's arm. ''You get some rest, young man. I'm gonna figure a way out o' this mess.''

He turned and walked to the door behind Iver Olson and the boy. Casting a backward glance, he saw Crystal lean down, touch her lips to Jody's, and press the cool rag to his forehead, whispering.

Stillman went into the other room, where Leon sat at the end of a table, a mug of coffee steaming between his hands. A big, iron coffeepot and a bottle of bourbon sat nearby. Leon was still in his snowy coat. "How's the boy?"

"Not good. He took a bullet in the lung. We got to get him to town."

"Not in this weather."

"Any sign of a letup?"

McMannigle shook his head, swallowing coffee. "Not that I can tell."

Stillman took off his coat, laid it by the fire, and tossed his wet hat on top of it. He sat across from Leon, poured coffee into a tin mug, and lifted it to his lips.

"Tomorrow," he said, "letup or no letup, I'm getting that boy to town."

23

Stillman lay awake on his cot near the potbelly stove, hearing the wind in the flue and Leon McMannigle mumbling and sighing in troubled dreams.

I'll say good-bye to Mrs. Hobbs for you, Cole had said, grabbing his crotch.

Stillman flinched. The gunman knew about him and Fay. How? He must have tracked one of them. Why? Had Hobbs, suspecting, put the gunman on her trail? Or was Cole working alone, tending his own goatish fever?

Stillman swung his feet to the cold floor, leaned over, and retrieved a log from the wood box. The wind creaked the ceiling timbers and rattled the damper. Snow blew against the walls—probably piling up pretty good outside.

Using an iron poker, he opened the door slowly so the squeaky hinges wouldn't roust Leon, and added the log to the conflagration. He adjusted the log with the poker, then sat on the cot, pulled his wool socks over his long johns, and ran a hand through his hair, agitated.

Fay was in trouble.

He lay there for several hours, sleeping fitfully and tending the fire. It was still dark when he woke to the smell of frying bacon and the sound of Iver Olson knocking pans around in the kitchen. The fire had recently been banked, and the stove fairly glowed.

He dressed and went outside to check the weather.

Drifts curled two feet up from the cabin's base and around the corral posts, but the wind had died and the snow had stopped. He guessed six or eight inches had fallen, and from the cold air's nip on his nose, he judged the temperature to be around zero.

It would be a long, hard trip into Clantick, which lay about seventeen miles north. They'd have to rig a wagon for Jody and keep as undercover as possible, which meant a slow trip as well as a hard one. If Hobbs found them out here, they'd all be killed, buried, and forgotten—no questions asked.

Their only hope was to make Clantick and mix with the townspeople. And get Jody to a doctor.

Inside, Leon was up, stepping into his trousers. Olson's grandson was setting a breakfast table. Stillman crossed the room, tapped on Jody's door, and opened it a crack.

Crystal, squeezed in beside Jody on the narrow cot, stirred and looked around, half-asleep. Then, waking, she turned quickly to Jody, cupped her hand to his face, and listened.

To Stillman, she said, "He's alive."

Jody's foot moved and he wagged his head, opening his mouth. "I . . . I'm alive," he mumbled.

Stillman and Crystal shared a smile. "Let's see if we can get some food in him and get moving. The storm's stopped," Stillman said.

After breakfast, he and Leon harnessed Iver Olson's ancient prairie schooner to two good horses in Olson's corral and stretched a tattered canvas over the hickory bows. In the twelve-by-five box, Crystal fashioned a bed of straw, adding blankets and several buffalo robes.

They situated Jody into it, burying him in the robes so that only his black hair was visible, sliding in the breeze funneling through the moth-eaten canvas.

Crystal had gone back in for the rifle they had escaped with when Jody said weakly, "Mr. Stillman, I ain't gonna make it."

"Sure you are."

"I can feel it. I'm losin' all my energy."

"That's why you need to sleep. Conserve that energy."

Jody touched the hand Stillman had draped over the end of the worn maple wagon box. "I know you already done me one favor too many, but when you leave here, will you do me one more?"

"Son, that kind o' talk—"

"Take Crystal with you? She doesn't have anyone else here . . . just a crazy sister . . . and I'd worry about her."

Stillman looked at him glumly. He tucked the robe under Jody's chin, pursing his lips and nodding. "Okay, son. I'll take her with me. Now you get some rest."

Stillman and Leon went to the corral, saddled their horses, and led them into the yard. Crystal had climbed onto the quilts she'd folded over the buckboard's seat while Iver Olson set bags of food in the wagon box and offered words of encouragement to Jody.

Turning to Stillman, he said, "There's a ravine just east of here. Crystal knows it. There's a trail north that not many know."

Stillman nodded. "Much obliged. You gonna be all right?"

Olson's Norwegian-blue eyes twinkled, but he smiled sadly. "Hobbs and his won't mess with me. They like my cookin' too much." He lowered his gaze to where the snow was pocked with hoofprints. "If they stop by, I'll try to stall 'em, but you'll be easy to track. Best get a move on."

• • •

When the sun first pearled the clear, cold sky, they were crossing the shoulder of a butte near Heron Gulch. An hour later the sun shone gold on the new-fallen snow, etching the knobs and ridges in salmon, cloaking the western slopes in shadow.

As the wagon bounced along the rough bottoms of Heron Creek, Stillman and Leon McMannigle took turns scouting ahead and behind, breaking trail for the unwieldy schooner that rattled like a half-empty lumber dray.

Stillman rode up after scouting their backtrail. "How you doin', son?"

"I'm all right." Jody looked pale, and his eyelids drooped.

"Warm enough?"

Jody only nodded and closed his eyes. He was taking a beating on the rough trail, but if they ventured onto less sporting routes to town, odds were Hobbs would find them.

"How 'bout you, miss?" Stillman asked Crystal.

Crystal tried a smile and nodded, her breath puffing around her face, thick wool cap, and scarf.

"I don't think we're bein' followed. We might make it, after all," Stillman tried to assure her.

Looking straight ahead, she didn't seem to hear. "Mr. Stillman?" she said stiffly.

"Yes, ma'am."

"My father was riding with those men who burned us out and shot Jody."

Stillman knew what kind of man Warren Johnson was. Still, the information surprised him. Keeping his horse even with the wagon, he watched Crystal sadly. He was not an emotional man, but he suddenly wanted to take the girl in his arms and hold her for a long, long time.

"You know," he started, feeling awkward, "I've been

disappointed in life, but I've never had too many regrets. After meeting you, though, I regret not raising a whole passel of girls.''

She turned to him quickly, shocked by his uncharacteristic candor. Embarrassed, he looked away, then spurred Sweets ahead toward Leon.

Mid-morning, Donovan Hobbs, Weed Cole, and eight other riders cantered up to the roadhouse. The snow around the corrals and near the cabin had been pocked and scraped by several sets of hooves, and wagon tracks angled northward through a crease in the mountains.

"Looks like a goddamn caravan been through here," Cole said.

"Indeed." Turning to the others, Hobbs said, "Spread out. No use sitting here like ducks on a pond.''

Cole laughed. "Hell, they're long gone.''

"Or so they may want us to believe," Hobbs said self-importantly.

He waited for the riders to take positions in the trees and behind the outbuildings, then yelled, "Hello, the cabin!"

The door remained closed, windows dark.

"I say, hello the cabin! Olson, are you there?"

The door opened. Iver Olson stepped out, forcing a smile. "Didn't hear ya ride up in all this snow. My stew ain't ready yet.''

Hobbs tipped his hat back and leaned forward in the saddle. "We didn't come for the stew, Mr. Olson. We came for your guests.''

"What guests?"

"The ones that made all these tracks in the snow.''

Olson dropped his deep-lined face, pondering the tracks as though seeing them for the first time. "Those were some freighters out of Virgelle. They left at sunrise." He hooked

his thumbs under his suspenders and rolled onto the balls
of his feet in an unconvincing attempt at nonchalance.

Hobbs sucked his cheek and sighed, as though dealing
with a disappointing child. "Hold your positions, men.
Cole, come with me."

"My stew ain't ready yet," Olson repeated as Hobbs and
Cole brushed past him through the cabin door.

"Check the back room," Hobbs ordered Cole, looking
around.

He took off his hat, tossed it on a table, and sat down,
shaking his hair out from the collar of his fur-lined coat.
"Listen, Olson—we know Stillman and the Harmon boy
were here last night. We can track them, but you'd be sav-
ing me some time if you told me when they left and where
they're headed."

"I don't know what you're talkin' about. I told ya—"

"Stop with the lies, old man!" Hobbs yelled, his voice
shrill, his face red with exasperation. "We are neighbors,
Mr. Olson—it is in your best interest to act neighborly."

Nervously Olson lifted the globe off a table lamp and
cleaned it with his apron. "Those freighters—they come
all the way from Virgelle last night, got caught out in the
snow."

Cole walked out from the back room and tossed a blood-
smeared sheet on the table. "One o' those freighters musta
got himself hurt."

Olson slowly replaced the globe, frowning, lips moving
but not saying anything. In the kitchen, a pan clattered to
the floor. The old man started at the noise, knocking the
globe off its copper pedestal. It shattered on the table, glass
shards flying onto the floor.

Hobbs smiled. He skidded out his chair, got up, and
walked into the kitchen. A boy yelled. There was a brief
scuffle. Then Hobbs reappeared in the doorway with Ol-

son's grandson squirming and fighting against the ironlike grip on his arm.

"Ow—that hurts!" the boy squealed.

"Homer!" Olson blew through taut lips. He staggered forward. Weed Cole casually reached out and grabbed him by the waistband of his trousers, holding him back. "Let him go—he's just a boy!" Olson barked.

"Where did they go? Big Sandy or Clantick?"

Olson stared, old eyes horrified.

Hobbs pulled a knife from the sheath on his belt, showed it to Olson, then pulled back the boy's head with a handful of hair. The boy yelped, arms flailing forward. He panted, rasping, the breath gurgling in his throat.

The young neck shone white in the harsh light from the window.

"Grampa!"

"Homer!" The old man lurched forward again, but the gunman yanked him back.

Hobbs laid the curving blade point at the base of the boy's throat. "Big Sandy or Clantick?"

Olson took a deep breath and licked his lips, crestfallen. "Clantick."

"Which way?"

Olson's eyes widened at the knife blade pressing at his grandson's neck. "Heron . . . Heron Creek trail. Let him go."

Hobbs looked at Cole. "You know it?"

Cole, grinning at the show, nodded.

"When did they leave?" Hobbs said.

"Sunrise," Olson replied.

Hobbs raised his eyebrows at him. "If you're lying . . ." He withdrew the knife and pushed the screaming boy to the floor.

To Olson, he said, wagging the knife, "You're here because I allow you to be here. If there's any more of this horsing around, I'm going to cut off that boy's head and mount it above your door. Understood?''

Olson lifted the crying lad to his feet, giving Hobbs a hard look.

Hobbs stepped toward him, eyes bright with anger. ''I said, is it understood?''

''Understood.'' Olson choked under his breath, surrendering his gaze to the floor.

When Hobbs had walked out of the cabin, he added, kneeling and holding the howling boy to his shoulder, ''Ya plug-ugly bastard.''

24

Unable to sleep through the storm, Fay sat up and read by the living-room hearth. The words were a blur. She couldn't concentrate. Where was Ben? Where was Donovan? She kept wondering if their paths had crossed, and shuddered at the thought.

At nine the next morning, the wind ceased and the clouds parted, laying an eye-piercing carpet of gold light upon the new-fallen snow. Against the Bodios' protestations, Fay ordered her horse saddled. Then she bundled up in her warmest winter gear and headed for the barn. She had to find out for herself what was happening.

Spying movement in the distance, she stopped in her tracks. A lone rider was approaching on a gray, swaybacked nag. Fay watched the man come through the gate, dressed in a bulky wool coat, his breath frozen in the scarf around his hollow cheeks. His eyes were dark and wild with suppressed emotion, and he held a rifle across his saddle as though eager to use it.

"You Mrs. Hobbs?" he said as he halted the winded nag, spitting out the name like a sour prune.

"That's right."

"Where's your man? Where's Hobbs? I wanna talk to him."

"I don't know where he is."

The man jerked his head around nervously, scanning the buildings with a suspicious gleam in his eyes. The eyes and the long, thin, hooked nose gave him a predatory air. His frosted eyebrows rose like a bat's wings.

"Don't know, huh?" he said, as if to someone else.

"Your guess is as good as mine."

The man's gaze took in the nearly empty corrals and the quiet bunkhouse and cookshack. Frustrated, he turned to Fay. "I reckon you're right. I reckon he wouldn't be hidin' from the likes o' me." The man gave a woeful chuff.

Then his voice rose, shrill with anger, and his eyes filmed. His breath clouded about his head, nearly hiding his face. "But he's gonna want to hide his sorry ass the next time he sees me, 'cause I'm gonna be bearin' down on him good—with one of these!" He lifted the rifle from his saddle and jerked it at Fay.

She heard the house door open behind her and turned to see Ernesto Bodio walk onto the veranda with a pistol in his hand. Fay gestured for him to stay where he was.

Turning back to the visitor, whose eyes were blinking back tears, Fay asked with a sharp sense of foreboding, "What's happened?"

"He killed my brother, that's what happened—the son of a *bitch*!"

Fay's face blanched. She swallowed and took a breath, trying to organize her thoughts. "Who . . . why . . . ?"

The man turned his head to spit. Beneath him, the nag coughed and blew. "I rode out from Big Sandy to see how they faired in the storm—my brother and his hired man—and I found them dead in their cabin. Shot in the head, both of 'em."

"How do you know it was my husband who shot them?"

The man took off his right glove, reached into his coat

pocket, and produced a check. He handed it to Fay with an angry snap of his wrist. It bore Donovan's signature. "My guess is he used that dummy note to get into the cabin so he could shoot my brother, Gunther Van Orsdel, and Jackson Cooper at close range."

Fay stared at the check, feeling her heart throb in her temples. She felt like an accomplice in Donovan's brutal game, and she guessed that in a very real way she was indeed.

Her brow ridged with sorrow, she gazed up at the man, shaking her head. "I'm so sorry. . . ."

Her sympathy was lost on the man. "Your husband's the one's gonna be sorry," he said tightly. "I know the law's on his side, but it can't protect him forever from *this*." The man lifted the barrel of his rifle again, reined the old nag around, and cantered away through the snow.

"Your horse is winded," Fay called to him, squinting against the harsh light. "At least let me offer you a fresh mount. . . ."

But the man rode on without looking back. Fay lowered her eyes to the check in her hands. She fingered it thoughtfully, then ran to the barn for her horse.

The day was cold and clear in the wake of the storm, the temperature not climbing much above zero. The snow glittered like sequins, making it hard to see, and the pines that occasionally crawled into the ravine looked black. The brushy bottoms teemed with deer and coyote tracks, nearly obliterating the snow around ice-fringed springs.

The ride was hard on Jody, but there was little to do about that. If they'd left him at Olson's, he might have been discovered by now, or died before they brought the doctor back. Crystal trotted the two harnessed sorrels when the

trail was good, and they made better time than Stillman had
expected.

As they rode he tried to figure out the best trail ahead
around cutbanks, boulders, dry washes, scrub thickets, and
fallen trees. Getting the wagon hung up or stuck, or losing
a wheel, would cost them dearly.

A keen sense of urgency gnawed at him and dictated his
every action. He knew that if Hobbs's men were coming,
they'd found their trail by now, and there'd be no mistaking
it. Before noon, he hoped it would warm up enough for the
snow to melt, but by midday there seemed little chance of
that. He hoped then for a wind that might obliterate their
sign.

A breeze lifted in the late afternoon, but by then it was
time to stop. They made a rough camp in a brushy hollow
in a side canyon off Juniper Creek.

With the rising wind, the air turned colder. They nestled
Jody under the cutbank of a dry creek thick with wild rose
and willows, covered him with the buffalo robe and blankets, and built a small fire.

Then Stillman rode up the ridge behind them and drew
rein in a notch where the sky couldn't outline him. Shading
his eyes from the west-falling sun reflecting off the snow,
he watched down Juniper Creek, tracing every knob that
bulged nearby, every draw lip, and every mesa.

They had left the trail that followed Juniper Creek about
a mile back, crossing a frozen spring embedded in dog-
woods and scrub willows, and took to the side canyons.
Leon McMannigle lagged behind, covering their tracks
with pine branches and deadfall.

Now, plain as the cedars dotting Buster Butte, he saw
the riders curling single file around the anvil-shaped rock
below the second mesa south. There were ten men, maybe
more. They rode on down the point, up and over a narrow

saddle, then down again to the creek bottoms and out of sight.

It was shading into dark when Stillman got back to the camp and picketed his horse in the willows with the others. The buckboard stood above the cutbank in plain sight. There was little they could do to hide it. In the shallow ravine, Crystal sat cradling Jody to keep him warm. Her face was drawn, her eyes wide with worry.

While Stillman stripped the saddle from Sweets, Leon came over. "How's it look?"

"They're coming. Two, two and a half miles south."

Leon punched his fist and gritted his teeth. "Shit!"

"Well, we knew they'd come."

"I thought they'd hold off till tomorrow, but it makes sense to track us in the snow."

Stillman draped his saddle on a deadfall willow trunk next to Leon's. "They'll hold up soon if they haven't already. We'll have to get an early start again tomorrow." He straightened his back, looking off speculatively, and sighed. "Or . . ."

"Or what?"

"I was thinkin' . . . we could try to find their camp later. . . ."

Leon smiled without humor. "That's crazy talk, Ben. You know it. There ain't no way we could take out ten men in the dark."

Stillman looked at Jody. "I just want to get 'em off our backs. How is he?"

"He's in bad shape. We have to get him to town by tomorrow. I doubt he'll last a third day like today."

Stillman stuffed his mittened hands in his pockets, slumped down on the willow log, and closed his eyes, feeling as hollow as an old tree stump.

He remembered when he and another soldier had left

Fort Keogh one winter Saturday to hunt deer along the
Powder River. On their way back in the afternoon, a storm
came up—a whiteout with howling winds and bone-
splitting cold. Huddled in a buffalo wallow, they wrapped
themselves in blankets and slapped each other to stay
awake. Stillman's feet had long since numbed, and he and
his partner were nodding off when Bill Harmon's voice
boomed above the wind, calling their names.

Now he opened his eyes to gaze at Bill's son, lying still
and frail in the robes beside Crystal. The firelight played
across his sallow cheeks, creased with pain. He had to get
him to town. Tomorrow. If he died, the ghost of Bill Harmon would haunt him forever.

When he moved over to the fire, Leon handed him a cup
of hot coffee. "Let it go now," his partner said. "You'll
wear yourself out frettin'."

Stillman dipped up a plate of boiled venison heart and
ate slowly, taking comfort in the warm food and coffee,
feeling his strength return.

When he finished the meat, he wandered behind the fire,
scrubbed his plate with snow, then returned it to the bag
Olson had packed and poured a fresh cup of coffee from
the black enamel pot perched on a flat rock amid the flames.
Having been boiling for a half hour, it was strong enough
to peel the paint off a barn, but that was fine. Coffee perked
on a stove couldn't equal snowmelt java boiled over pine.

"You get some rest, Leon. I'll take the first watch."

Coffee in hand, he walked up the bank and kicked along
the trail to clear his head. He sipped his coffee and stood
looking around.

The ravine walls swept back against the twilight, gauzy
with snow. Above, the sky was clear, the first stars glowing
so brightly that Stillman could imagine their heat. An owl
hooted, breaking the eerie quiet. The wind had died, but it

was cold. They'd need to keep the fire banked tonight.

He sipped the quickly cooling coffee again, found a boulder to perch on, and thought about Fay. She'd be safe until he came for her. She was strong, like Crystal. A survivor.

After a while, his cup empty, he stood up stiffly, favoring his saddle-sore butt and back, stamped his feet, and wandered back down to the fire.

Crystal had sliced off some venison and was staring at her plate.

"Jody eat?" Stillman asked, startling her.

She shook her head. "I'm not hungry, either, but I know I'll need it tomorrow. I heard you tell Leon they were behind us."

"We'll make it."

"I don't think Jody will," she whispered, but her voice was matter-of-fact. She bit into the meat and chewed without vigor, staring stonily into the flames.

"We have to believe he will."

"It's too hard, and I'm too tired."

"You're strong." He looked at her across the fire. "You're one of the strongest people I know. Not many girls could be raised by a father like yours and turn out like you."

She raised her eyes to meet his and smiled. "That's the second compliment you've given me today, Mr. Stillman."

Flushing, he refilled his cup. "This cold air—it makes me sappy."

Several constellations had passed over the horizon when he at last turned in. Leon had to shake him several times to roust him. "It's five," he said.

"Jody?"

"Still kickin'."

Stillman stamped into his boots and grabbed his saddle. "Let's go to Clantick," he said.

25

Puffing on a cigarette stub, Weed Cole climbed up the bank and took back his horse's reins from Jimbo Tonneson, who'd wrapped them around his saddle horn.

"Yep, they camped here last night," Cole said to Hobbs, who sat straight-backed on his silver gray.

Cole regarded his boss and stifled a smirk. With his red locks, red goatee, fringed buckskin coat, the Englishman no doubt fancied himself General George before the Big Horn. He needed a fence post wrapped in barbed wire shoved up that tight ass o' his.

"Ashes are still warm. I'd say we're not much over an hour behind 'em," Cole added, looking away so the spectacle of the Brit wouldn't make him throw up his breakfast.

Hobbs turned to him sharply, eyes shaded by his hat brim, chin sticking out. Looks like a wart on a bullfrog's ass, Cole thought. "Not much over an hour behind them?" Hobbs said with strained reserve. "If we hadn't gone off on your wild-goose chase, we'd have them by now."

Cole lifted his hat and scratched his head, sheepish. "I thought for sure they were gonna try and ambush us in those rocks. You gotta watch yourself, trackin', or you'll ride up under their noses and get yourself shot."

"Do I detect a note of . . . fear, Mr. Cole?"

Cole's face flushed. The other men watched him nervously. He watched Hobbs, releasing cigarette smoke in short bursts.

It would have been easy as pie to blow the little high-falutin ferret out of his stirrups right then and there. His left eye closed and his right hand twitched. Then he caught himself. Not yet, he cautioned. Everything in its own good time.

Morris Whitley cleared his throat. "You know, they're prob'ly gonna keep to the canyons until they're just about to town—followin' one creek bottom or another all the way to the Milk."

"What are you saying, Mr. Whitley?"

The cowboy's Adam's apple bobbed in a neck covered with two-day stubble. "Why don't we split up? Half of us take the short route to town and try to cut 'em off. The others keep on their asses, pushin'. That way—"

"Yes, we'd box them in," Hobbs said, rubbing his chin. Turning to Cole accusingly, he said, "I thought ten men on horseback could overtake a buckboard. But now that we've lost so much time due to Mr. Cole's . . . Yes, Mr. Whitley. Yes, we shall do just that."

Hobbs pointed his sparsely whiskered chin at the lanky cowboy and said, "You and I and two others will lead them on the shortest route to Clantick, Mr. Whitley. Cut them off at the pass, so to speak."

"Yes, sir, Mr. Hobbs," Whitley drawled. "That's just what I had in mind."

Hobbs took the man's ears in his two soft hands and squeezed. "You're brilliant, Mr. Whitley. Brilliant!"

Turning to his ramrodder, he said, "Cole, you and the others keep hounding their asses. Don't let them turn around and get past you. Another slipup on your part and

Mr. Whitley here will be snoring in your bunk. Understood?''

Cole gave Hobbs a cold smile.

Not willing to press the issue, Hobbs clapped his hands, called the names of two men, and spurred away, making a beeline toward town.

Cole leaned on his saddle horn and watched the men ascend a notch in the ridge. His eyes were black.

That fucking Brit was getting just too goddamn big for his britches.

Fay galloped into town at noon and cantered down Main Street, raising the eyebrows of several merchants sweeping slush from their boardwalks. Well, what do we have here?

They'd never seen Donovan Hobbs's wife in an oversized sheepskin coat and riding pants, her hair bouncing on her shoulders—indeed, had never imagined her in anything less than pearl chokers and feathered hats.

Exchanging hangdog glances, they watched her canter west on the tall, white-socked black, and turn the corner around the big cottonwood at the edge of town.

What do you make of that? Not even a sidesaddle!

Outside the business district, Fay spurred along a buggy path curving up a butte face and halted at the massive stone house perched on top. Beneath the stone turrets and outside the white picket fence, two black buggies each stood harnessed to a black stallion, their horsehide upholstery fairly glistening in the cold sun.

Fay tied her nickering gelding to the hitching post, strode up the wide wooden steps, and knocked on the carved cherry-wood doors. A second later she rapped with her fist until the stained glass rattled and a gray-bunned maid appeared frowning.

''I have to see Mr. Anderson,'' she said firmly, striding

past the maid, who had only just closed the door as Fay
marched out the foyer and into the living room.

Mrs. Anderson appeared in the kitchen door, a young
maid peeking around her shoulder, dressed for guests in a
quiet blue gown, wrinkled cheeks smeared with rouge. ". . .
Mrs. Hobbs?"

"I have to see Mr. Anderson," Fay repeated with the
same urgency, following the smell of roast beef and the
sound of men's voices to the dining room.

Sophus Anderson and three men in suits sat around an
oval table bedraped with white linen and adorned with Aus-
trian crystal, crouched over plates of mashed potatoes and
gravy and thick slabs of marbled, pink beef charred at the
edges. Mr. Hall from the mercantile, who faced the doorway, saw her just as he forked a load of gravy-drenched
potatoes into his mouth. He did a double take, probably
thinking for a moment she was one of the stable hands.
Then he froze, bewildered.

Turning to look at what had suddenly enraptured Mr.
Hall, the others fell silent.

Wiping his mouth with an embroidered napkin, Anderson said, "Mrs. Hobbs!"

Fay swallowed and nervously swept stray strands of hair
from her cheek. "Mr. Anderson, may I have a word with
you?"

"Uh . . . well, I'm . . ." He hesitated, looking at his
guests with an expression of frantic confusion.

Fay's voice rose. "If you want, I'll take a seat and have
a word with you here, though I doubt your associates will
be pleased with what I have to say."

"All right, all right, Mrs. Hobbs," Anderson said, rising
and smiling at the others. "This, gentlemen, is Donovan
Hobbs's lovely wife, Fay. She's quite the equestrian." He
chuckled, indicating her garb. "I'll just step out for a mo-

ment and clear up Mrs. Hobbs's concerns. Please, help yourself to more wine!''

When Anderson had led Fay to his oak-paneled study and closed the door, he said, ''Mrs. Hobbs, what could possibly provoke such an intrusion? Those men are partners of your husband's and mine in—''

''Murder, Mr. Anderson?''

''Pardon?''

''Have you taken a ride through the Clear Creek lately? It looks like a battlefield.''

''Mrs. Hobbs! . . . Please keep your voice down. Who?''

''Van Orsdel and his hired man. His brother found the two men in their cabin—dead. Shot in the head. And the Harmon ranch has been burned. I rode out looking for Ben and saw it myself.''

Anderson's face softened.

She said worriedly, looking down, ''There's no sign of Ben and Jody.''

Anderson turned and planted his fingertips on his broad, mahogany desk. ''I had no idea he was going to go this far.''

She tipped her head and looked at him directly, her dark eyes lit with incredulity. ''Sure you did. We both did. We know what kind of man my husband is. It was just more convenient to ignore it.''

His back to her, Anderson squeezed his eyes closed. ''If he's ruined, I'm ruined.''

''We're already ruined, Mr. Anderson. We both have blood on our hands.'' Laughing angrily at an afterthought, she added, ''Hell, we're bathing in it.''

When Anderson didn't move or reply, Fay slumped down on a cowhide settee beneath an old Regulator clock whose pendulum reported the passing seconds with hollow, wooden knocks. She took her hat in her hands and worried the brim. Her thick hair fell around her face.

"What's he doing?" she asked after a time. "What's he trying to get away with?"

Anderson moved slowly around his desk and sat heavily into his overstuffed swivel rocker. He set an elbow on the desk, rested his chin in his hand, and told Fay about her husband's determination to have the whole Clear Creek Valley to himself, and about his selling the rustled stock to Goodnight.

"It was hellishly efficient," Anderson said with a mirthless laugh. "The Indians weren't going to ask where their free beef came from, and shipping it on the river—separate from his own stock—who was going to know?"

"What about the dead nesters and burned cabins?"

Anderson shrugged. "It's a big country, and 'nester' is a dirty word."

They sat listening to the clock for several minutes. Then Anderson tapped his fingers on the desk and sighed. "Well, greed is my excuse," he said slowly, a curious smile growing on his long face. "You're a beautiful woman. You could have married anyone. Why did you get involved with Donovan Hobbs?"

"Greed," Fay said, undaunted, as though she'd considered the question at length. She nodded, lips pursed. "It was all arranged, you see. It was safe and tidy, and a good place to hide."

"From what?"

"The memory of Ben Stillman, I guess."

Anderson nodded. "Well, you can run," he murmured.

"Yes. But you can't hide." Fay got up slowly and moved to the door.

"Where are you going?"

She turned to him, placing her hat on her head. Her eyes were determined. "To put my life back together."

26

Stillman halted his bay on the leeward side of a hillock and waited for the buckboard to catch up. Fishing his tobacco pouch from his shirt pocket, he studied the ravine on his left.

A creek meandered through willows and cattails burdened with soggy snow. Here and there a dead box elder poked its barkless branches skyward. The water was black under the purple sky; the silky chinook wind fingered it, combed it to a light froth. The air was fresh with the smell of wet earth and sage.

The country ahead was empty except for an occasional hawk drifting under the cloud-heavy sky, and the sudden leaps and bounds of pronghorn antelope, hooves casting up gouts of melting snow and grass.

The unscarred vastness reminded Stillman of the time he and Bill Harmon rode with a herd up from Texas. Working the point, he and his partner were at times a day or two ahead of the herd, waiting for the drovers at some watering hole with fresh buffalo tongue roasting over a fire and a pot of Arbuckle's gurgling and steaming on a charred rock. Sometimes they hung the meat from a river-bottom tree, moving on to scout the next butte or creek, trigger fingers twitching in anticipation of Red Cloud's Sioux.

That wide-open country had given him the jitters. What lay behind the Pumpkin Buttes or beyond the dry fork of the Powder River only God and the Teton Sioux knew.

The Hi-Line gave Stillman the same feeling. It was as raw and as wide open a land as the Bozeman Trail twenty years ago. The Indians were gone, but they'd been replaced by land-hungry cattlemen armed with cowboy mercenaries.

Stillman ran the edge of the cigarette paper along the tip of his tongue, then folded it closed. The run toward Clantick had been too easy thus far, too quiet—like a held breath. Crystal would be pulling the buckboard onto the tableland soon, where she'd stand out like an open barn door. Stillman could use some of those Rees old Burl Magnusson from his trail-driving days had hired to poke around knobs and mottes, to scour draws, and to scout that curling creek line out yonder.

He turned as the buckboard clattered up the grade behind him, its wheel hubs barking for grease.

"Better stop and blow the horses," Stillman told Crystal. "Where's Leon?"

Frowning, Crystal turned to look behind her. "I thought he was just . . . I don't know."

Stillman took another drag off his cigarette, then mashed it against his boot sole. "We better wait for him. Something might be up." He climbed down from the saddle and reached under the wagon's jockey box for the grease bucket.

He was lubricating the second hub when Crystal said, "Here he comes."

Stillman turned to watch Leon gallop across the ravine bottom. He approached in a clap of hooves, his horse blowing and shaking its bridle, its neck lathered.

"They're only about a mile back," McMannigle said,

pulling on the reins. Beads of sweat streaked the dust on his black cheeks.

Stillman scowled. He walked to the wagon and looked in the box. Jody lay with his chin tipped to his chest. He was asleep, but pain registered in the lines around his dark, sunken eyes.

Stillman winced and shook his head. "We don't have time to try and lose 'em in the ravines. We have to make a straight run to Clantick."

"The buckboard will never make it," McMannigle warned.

"You got a better idea?"

McMannigle rubbed his forehead and twisted around to look behind them. After a few seconds he looked at Stillman. "You take the boy on your horse. I'll give Crystal mine. You all make a beeline for town. I'll take the buckboard and head on down the draw. They'll follow the wagon tracks."

Stillman quickly considered it, returning the grease bucket to its hook below the jockey box. The hard ride could very well kill Jody, but Leon was right. Hobbs would catch the buckboard and kill them all.

Stillman looked at Crystal. She'd grabbed the rifle from the wagon box and was holding it across her knees. "Sounds like a plan. But I'm going with Leon."

"Oh, no you're not, miss," Leon said, wagging his head.

"Ben and Jody'll have a better chance without me. It's easier trackin' two horses than one. And you're gonna need somebody ridin' shotgun. We don't have all day. Let's get a move on."

Leon looked at Stillman. "She's got a will on her, don't she?"

Stillman raised his eyebrows and wagged his head with dismay.

He and Leon lifted Jody out of the buckboard and onto Stillman's saddle. Then Stillman pulled his pistol and spun the magazine, making sure all six chambers showed brass. He mounted Sweets behind Jody, who sat like a rag doll cloaked in a buffalo robe, his chin grazing his chest. Crystal, standing beside Sweets, squeezed Jody's hand and kissed it.

"I'll see you soon, my love. Okay?"

"I'm so . . . *tired*," Jody groaned.

Stillman looked at Leon. "You two hightail it."

"Don't worry about us," McMannigle said. "It's you they're after."

Stillman poked Sweets with his spurs. The horse sprang into a trot and quickly rocked to a gallop. Stillman had rested the animal several times throughout the day, never spurring him beyond a canter. Sweets was happy to have his head now, snorting and laying his ears back with the feel of the wind against his face and the warm blood coursing through his shoulders and thighs, the grassy turf meeting his hooves with a satisfying thud.

Happy as the horse was to have his way, when Stillman felt him tiring, he reined him to a halt atop a camelback and jumped down. He held Jody on the saddle and surveyed the ground behind them—a dun-green expanse of rolling prairie gently lifting to the first front of the Two Bear Mountains capped in sunny clouds.

"Where . . . where are we?" Jody asked, weakly coaxing his head up to look around.

"About two miles from town."

"Where's Crystal?"

Stillman turned to answer the boy when, from far off behind them, he heard gunfire muffled by the wind. *They've spotted the wagon*, he thought with a heavy, sick feeling in his gut.

Mounting up, Stillman said, "She's all right, son. She'll be along soon."

When the Milk River buttes and the first clapboard shacks and stock pens of Clantick appeared on the horizon, three riders rose up from the prairie on Stillman's left. Galloping and standing in their saddles, hats tipped into the wind, they were angling northward between Stillman and town.

"Son of a *buck*!"

The lead rider was Donovan Hobbs. Stillman placed the Englishman by the stiff head and back, bouncing curls, and by the way his knees gripped the saddle—as though he felt no more at home on a horse than on the back of a charging rhino.

"Okay, you bastard," Stillman muttered. With one hand on Jody's shoulder, he reached down and shucked his rifle from its boot and levered a shell into the chamber.

"Son, can you take the reins?"

Jody nodded, blindly reaching for Stillman's hand. Stillman wrapped the reins over Jody's fist. "Now lean forward so I don't blow out your eardrums."

The boy hunched down. Stillman raised the rifle to his shoulder and squeezed off three quick shots. The riders flinched and pulled up a bit but kept coming just the same.

"Okay, you bastard," Stillman said, squeezing off three more rounds. "I've had my goddamn fill o' Donovan Hobbs!"

He laid the Henry's sites on Hobbs's buckskin coat and squeezed the trigger. Hobbs's silver-gray gelding took a dive. Hobbs flew over its head. He landed several feet beyond the horse and lay there for several seconds before rising to a knee.

He looked around, hatless and stunned. The horse stayed down, kicking its legs.

The other two riders pulled up to appraise the state of their boss and squeezed off several rifle rounds in Stillman's direction. It bought him the time he needed to make an arc around the riders and turn Sweets toward Clantick, splashing through puddles and mucking through slushy snowdrifts.

He halted the horse near a chicken coop at the scraggly edge of town and turned to scan his backtrail. No riders. At least, not yet. He traced a wandering course around outhouses, stock pens, and low, clapboard shacks until he found his way to Main Street.

It must have been near six o'clock. The shades were drawn in several storefronts, the streets practically deserted, except for several cow ponies and a lumber dray congregated outside Howell's Saloon. Stillman stopped a leathery toothpick of a man headed that way.

"Mister, where might I find Doc Nelson?"

The man tipped back his sugar-loaf Stetson. "Two blocks down and to the right, but I don't think he's in. Mrs. McQueen's having her baby out to Zurich. What's with the boy?" The man jerked his head around, giving Jody the twice over.

Ignoring the question, Stillman scowled. "Where's the banker's place—Anderson's place?"

The man took his hand from his denim pocket and pointed. "Atop the butte over yonder. Big stone house. But I thought you was lookin' fer a doctor?"

"Any more in town?"

"No."

"Then I guess the banker will have to do."

Stillman reined Sweets around and spurred him up the street. If he had looked left down Second Avenue, he would have seen Fay's black horse tied to the hitching post before the sheriff's office. But he kept his eyes straight ahead, intent on Anderson's, whom he hoped he could trust in spite of the banker's ties to Donovan Hobbs.

Stillman found the place—easily the largest, most distinctive house in town, it was hard to miss—and eased Jody out of the saddle. As he was carrying the boy up the wide wooden steps, the cherry-wood doors opened. Anderson stepped out with a cloth napkin hanging from his collar.

"Oh, for Christ sakes!" he complained with a pained expression. "What happened?"

"Hobbs," Stillman grunted, carrying Jody through the doors. "The doctor's out of town. He needs a bed."

"This way," Anderson said.

He led Stillman up a staircase, down a hall, and into a papered bedroom with a canopied, four-poster bed and lace curtains. He threw the covers back. "Lay him down here. How bad is he?"

"Bullet in the chest."

Anderson winced and shook his head. "I'll go tell Carl to have Mrs. Nelson send the doc over here as soon as he gets back to town."

When Anderson had left, Stillman worked the buffalo robe off Jody and nestled him under the sheets and blankets. He checked his wound and found the bandage soaked with blood.

Jody was out, sleeping deeply, throat rattling with short, barely audible breaths. His face was pale and drawn. His cheeks were hollow, eyes ringed with dark circles of pain and exhaustion.

Stillman said, "Jody."

The boy didn't even stir.

"Damn," Stillman said, tucking the covers under his chin and backing up to a chair. He sat down with a sigh. "I hope I haven't gone and killed you."

● ● ●

Sheriff Ed Lewis squirmed around in his cane-back office chair behind his rolltop desk covered with wanted posters, dirty coffee cups, cigar butts, and mouse turds. He regarded Fay with his fishy blue eyes strangely magnified by thick-lensed spectacles. He pursed his lips and folded his small, wrinkled hands over his wool vest. Frowning, he said, "Mrs. Hobbs, I'm not sure what it is you *want*."

"I want you to find my husband and arrest him. He's been murdering people in the Clear Creek Valley," Fay said urgently, carefully enunciating every word for the old fool's torpid brain.

She'd come here only after riding around for several hours, searching for sign of Ben and Jody, wondering what to do. She knew the sheriff was in her husband's pocket, but certainly he didn't know about the murders!

Slowly the sheriff gave his eyes to the deputy sitting against the wall on an upended apple crate. The deputy's fleshy, sun-cured cheeks inched upward with a grin. He met Lewis's gaze. Fay thought it was the first time he'd taken his ogling eyes off of her since she'd entered the office.

"Are you sure, Mrs. Hobbs, you and your husband didn't just have ya a little spat, and you—"

"Sheriff," Fay snapped, leaning forward in her chair, taking a deep breath, "earlier today I learned that a Mr. Van Orsdel and his hired man were found dead in their cabin. They were each shot in the head."

"Why do you think your husband did it?"

"Because this was found near the bodies." She took the folded paper from her coat pocket and set it on the desk. It was the fake check Hobbs had drawn for Van Orsdel, complete with Donovan's ostentatious signature.

Fay leaned back wearily and sighed as the sheriff studied the document, squinting his eyes and moving his lips, occasionally mumbling a word to dope out its meaning.

"Want me to read it fer ya, Sheriff?" the deputy offered with a smirk.

"When did you learn to read, Todd?" the sheriff snapped. Turning to Fay, he said, "It looks to me like your husband offered this man a very handsome price for his land. He no doubt would have made good on the deal if this Van Orsdel hadn't been killed—by rustlers, no doubt. Or highwaymen."

Fay rose and planted a fist at the edge of the rolltop desk. "Sheriff, I know that my husband has supplemented your income very generously. For that I'm sure you're grateful. But are you going to sit there and let him get away with murder!"

The sheriff's eyes darkened. "Mrs. Hobbs, are you accusing me of taking bribes?"

"I'm not accusing—" Fay stopped, closed her eyes, and licked her lips. She tried again, slowly. "I simply want you to stop my husband before he kills Ben Stillman and Jody Harmon."

"Stillman? How do you know Stillman?"

The deputy gave a clipped laugh. The sheriff looked at him, frowning.

Ignoring them, Fay said, "He's burned the Harmon ranch. Ben was staying there. Ben and Jody are both gone, and I'm almost *positive* Donovan is hunting them."

"How do we know it's Donovan?" the sheriff asked impatiently.

"Because neither he nor his men have been home in two days."

"Well, good Lord, woman—it's roundup!"

Fay took another deep breath and spread her hands. "Okay, what about Ben Stillman and Jody Harmon? They are missing. Would you please look for them?"

The sheriff glanced at the deputy and cocked his head at

Fay. "How did you say we know Stillman?"

Stiffly, with exaggerated calm, Fay nodded. "Okay, Sheriff. I get the idea. I'll take the check back from you now and find a different angle."

Lewis leaned back in his chair, folding the draft and stuffing it inside his coat. "No, I think I better hold on to this for safekeeping. Evidence, you know."

Fay's chest heaved. Her face flushed. "You *bastard*!" she screamed, sweeping his desk with her arm. Papers and cigars flew across the room.

The sheriff jumped to his feet and shouted, "Mrs. Hobbs!"

The deputy lunged for Fay, restraining her with his massive arms as though she were a doll. He laughed and whooped as she struggled, knocking his hat off.

"What should I do with her, Sheriff!"

"Escort her to the door," Lewis ordered. To Fay he said paternally, "I'm sorry, Mrs. Hobbs, but it appears you've had a bit too much to drink. I think it best you go home and explain your behavior to your husband."

Struggling as the deputy turned her toward the door, Fay yelled in a deep, rasping voice, "You're a small man, Lewis. A very, very *small* man!"

The deputy opened the door and shoved her through— into the arms of Donovan Hobbs.

"Mr. Hobbs!" the deputy said with a harebrained laugh. "We were just talkin' about you."

27

"What is the meaning of this?" Hobbs barked.

He cut his small, narrowed eyes between the deputy, Fay, and Lewis, as though they were kids caught roughhousing in school.

The deputy scratched his head and gave the sheriff, standing tongue-tied before the desk, a wry, sheepish grin.

Hobbs turned his interrogative eyes on his wife. "What's going on?"

With cold exasperation, Fay replied, "Donovan, what have you *done*?"

The answer was so unexpected it didn't register. Disregarding it, Hobbs looked beyond her to Lewis. "What's going on here, Sheriff?"

Lewis's cheek twitched; he hesitated, cleared his throat. "Uh . . . the missus here, Mr. Hobbs—she wanted to report a murder."

Forehead creased like crumpled paper, Hobbs turned back to Fay. "What?"

"You're a murderer, Donovan," she said flatly. "You killed those men in the Clear Creek. And you burned the Harmon ranch."

Hobbs looked at her, stupefied.

"What did you do to Jody Harmon and Ben Stillman?"

Hobbs's eyes blazed. He glanced around, then moved stiffly forward and shoved Fay into the office. The deputy followed and shut the door behind them. The sheriff hesitated, removed the document from his inside coat pocket, and handed it to Hobbs.

"She said she found this in Hungry Hollow."

Hobbs grabbed the bank draft. His eyes smoldered over it, the idea of his wife betraying him going down like camphor.

"What did you do to Jody Harmon and Ben Stillman?" Fay implored.

Hobbs looked into her wide, lovely eyes, lit with a passion he'd never before been privy to. It excited him as it enraged him.

He crumpled the document, opened the door of the potbelly stove, and tossed it in. "Why are you so concerned about Jody Harmon and Ben Stillman?" His voice was cold as the English winter.

Behind Hobbs, the deputy snickered.

Hobbs turned sharply and squinted his eyes at the man. "What? Out with it!"

The deputy took a long look at Fay. Then his gray eyes slid to Hobbs, a half smile curling his scarred upper lip. He'd never been taken seriously by important men, and the sudden attention was intoxicating. "Nah . . . it ain't no business o' mine."

"What is no business of yours, Deputy?"

The man scowled with feigned reluctance, said to Fay, "Sorry, ma'am . . . Weed Cole got to drinkin' in the saloon the other night, and said he seen her—your wife—and Ben Stillman together."

"Together?"

The deputy scowled again and shook his head as though

this were the hardest thing he'd ever had to do in his life.

"I'm awful sorry, ma'am. They were together in the . . . biblical sense, I guess you could call it." The deputy snorted accidentally, stifled it, flushed, and feigned a look of diffidence.

Hobbs stared at the deputy as though the towering brute had just fallen from the sky. After a long time he turned to Fay. His eyes were flat, his brow furrowed. "Tell me this man is lying," he said. It was like a plea. His voice almost cracked.

Fay said nothing. Her fear for Ben and Jody was now coupled with a heart-pounding fear for herself.

"How do you know Stillman?"

Fay cut her eyes to the door behind Donovan, then sprang for it. She realized it was hopeless even before Hobbs grabbed her and threw her back into the room.

He stepped casually toward her, almost swaggering, his thin, effeminate lips pursed inside the red goatee like a rodent peering from its hole. She sensed that the memory of her past reluctance to share his bed was mingling in his mind with the image of her and Ben, stoking him toward an explosion.

"How do you know Stillman?" Hobbs repeated with a casual air.

She licked her lips, tasting fear. "I don't. The man is lying."

"Todd," Hobbs said to the deputy without looking at him, "step over here."

The deputy, who'd been leaning next to the door with his arms folded self-importantly, moved slowly forward. His six-and-a-half-foot frame dwarfed the buckskin-clad rancher. Nervously he tipped his soiled Stetson back from his broad, white forehead.

"Tell me again what Cole told you about my wife and Stillman."

The deputy's smile had faded, his eyes turned cautious. He hesitated. "What do you mean?"

"Tell me what Cole told you in the saloon," Hobbs said.

The deputy chewed this for a second. Wondering if he wasn't in over his head, he suddenly felt himself yearning for a saloon table, a bottle, and a quiet whore. "I told ya— he seen 'em together."

Hobbs squeezed his eyes shut. "How?"

"Naked."

"Doing what?"

The deputy sucked his upper lip, cutting his eyes between Hobbs and Fay. He gave a nervous chuff. "They were . . . ruttin'." The big man, flushing with confusion, glanced at the sheriff for help. The sheriff, offering none, stared at the floor.

Hobbs opened his eyes at Fay. Fear had turned her to stone. "Do you think even a dull brute like the deputy here would tell me such a thing if it weren't true?"

Fay's breast heaved. "What have you done to Ben and Jody?" she asked, her voice thin with desperation.

Hobbs blinked, lifted his chin. "Do you know what the Mexicans do to adulterous wives?"

"Are they dead?" Her voice rose to a shriek. "Tell me, you son of a bitch!"

"They beat them, slash their lovely faces, and throw them to the savages like the deputy here." Hobbs chuckled dryly. "If there's anything left of them after that, they blow their lying, deceiving, cuckolding brains out." He gave an evil smile and, with his left hand, pulled his pearl-handled Bisley from his right holster, clicked back the hammer, and raised it to Fay's forehead.

"Easy now, Mr. Hobbs," the deputy said self-importantly. He reached out his big hand and laid it on Hobbs's shoulder.

Hobbs turned, his face ashen, and stared at the hand until the deputy removed it. "What did you say?" he said through clenched teeth.

The deputy swallowed. "I said . . . come on now, that's enough."

Hobbs pressed the barrel to Fay's forehead. The deputy stepped forward. Hobbs yelled, "Don't *touch* me!"

He swung the pistol left. Just as the man's lips parted to yell Hobbs blew a bullet through his head. The temple exploded like a ripe melon, spraying brains and bone. The man folded against the wall. Falling, his body jumped and twitched as Hobbs emptied the Bisley as deliberately as if he were target-shooting into the big man's blood-soaked frame.

Fay had sunk to her knees, screaming and holding her ears against the deafening shots.

"Hobbs—what the hell!" Lewis yelled, watching the exhibition with white-faced, wide-eyed horror.

Fetid smoke hung in the air, cloudy and blue-veined. The rich, coppery smell of blood and viscera tightened Fay's stomach and made her retch.

Hobbs holstered the smoking Bisley. "Now, then," he said with a sigh. "You get the idea."

He grabbed Fay by the hair and, as she screamed and struggled against him, dragged her through an open cell door. "Sheriff, my wife has been naughty. Until I can decide what to do with her, I want her locked up." He closed the door with a loud, metallic boom.

The sheriff was looking at the deputy uncomprehendingly, blinking his rheumy blue eyes behind lenses as thick as shotglass bottoms. Then, wits returning, he went to his desk, rummaged in a drawer for a key ring, and locked the cell.

Fay lay with her shoulders against the cinderblock wall, her hair a raven cloud around her face, staring at Hobbs. Her big, brown eyes were fairly glistening, her oval face ashen with unmitigated hatred.

Meeting her stare, and aroused to a frenzy, Hobbs clapped his hands and squeezed them together. "Now, shall we go find her . . . her . . . *friend*?" he said to the sheriff with psychopathic cheer.

In the chair by Jody's bed, his boots propped on the bed frame, Stillman had nearly nodded off from exhaustion when he heard someone on the stairs. His eyes opened and he shucked his Colt so quickly he surprised himself.

"Just me," Anderson said, entering the room with an enamel washbasin. "I sent Carl to the Nelson place. Doc should be sent here as soon as he gets back to town." He looked at Stillman. "You can leather that iron anytime now; you're making me nervous."

Stillman regarded the gun in his hand, then holstered it. "Sorry—my brain's gettin' as heavy as my eyelids. I want to thank you for what you're doin'. I wasn't sure I could trust you, but I didn't have a choice."

Anderson pulled back Jody's blankets and, wincing, slowly removed the bandage on his chest. "You can't trust fence-straddlers, that's for sure."

"You still straddling?"

Anderson's jaw tightened as he worked. "Stillman, my livelihood is that bank and Donovan Hobbs. His money built it, built this house, carpeted these floors—hell, bought the damn rag I'm using to dress his handiwork!" He turned to Stillman, his gray eyebrows raised like wings, spectacles hanging low on his ax-handle nose. "But if Hobbs came through that door right now, I'd blow his fucking brains out." He narrowed his eyes and punctuated the thought with a nod, then turned back to Jody.

Thoughtfully Stillman dropped his eyes to the floor, then raised them. "I have another favor to ask you."

He reached inside his buckskin coat and pulled out Goodnight's ledger book. "This here will hang Hobbs and his crew. Can you hold it for me until I leave town?"

The banker rung out the rag in the basin, then set the basin on the table beside Jody. "Love to," he said.

"You got a safe?"

Anderson pulled the covers up to Jody's chin. The boy slept restlessly, jerking his head in pain. "That's all I know to do. Now we'll have to wait for the doc."

With his middle finger, the banker shoved his glasses up on his nose and studied the boy for a moment, shaking his head. He regarded the ledger in Stillman's hand and said, "Follow me."

Stillman followed the old man downstairs to his study, a quiet room where the Regulator clock ticked and two long windows spilled washed-out light on the gray-carpeted floor. An old black cat as big as a badger snoozed on a hearth cushion before a crackling fire.

Anderson pulled his slacks up his thighs, knelt down to the safe behind his desk. He jerked the combination dial back and forth, dropped the bar, and opened the door. Stillman handed him the ledger, and Anderson set it inside.

Stillman said, "You realize what Hobbs would do to you . . . ?"

Anderson shut the door and spun the knob, rose awkwardly to his feet. "Oh, to hell with Hobbs!" Gazing at Stillman, he said, "You look like walking death. Why don't you go upstairs and lie down? I'll keep an eye on young Harmon."

"No, Crystal and Leon are still out there. I've dawdled away too much time the way it is."

"You go back out there now, you'll get lost. It's turnin' dark and another storm's blowin' up."

Stillman looked out the window, where a gunmetal sky hung low over the Milk River buttes and snowflakes swirled. The banker was right. If Leon and Crystal were going to make it, they'd have to make it on their own.

Stillman ran a hand along his jaw. "Well, I can't just sit here. I'm gonna go down and see if I can wire Dale True in Helena, get some help up here." He made for the office door, then suddenly stopped and turned.

"Where's your wife?"

"I sent her over to her sister's in Shelby," Anderson said, looking down. "After what happened this afternoon, I had a feelin' hell was comin' down. I suppose it was just a matter of time with a man like Hobbs."

"What happened this afternoon?"

"Your woman—or Hobbs's woman . . . or whoever the hell's woman she is—came callin'. She found the Harmon cabin burned."

"Fay's in town? She's all right?" Stillman's voice rose.

"She was full of vim and vinegar a couple hours ago. As long as she don't run into her husband, she should be just fine."

28

It was near dark, and the weather had turned cold once again.

A sky the color of bruised plums dropped low and swollen over the false fronts of Main. The wind groaned in from the northwest, and Stillman felt it pressing him sideways as he rode the bay up to the telegraph office.

A lamp shone inside the small, gray cabin. Stillman quickly tied Sweets to the hitching post and, after scanning for Hobbs and his crew, shucked his rifle and stepped inside.

A stout, pig-faced man in green eyeshades stood behind the counter, counting money and tallying figures in an account book.

"Sorry, I'm closed," he said.

"This is an emergency."

The man shook his head, counting bills from one hand into the other. He stopped, plucked a pencil from behind his ear, and scribbled a figure on a tally pad. "If Joseph wanted to get word out that Mary was about to pop, I couldn't do it. Lines are down."

Stillman cursed. "For how long?"

"Hour, hour and a half."

"What happened?"

The man wrapped a bundle of one-dollar bills with a rubber band and shrugged. "Beats me. The storm or those damn Crees. Come back tomorrow. I'll send someone out at first light."

Stillman dropped an elbow to the counter and kneaded his forehead. "Are you sure?"

The man sighed and smiled sympathetically. "Mister, go have yourself a few drinks over to the saloon. It'll be mornin' before you know it."

"I don't think so, friend."

On the boardwalk he stopped. Sweets was gone.

He glanced around, feeling a wet chill leapfrog his spine. Through the snow, he could make out three men facing him on horseback across the street, rifle butts snugged against their hips. Above them, another rifleman lay on the porch of Mugridge's Dental Parlor.

Hearing footsteps, Stillman turned and saw Donovan Hobbs and Sheriff Lewis walking toward him, Lewis packing a double-barrel shotgun.

Stillman backed up a step, turned, and bolted through the door of the telegraph office, diving over the counter as the plate-glass window shattered in a fusillade. He hit the floor and looked up at the pig-faced man sitting at a small, pine desk buried in paper.

"Get down!" he yelled.

But the echo of the yell hadn't died before a slug took off the top of the man's head. He jerked violently backward, slumped to the desk, and slid to the floor. Stillman scrambled to his feet, gripping his Henry, and ran to the back, where a narrow plank door defined itself in the log wall.

He crashed through the door shoulder first, bulling it off its hinges, and hit the ground on top of it. A plank from the frame fell across his legs. Pain from the impact numbed his shoulder and shot through his neck.

Wincing, he lifted his head and took a quick survey of the alley. To his left was a chopping block and several cords of neatly stacked stove wood. To his right was a trash heap smelling like rotten eggs and coffee grounds. Beyond, a snow-flecked Airedale was trotting away, casting wary glances behind him.

Stillman got to his feet, keeping his eyes on the rooftops. Intermittent rifle fire punctuated the snowy silence. Apparently Hobbs hadn't thought to cover the building's flank. Whoops and yells rose from Main Street. Stillman looked back and saw Hobbs and Lewis sidestepping through the telegraph office.

At the same moment they saw him. Levering a shell, he swung the Henry and fired. The men dropped. Stillman turned to run, but not before Lewis tripped both triggers on his scattergun. The big gun boomed like a cannon, and buckshot whined like hornets through the doorway.

Stillman bolted past the trash heap. Cans clattered and hooves pounded behind him. Ahead of him a two-seated surrey sat harnessed to a gray mare. Stillman ran, untethered the horse, and jumped aboard. He released the brake and gave the horse the reins. The startled animal crow-hopped and twisted its neck, finally moving forward at a canter, then a gallop.

At the end of the alley, Stillman turned sharply up Second Avenue and saw Fay's white-booted black tethered to the hitching post before the sheriff's office. The horse's mane and saddle were dusted with snow, as though it had been standing there for a long time. His brow stitched with worry, he stared at the horse, craning his neck as it slipped farther and farther behind him.

He swung his gaze forward when he heard gunfire and

bullets zinging off posts and punching through windows. He took another right. A grizzled old bear of a man in a red plaid mackinaw on a buckboard wagon dead ahead yelled, "Rein away, fool!" But the surrey smacked the buckboard's back wheel, bounced several feet in the air, and tipped.

Stillman rolled clear and watched the overturned buggy bounce down the street behind the mare, who shook her head from side to side as though she'd been told something she just couldn't swallow.

"Ohhh!" the buckboard driver groaned. "Look whatcha done to your buggy, boy!"

Pushing himself to his feet, and feeling as though a metal spike had been hammered through his hip, Stillman limped over to his rifle. He jacked a round into the chamber and squeezed off a shot at the four riders pounding toward him. The buckboard driver berated him for his poor driving until, realizing the score, he whipped his mules down a side street.

Dragging his right leg, Stillman stumbled into the walkway between the feed store and Buckman's Card Palace. He turned, fired three quick rounds to hold the riders at bay, and dodging shipping crates, continued down the walkway, across the alley, and between two open barn doors. He heaved the doors closed. Feeling his way between the stalls in the semidark, heavy with the smell of horses and ammonia, he reached the wall ladder and scrambled up to the loft.

Using his rifle as a cane, he climbed through the hay shocks toward the gable and cracked the loft doors. The Henry gripped firmly, he peered down on the alley. Swirling snow covered the wagon boxes, spools of barbed wire, and rabbit cages below. Trash swirled against the buildings, growing fainter in the darkening night.

Three men with rifles crept down the walkway, their dusters blowing, hat brims flopping in the wind. The others would be coming from another direction. They'd tighten their circle till they had Stillman hung out to dry like the afternoon wash.

He cursed. Trapped in a friggin' barn like a rabid dog.

Sucking in his breath, he poked the Henry between the loft doors, lifted the target site, aimed at the rifleman stepping around a beer barrel, closed his first knuckle over the trigger, and squeezed.

The Henry barked. The man slammed back against the brick wall, fired his rifle into the air, and slid slowly down the wall.

The other two crouched and returned blind fire, frantically looking around. One retreated up the alley. Stillman shot the other as he turned to follow. He lurched forward, clutched his side, and crumpled to the ground.

Suddenly a whoop arose like an Indian war cry. Stillman looked left, and a bullet creased his earlobe. He dropped, tossed off his hat, and peeked down at Weed Cole standing in the alley with his arms spread. Even in the fading light, Stillman could see a smile straightening his mustache in a line above his mouth.

Like a warlock sprung from hell, Cole screamed. "We're comin' for ya, Stillman. You ain't gettin' away this time, ya old fool!"

Stillman raised his rifle, levered a shell, and fired. The gunman bolted to the barn doors and heaved them wide as Stillman's third shot hit the alley.

The doors at the other end of the barn scraped open. "Where is he?" It was Hobbs's high, nasal accent.

Stillman scrambled away from the loft doors, pressing his back against the wall and listening.

"In the loft," Cole said. "He's mine."

"We'll see."

A shell kicked into a rifle breech. Five shots broke the silence. The bullets cracked through the loft floor and into the ceiling.

Shattered swallow's nests rained mud. A cat hissed and disappeared through a crack. It was too dark to see the holes, but Stillman had felt the impact of one slug about a foot away from his boot.

"Come on down, Marshal. Fay's waiting for you at the jail," Hobbs said.

Stillman's ears rang and his pulse quickened.

He thought for a moment, then said, "She's your wife, Hobbs—why should it bother me?"

He jumped and ran as Hobbs, keying on Stillman's voice, fired three shots through the floor. He stood in the gathering dark, gripping his rifle, trying to see through the floor cracks.

"I know," Hobbs said darkly.

Stillman dropped the Henry's barrel and fired three bullets through the floor, then skipped to another position.

"Know what?" Cole asked in a low, guarded voice.

"Shut up," Hobbs ordered. His voice rising, he said to Stillman, "You know what I'm going to do with her? I'm going to give her to Cole." He laughed. "What do you think, Mr. Cole? You've been wanting a night with my wife, haven't you?"

Stillman fired another round at Hobbs's voice in the floor, then switched positions. "I think Cole would rather spend a night with you, Hobbs."

Stillman jumped as three pistol shots tore the floor.

Hobbs laughed. "Well, maybe I'll throw her in the bunkhouse." He stopped, waiting for a reply or a bullet. "Imagine that, Stillman—a treat for my men."

Stillman heard a heel catch on the floor beneath him, and

fired. Hobbs cursed. Through clenched teeth he said, "Get him!"

A long silence followed. Stillman listened. Only the faintest crackling of straw as Cole maneuvered toward one of the ladders. The darkness had grown impenetrable. The hair on the beck of his neck prickling, Stillman crouched on his haunches, brought the rifle across his knees, and waited.

Something clattered across the floor. Stillman started and lowered a hand for balance. It was a decoy. Cole had thrown a nail from the loft. Stillman sucked in his breath, released it slowly through his mouth.

In one motion, he levered a shell and sprayed the darkness, the Henry jumping in his hands until the hammer clicked tinnily. He dropped the empty carbine, dove to the floor, and rolled as Cole returned fire. Bullets thumped and twanged around him, dust rose. He pulled his Colt and fired toward the flames jumping from Cole's pistols.

When the Colt was empty, he rolled into a haystack, broke open the pistol's magazine, and thumbed shells from his cartridge belt. Cole, moving around, shot into a corner. Stillman closed the magazine and was about to start firing again when he heard rifles outside.

A familiar voice sounded. "Yo, the barn! Federal marshals. You're surrounded."

It was McMannigle.

Cole had moved to the other side of the loft and shot at a mouse scuttling in the hay. Stillman fired, emptying the Colt, and waited for a scream, the sound of a body hitting the floor.

None came. Boots pounded across the loft, passing only a few feet in front of Stillman, who was thumbing shells into his pistol.

Slamming the cylinder home, he looked to the north side

of the loft, where the doors yawned open against the snowy sky. A shadow passed. He heard a crash and remembered the rabbit cages piled below.

"Son of a *bitch*," Stillman said out loud.

He ran to the loft doors and looked out. A figure ran up the alley and disappeared in the dark. Stillman thrust his pistol out and emptied his magazine. But Cole was gone.

"Stillman!" McMannigle called.

"Here."

Stillman retrieved his rifle and made his way to the ladder hole filled with soft yellow light and climbed down. Leon stood holding a lantern in one hand, a rifle in the other.

He grinned. "I do believe I saved your ass *again*."

Stillman smiled cheerfully. "How'd you make it?"

"We led 'em into a box canyon and dry-gulched the hell out of 'em. That girl, she can shoot better'n most fellas!"

"She made it, too—thank Christ. Where is she?"

"Here," Crystal said. She ran to Stillman and threw her arms around his neck. She clung to him for several seconds, then slowly pulled away, lifting her chin to look into his eyes. She shook her head fearfully. "Please tell me Jody—"

"He's at Sophus Anderson's place, waiting on the doc."

She turned and ran for the door.

"Crystal, wait! Hobbs's riders—"

But she was gone.

Leon said, nodding, "There ain't *too* many of 'em left. We killed two on the way into town, and two more here."

"Hobbs?"

Leon shook his head. "Never seen him."

"Cole's out there, too."

Stillman laid his Henry on a stall partition and filled the magazine from his cartridge belt. He told Leon to look after Jody at the Anderson house and gave him directions.

"I got business at the jail."

29

Hearing hoofbeats outside his office, Sheriff Lewis turned to the window, blocking the light of the oil lantern behind him. Three men galloped past, shoulders bent to the wind and blowing snow, heading out of town.

What in hell was going on? The sheriff felt queasy, and he wasn't sure if it was from the deputy's innards on the floor, or fear.

Feeling vulnerable before the window, Lewis walked to his desk and sat stiffly in his creaky chair. He glanced behind him at Hobbs's wife, sitting on a cell cot in the shadows, head on her knees, and shrugged. The more pleasant they were to look at, the harder they were to live with—that's what he'd always heard.

He laid the shotgun on the desk and sat staring at the single, dark window in the brick wall, chewing his mustache and fingering the old Loomis's triggers.

Finally he opened a drawer and got out a tobacco pouch and papers. He leaned forward, creasing a paper between the index and middle finger of his left hand, and shook tobacco from the pouch. His hands trembled, dribbling Bull Durham on a wanted dodger.

Damn. He wished he could just ride to the boardinghouse, crawl into bed with one of Peg Emerson's girls, and weather the storm. This was Hobbs's fight, not his.

He was bringing the paper to his lips when the window shattered and a brick bounced off his desk and chinked against the wall. Startled, Lewis jerked the shotgun to the window and tripped a trigger.

Before the thunder of the shot had died, the door blew open in a rain of splinters and a gust of wind and snow, snuffing the lantern. Lewis tripped the second trigger. The cannon roared, sending buckshot through the black opening.

Lewis squinted his eyes. No one was there.

"You're empty, Sheriff," said a quiet voice above the wind. "Set that heater on the desk and follow it up with your six-shooter, nice and slow."

Lewis could make out Stillman's dark outline. He'd come in low, under the shotgun blast. With one knee on the floor and his pistol aimed upward, he'd drawn a bead on Lewis's face.

The sheriff did what he was told. Stillman stepped back and closed the door, then called into the dark at the back of the office for Fay.

The cot creaked and a shadow moved. "I'm here. Where's Donovan?"

"I thought he'd be here." Stillman spoke quickly, with an urgent edge. To the sheriff, he said, "Let her out."

The sheriff did not hesitate. Wanting to get the hell out of there himself, he retrieved his keys from a desk drawer, unlocked the cell, and threw the door wide.

Fay walked quickly to Stillman's side, placed her hand on his chest, and said quietly, her voice thin with fear, "He's here . . . somewhere."

Stillman nodded. He turned to the sheriff. "Where's Hobbs?"

Lewis shrugged. "Don't ask me. I just retired."

Stillman could tell he meant it. "There a back door to this place?"

The sheriff shook his head.

Stillman cursed. To Fay, he said, "Stay close to me."

"Where are we going?"

"Somewhere safe."

He took Fay's hand, and they walked up the street, keeping to the building fronts for cover. Stillman held his rifle loosely in his hands. Moving sideways, he kept one eye ahead of them, another on their backtrail. Hobbs could be anywhere, and so could Cole.

Stillman felt exposed. His back prickled. The snow whipped under the awning, and the wind cut like a knife.

Hand in hand, they turned behind a lumber dray and hurried across the street. The Windsor Hotel was dark. Stillman tried the front door. It opened.

Inside, a lamp burned on the front desk no brighter than a match. Stillman had to pound the bell several times before a skinny young man in pince-nez glasses and sleep-mussed hair appeared on the stairs. He pulled suspenders over a wrinkled shirt, blinking weary eyes.

Seeing Stillman's rifle and countenance, he stopped, one hand on the banister. Apparently he'd heard the shooting at the livery barn.

"It's okay, kid," Stillman said, "I'm one of the good guys. The lady needs a room."

He didn't sign the register, and the kid didn't push it. Key in hand, Stillman led Fay to a room on the third floor. Inside, he touched a match to a mantle, then replaced the flame-blackened chimney.

Fay removed her hat, threw her arms around Stillman, and pressed her lips to his. Her breasts swelled against his chest. Her lips opened. He felt the want in her, the need, as she urged against him, pushing him back toward the bed.

"No," he said at length, easing her away. "I have to go."

"Stay," she breathed.

Nothing would have been easier. Or harder. She smelled like desert rain. Her body warmed him. Fighting his desire, he shook his head. "Jody . . . Crystal—they're at Anderson's."

Taking her elbows in his hands, he pulled her to him and kissed her, then walked to the door. "I'll be back soon. Don't you open that door for anyone. Here—" He shucked his Colt from his holster and set it on the table beside the bed. "Anyone crosses that threshold, you empty the cylinder."

She looked across the room at him, her dark French eyes creased with worry. "You be careful," she ordered.

Downstairs, Stillman found the night clerk behind the desk staring warily across the lobby to the broad, curtained windows lining the boardwalk. Stillman blew out the lamp and walked to the door. "Lock up behind me. You're closed for the night."

He walked up the street and found Sweets standing with his rump to the wind, reins dangling on the snowy ground. He mounted and rode up the hill behind the Anderson house, standing ghostly dark in the stormy night. Halfway up the grade, Stillman tethered Sweets to the corral, shucked his rifle, and walked carefully toward the house, blinking his eyes against the snow and gritting his teeth against the cold wind.

He crept up the back-porch steps, opened the screen door with painstaking slowness, tried the inside doorknob, and stepped inside. He stood against the wall, looking around and listening.

Hobbs was here. He could sense him in the heavy silence.

"Ben . . ." The voice was raspy and tight.

Stillman looked to his left. Leon lay against the wall on the other side of the door. Stillman knelt down and saw blood staining the man's coat. "What happened?"

"Hobbs," McMannigle grunted. "He's down the hall. I think he's got Crystal."

Stillman looked down the hall, where shadows played. It was too dark to see anything. He squeezed Leon's arm, then rose and crept ahead, biting his lip and bringing the Henry to bear.

A figure appeared twenty feet ahead. Stillman jumped under the stairs to his right as three quick shots pierced the silence. One slug tore into the railing above him. The other two shattered the glass in the door behind, letting the storm in. Stillman felt the cold on his neck.

"Come on in, Marshal, we've been waiting for you," Hobbs said.

Stillman peered down the hall. It was empty. Anderson's study lay ahead. Soft yellow light shone in the open doorway.

"Come on," Hobbs said tightly. "Don't be shy."

Crystal screamed. Stillman jacked a shell and ran past the open doorway, glancing inside. Hobbs stood before Anderson's desk, holding a gun to Crystal's head. Stillman pressed his back to the wall beside the door, thinking.

"Drop the carbine and come on in, Stillman, or the girl swallows a bullet."

Stillman winced and dropped his chin. There was no other way.

He turned and stood in the doorway, holding his rifle toward the ceiling. Hobbs and Crystal stood before him. The Englishman held the girl with his left arm. He pressed

the business end of his nickel-plated Bisley to her throat
with his right hand.

Crystal's green eyes narrowed with fear and anguish. The
old Regulator clock above the settee ticktocked with re-
lentless vigor. The girl's face was pale, and her chest
heaved.

Behind them, Sophus Anderson sat in the chair behind
his desk, legs stretched before him, arms dangling, head
thrown back. A hole in his forehead leaked blood. His open
eyes seemed to regard Stillman apologetically. Several feet
away, the safe door hung open.

Stillman felt so ill his knees almost buckled. "Good
Christ, Hobbs."

Flushed and menacing, Hobbs grinned. "Yes, well, I
caught the banker with Mr. Goodnight's ledger. It's mine
now. Your case is closed."

"Mr. Anderson gave it to him 'cause he threatened to
kill me, Mr. Stillman," Crystal explained, choked with
emotion. Lips trembling, her eyes tearing, she added, "He's
a son of a *bitch*."

"That's me," Hobbs said with cheer.

"How'd you know he had the ledger?" Stillman asked.

Hobbs pursed his lips. "Just a hunch. I didn't think
you'd keep it on you. When I followed the doctor here and
found the boy and her, well . . ."

Following Hobbs's gaze, Stillman turned to see a man
in a black suit and vest sitting on a leather davenport, a
black bag at his feet. The doctor worried a ring on his left
hand and regarded Stillman anxiously.

Turning to the Englishman, Stillman said, "Let the girl
go, Hobbs. This is between you and me."

Hobbs ignored the plea. Flushed, he faked a smile. "Ah,
we meet at last—the cuckold and the cuckolder."

"Let the girl go."

Hobbs tipped his head at Crystal, fingered her hair, nuzzled her neck. "What do you say we make a trade? Fay for this hearty, nubile—"

"Shoot him, Mr. Stillman." Crystal's eyes darkened with fury. "Shoot him!"

Lifting his eyes to Stillman, Hobbs wrinkled his nose and jabbed the Bisley under Crystal's chin. "Drop the rifle, or she'll require a coffin."

Stillman set the Henry on the floor.

Crystal said, "*Shoot* this slime!"

"Shut up!" Hobbs shrilled, shoving her to the wall and pressing the Bisley to her left eye.

"Hobbs!" Stillman protested.

The Brit gave him a daring look, eyes flashing. Crystal looked at Stillman, silently begging him to shoot.

"You have the ledger—what else do you want?" Stillman said.

Gritting his teeth, Hobbs hissed at Crystal, "I want you to see how Fay's going to die!"

Crystal brought her leg up between Hobbs's, slammed her knee into his groin, and chopped the gun away with her arm. Hobbs groaned and crumpled. The Bisley cracked. Crystal screamed, brought her hands to her head, and slumped down.

Stillman jumped, sprang off a footstool, and slammed Hobbs to the floor with his hands around the Englishman's neck. The Bisley hit the carpet and slid under a chair. Hobbs squirmed out from under Stillman and gave the ex-lawman a collegiate upper cut with his right fist. Stillman fell back, fuzzed by the pain in his jaw.

Hobbs crawled across the room and grabbed the Henry. Stillman reached under the chair for the Bisley, thumbed back the hammer, and as the Englishman lowered the Henry's barrel, plugged his left shoulder.

"Ah!" the Englishman screamed, the impact of the slug slamming him sideways. Again, he brought the Henry to bear, eyes crazy with rage.

Stillman squeezed off another round. Hobbs shrieked as the bullet tore through his belly. He bent forward, knees buckling, tipped his head to peer at the blood spreading at his middle. He squeezed the Henry's trigger, and the bullet tore into the desk. The rifle fell. He raised his head and glared at Stillman, exasperated. "You—" he tried.

He stepped forward, fell against the desk. Pushing off with one hand, he turned and stumbled toward the door. He stopped, overcome with pain, leaned into the doorjamb, and slid to the floor.

His cloudy eyes swept the room until they found Stillman. "You and Fay . . . shall rut . . . in *hell*," he wheezed.

He dropped slowly to his knees, his eyes blank with pain. Slowly he set his chin to the carpet, turned on his side, and curled his legs. His chest heaved, and he was dead.

Stillman moved to Crystal, pulled her hand away from her forehead, and scowled at the blood. He turned to where the doctor cowered on the davenport, shielding his head with his arm.

"Doc, give her a hand."

"No, it's just a graze. Help Jody," Crystal said.

The doctor rose slowly from the davenport, expressionless, blinking his eyes, trying to digest what had just transpired. He picked up his bag and went upstairs.

Stillman picked up the Henry, glancing out the windows. "Cole, where are you?" he muttered.

"What?" Crystal said. She sat against the wall holding a bandanna to her forehead.

"Cole," Stillman whispered.

"What about him?"

"You seen him?"

She shook her head.

"Why wouldn't he be with Hobbs?"

"Maybe he's outside."

Stillman shook his head. "We would have heard from him by now." Again he remembered what the gunman had said at the burned-out Harmon ranch: *I'll say good-bye to Mrs. Hobbs for you.*

Stillman looked at Crystal. "You gonna be okay?"

She nodded, quizzically meeting his gaze.

Stillman turned and hurried down the hall. He helped Leon to his feet. "I think Cole's after Fay," Stillman said, helping McMannigle into the study.

"What you doin' here, then?"

Stillman eased the man onto the davenport, where he lay back, holding his shoulder. He'd plugged the wound with his scarf. "You gonna be all right?"

"Go," Leon grunted, waving him off. "Go!"

30

Weed Cole stepped out from Hall's Mercantile carrying a gunnysack of trail supplies, ammunition for his pistols and carbine, two boxes of Cuban cigars, a bar of good castile soap, a Waltham railway watch, and a bamboo fishing rod with nickel ferules.

The unlatched door teetered behind him in the wind. He'd broken out the glass when he'd entered fifteen minutes earlier—after watching Stillman walk out of the Windsor, leaving Hobbs's wife snug as a bug in a rug.

Cole grinned.

He stepped off the boardwalk and tied the gunnysack to his horse. Lifting his collar, he tipped his head into the storm and ran across the street to the hotel, the wind flattening his woolly chaps against his legs.

He looked up and down the street, pulled his right pistol, and broke the door glass with the butt. He reached inside, threw the bolt, and walked in.

A young clerk met him at the top of the stairs, looking frumpy and frantic.

"What's going on?" he whined.

"What room's she in?"

"Who?"

"Who else?" Cole drew a pistol, pressed it to the kid's forehead, and clicked back the hammer. "What room?"

"Three-eleven."

"Go back to bed." Cole mounted the stairs and turned to the kid, who hadn't moved. "Go back to bed, or I'll cut your tongue out and hang it around my neck."

The kid turned into his room and slammed the door.

Cole climbed the stairs and walked down the hall, heels pounding the cedar floor. Stopping at Room 311, he tipped his head to listen.

Inside, Fay pressed her back to the door and closed her eyes. Her heart pounded so loudly she was certain Cole could hear. Her hands were slick with sweat. She could barely hold Ben's pistol.

Cole tapped once on the door. Fay caught a scream in her throat, jumped, and turned around.

"Hi there," Cole said.

With both hands, Fay raised the pistol and clicked back the hammer. She closed her eyes and squeezed the trigger. The gun barked and jumped. Smoke puffed. The smell of gunpowder burned her eyes.

Silence.

"Ain't you gonna let me in?"

She raised the pistol and blew another hole in the door.

Cole laughed.

She fired again and again, until the hammer clicked against the firing pin.

The door exploded. Fay screamed, threw the pistol at Cole, and ran to the window, clawing at the sash. Cole caught her by the hair and threw her to the bed.

"No!" she cried.

"Oh, yes!" Cole laughed.

Cole took her by the wrist and dragged her out the door. "Come on, honey. We're gonna take us a ride."

He dragged her down the stairs. She grabbed at the banister and called for help. Cole jerked her hand free and gave her a shove. She stumbled down the last three steps and fell to the floor.

Scrambling to her feet, she lunged toward the door, and tried to run. Amused, Cole grabbed her around the waist with one hand and opened the door with the other.

Outside, she screamed, but the wind sucked her breath away. Cole lifted her onto his saddle and brusquely tied her hands to the horn, cutting her wrists.

"What are you *doing*?" she cried, her voice thin with defeat. "It's *storming*!"

"Don't worry," he said, mounting behind her. "Won't be long before you're warmer'n you'd prob'ly care to think about."

He hooted and gouged the gelding's flanks with his spurs, and they cantered off through the storm.

Fay squeezed her eyes closed against the snow, head down, wincing at the pain of the cold reaching down her coat like a hand. She struggled against the twine, but the more she tried to loosen it, the tighter it grew.

They rode over the buttes southwest of town, then descended a ravine and followed it straight south for nearly an hour. Disturbed by the storm, the horse twitched its ears and shook its head. Twice it stopped, and Cole had to coax it on with his spurs.

Trees and brush pulled at Fay's coat and hair. She couldn't imagine where they were heading. She wondered if the gunman even knew. How would Ben ever find her? She hunkered down in her coat and tried to quell the paralyzing fear, tried to stop the tears freezing in her eyes.

Finally a cabin and corral appeared in the snowy dark. Its two front windows shed lantern light on two gutted deer hanging by the door. The carcasses turned in the wind.

Cole dismounted, led the horse into the corral, where four others stood rump to the wind, and released Fay from the saddle horn. Slinging the burlap sack over his shoulder, he led her stumbling through the deep-drifted snow past a barrel-laden freight wagon to the cabin.

The wind rattled a tin chimney. The air smelled like burning cottonwood.

Cole pushed open the door, jerked Fay in before him, and let her go. She grabbed a post where a lantern burned, and looked around.

Before her, orange flames danced around the rusty door of a potbelly stove. Two bearded men in shaggy, wide-collared buffalo coats played cards at a round table. One was thin and bald, with a long, horsey face. His eyes shone bright with alcohol.

The other man was tall, broad, and older, with carved marble cheekbones. Thick gray hair fell from a beaver hat. Seeing Fay, he smiled, revealing a gold front tooth and a light in his icy-blue eyes.

Fay turned to another man—stout, with a handlebar mustache and silvery, bristled hair—staring at her. An antelope carcass lay upon planks and beer kegs before him, and the knife he held dripped blood.

"Ja, vot haf we here?" said the big, gold-toothed Scandinavian.

Fay started at the man's baritone. "Help me," she said. The men laughed.

"You ever seen anything like that?" Cole asked them.

"Where'd you find her?" asked the bald man.

"My little secret."

"Fine, fine," said the big Scandinavian. "Not bad for a snowy night. How much you want for her?"

"She's not for sale, but when I'm done with her, you can have a poke for twenty greenbacks. I'm gonna take her

ONCE A MARSHAL 261

to Canada and sell her to a chink runnin' a hog pen in Medicine Hat.''

''Twenty!''

''Look at her.''

Fay gripped the post and closed her eyes, trying to keep from fainting and retching on the smell of wet buffalo hide and raw meat.

''But twenty dol-lors,'' the Scandinavian groaned, dipping his chin to his chest.

''Think about it, Pop,'' Cole said, taking Fay's wrist and leading her to a door.

The man carving the antelope called, ''Millie's in there with a customer.''

Ignoring the man, Cole rummaged around in his bag and produced three Cuban cigars. He threw two on the table and one to the man carving the antelope, and said, ''A stranger in a buckskin coat and a ten-gallon hat comes callin', you know what to do.''

He winked and threw the door open, pushing Fay in ahead of him. She caught herself on the tarnished bed frame. Before her, in the shadows cast by a hurricane lamp and a woodstove, a naked, tawny-haired girl straddled a man on the fur-mounted bed. She bounced on her knees as though riding for the gate, and her long, slender back curved over the customer's chest. He wore only a neat, red-brown beard and gold-framed spectacles, which slid down his nose when he lifted his head to see the intruders.

''Hey!''

The girl opened her mouth and looked at Fay, then Cole, with eyes older than her years. ''Whaddaya mean!'' she yelled in an East Coast accent.

''Out!'' Cole ordered.

''Whaddaya mean?'' the girl repeated, growing even more incredulous.

"Out, out, out!"

"We ain't through."

Cole drew his pistol and blew a widget from the ceiling. The man flung the girl aside, gathered his clothes, and ran cursing out the door.

A roar of laughter erupted in the other room.

Untroubled by her nudity, the girl reclined on the bed and gave Fay a cold appraisal. "I'm the only girl in this house. We ain't a hotel," she told Cole.

"Git before I braid your titties," Cole said, pulling her off the bed and throwing her out the door.

Another roar of laughter erupted in the other room.

Cole turned to Fay, then regarded the big oak tub before the woodstove. He scrubbed his mustache, thinking.

Fay clutched her coat closed and stepped back.

Grinning, Cole opened the door. "Girl, you bring me water for a hot bath, an' I'll pay ya what fancy pants owes."

He closed the door again and looked at Fay, his unclipped mustache spreading above his lip. "Alone at last, Mrs. Hobbs. Make yourself comfortable."

Fay's eyes blazed. "You sick son of a bitch. Ben Stillman will hunt you down like a dog. . . ."

Laughing, Cole moved to the small woodpile next to the stove. He grabbed a log, opened the door, and chunked it in.

Fay leaped past him for the door. He grabbed her ankle, tripping her. She slammed face-first to the floor and lay there, cloudy with pain. Her head throbbed.

"Help me," she cried softly, cheek pressed to the rough cottonwood planks. Her eyes filled with tears.

She was still lying there when the girl came and filled the tub from steaming water buckets. "What's her problem?" the girl asked Cole.

"She likes it rough," Cole said.

When the girl had left, Cole sat in the rocking chair and hiked a boot on a knee. He reached into his coat for a cigar.

"The bath is for you, honeypie," he said, lighting up. "Anytime you're ready."

Stillman stared at the half-open door numbered 311. He poked his finger through a bullet hole, pushed the door wide, and raised a lantern.

Shadows slid down the wallpaper. The room was empty, the bed rumpled. He stepped forward and picked his pistol off the floor, spun the magazine. His eyes narrowed and his lips trembled with rage.

The young night clerk stood beside him holding his robe closed at his throat. "I sure wish you people would take your personal problems elsewhere," he said through a yawn.

Stillman turned, gripped the scrawny neck, and shoved the kid against the wall. "Where'd they go?"

Pale and wide-eyed with fear, the kid stuttered. "Ha . . . how should I know?"

"West along Main," came a low voice down the hall.

Stillman raised the lamp. The hall was empty. A door latched softly.

Stillman released his grip on the shuddering neck and ran downstairs. Outside, he mounted Sweets and rode west, watching for tracks in the snow, discovering occasional, vague outlines of shod hooves being quickly erased by the wind.

The tracks led out of town. Stillman followed, leaning from his saddle. After fifteen minutes he lost them on the southern benches rising toward the Two Bears.

He rode in a wide circle but came up dry. Without trees or buttes, the wind had free rein, filling every gap and hollow, erasing every trace of man and beast with swiftly falling snow.

His heart hammering his breastbone, he halted Sweets on a knoll, tipped his head back, and yelled Fay's name until his throat felt like sandpaper. Only the wind answered, howling.

Stillman cursed and snugged his hat lower on his head and looked around, helpless. Had he ever felt so miserable?

He rode on. What else could he do? He wouldn't rest until he found her.

At length a dim figure approached on his left—a man on a brown horse holding a scarf knotted under his neck. His spectacles nearly covered with snow, he didn't see Stillman until Stillman yelled.

The man stopped and looked at him warily, wiping snow from his glasses. He wore a sealskin coat and a stocking cap. His beard was frosty white.

"You see a man and a woman out here?" Stillman asked him.

The man regarded him suspiciously, shook his head, and muttered, "No . . ." He clucked to his horse.

Stillman frowned. "Where'd you come from?"

"None o' your business," the man called, riding away.

Stillman rode after him and grabbed the bridle of his horse, drawing his Army Colt. "Mister, I asked you a question!"

The man gave a yell and cowered, startling his mount. "Easy, mister! Sandy Creek Roadhouse."

"Where?"

He jerked a thumb over his shoulder. "You'll come to a ravine. Follow it south."

Stillman turned the man's horse loose and gave Sweets the spurs.

●   ●   ●

Fay lifted her head from the floor, pressed her back to the log wall, and folded her arms. She shivered. "I'm not bathing in this weather."

"Sure ya are." Cole pulled his pistol. "Take your clothes off."

She stared down the Peacemaker's bore. "You won't shoot me."

"You know how many people I've killed?"

Fay's heart beat in her throat. She'd rather die than take her clothes off. She said as much with her eyes.

Cole bounded out of the chair, grabbed her by the hair, and threw her on the bed. She sank her nails into his neck. He slapped her twice, hard, then ripped open her coat and went to work on her blouse, rubbing his mustache on her cheek. His breath was pungent, revolting.

"Okay," she cried. "Okay I'll do it. Alone."

Cole lifted his head, breathing hard through his nose. "That's more like it." He crawled off of her and sat in the chair, filling the room with the smell of the harsh cigar.

Stone-faced, Fay sat on the edge of the bed and stared at the wall.

"Shed the coat and turn to me," Cole said.

She stood and shrugged out of her coat. Dropping it, she turned to the gunman.

She took a deep breath. With trembling fingers, she worked at the buttons on her shirt. Watching her, Cole's eyes turned to liquid. He licked his lips and grinned.

31

When Stillman saw the lights of the roadhouse, he tethered Sweets to a cottonwood along the creek.

Holding the Henry rifle in both hands, he trudged through the drifted snow to the cabin and peered through a window. Two men in buffalo coats played poker before a potbelly stove. A girl wrapped in a tattered quilt stood behind the bigger of the two men, appraising his cards.

In the shadows beyond the lantern and firelight, another man lay curled on a cot. Though Stillman couldn't see any hardware, he figured the men were armed.

Seeing Fay's hat on the floor, his blood rushed.

He ducked under the window and hid beside the door. He removed a cartridge from his belt and dropped it on a wind-cleared patch of porch. It clinked and rolled.

A few seconds later he skipped another bullet across the porch. A chair scraped the floor. Boots thumped. The door opened.

"Anybody there?" a voice called.

Stillman rushed around the door and thrust the butt of the Henry into the bald man's head. The man bounced off the door frame and fell on the porch.

Stillman stepped over him, jacking a shell. The big Scan-

dinavian jumped from his chair, wielding an old Walker
Colt.

The Henry boomed. Dust puffed from the man's buffalo
hide. He staggered back, shooting into the floor. Stillman
shot him again and he fell back on his heels.

The girl had backed against the wall, screaming. The
man on the cot lay frozen on his elbows, giving Stillman
a look of surrender.

Stillman ran across the room, bulled through the door,
and hit the floor.

Three bullets exploded in the wall above his head. He
looked up, raising his Colt. Across the room, Weed Cole
stood with a pistol in each hand. He fired twice, creasing
Stillman's coat collar.

Stillman returned fire, standing Cole against the wall.
Cole's Navy Colt clattered to the floor. Stillman shot him
again before he could lower the Peacemaker.

The gunman fell forward onto the woodstove, screaming.
Then the light in his eyes died. His chin fell against the
stove, and he lay draped over it, hands and face sizzling,
filling the room with the gut-wrenching smell of burned
flesh.

Stillman stepped forward and kicked the gunman off the
stove. He looked at Fay, who leaned against the oak tub,
half-naked, her head between her knees. Her back trembled
as she cried.

Stillman knelt down and pulled her head to his chest.
She cried louder and threw her arms around his neck. He
held her and rocked her, cooing to her softly.

"Get me out of here," she said.

"It's storming," he told her. "We should wait till day-
break."

She pulled back and looked at him with desperate eyes.
"I have to get out of this place, or I'll go insane."

Stillman nodded. "Get dressed."

He grabbed Cole by his feet and dragged his body out-side, smearing blood on the floor. In the cabin, the girl sat on the cot with her legs beneath her. Wrapped in a quilt, she chewed her nails and stared at the dead men, awestruck.

The stout, gray-haired man—the proprietor, Stillman fig-ured—was kneeling over the Scandinavian. He looked at Stillman accusingly. "Quite a show, mister."

"I'll pay for damages," Stillman said. "I'll send some-one out for the bodies when the storm lets up. In the mean-time I'll need to borrow a horse."

"You got cash?"

"How much?"

"Five dollars if you send it back tomorrow."

Stillman reached in his pocket and handed the man five dollar bills. The man stuffed them in his shirt. Stillman walked to the door.

"The woman—she yours?" the man asked him.

Stillman nodded. "Yes," he said, and walked out.

The storm had abated when Stillman and Fay followed the mail road into Clantick, the snow up to their horses' hocks. Dawn whitened the eastern horizon, and stars winked be-hind scudding clouds. Though the wind had died, the tem-perature had plummeted.

They road along Main Street, the frosted storefronts ap-pearing marooned in an ice age, and stopped at the hitching post before the Decker Hotel. Stillman figured they'd worn out their welcome at the Windsor.

"You go in," he said. "I'll be along soon."

Fay looked at him tiredly, her shoulders slumped in her big sheepskin coat. "Where are you going?"

"I have to check on the others."

"Don't leave me."

He sidled his horse next to hers and hugged her. "I won't be long, Fay."

"I don't want us to be apart ever again."

"I'm gonna hold you to that," he said with a weary smile. "Now go on in and get some rest. I'll be along soon."

As he reined his horse away Fay said, "Tell young Harmon the Hobbs ranch is his. I'm signing it over to him."

Stillman looked at her and raised his eyebrows.

She shrugged. "It's the least I could do."

His weary horse trudging through the deep-drifted snow, Stillman rode to the Anderson house, unsaddled Sweets, and stalled him in the stable with fresh oats and straw.

On the house's back porch, he saw the snow-dusted bodies of Sophus Anderson and Hobbs lying side by side on the floor, covers blown back revealing the top of Hobbs's head and half the banker's long, gray face.

Stillman felt a pang of sadness. He'd liked the sardonic old man, who would have recognized the irony of his fate.

Inside, he found Leon sawing logs on the study davenport, his right arm in a white sling. Cracking Jody's door, he found Crystal curled in a chair by the boy's bed. He closed the door softly and started down the hall, then heard a latch click behind him. Turning, he saw Crystal pad toward him, stocking-footed.

"Everything all right?" she asked.

"Fine," he said. "How 'bout here?"

She nodded. "The doctor said the bullet missed Jody's lung by a quarter inch. He just needs time and tending."

Stillman smiled. "That's good news."

Looking troubled, Crystal sat at the top of the stairs. Stillman sat beside her and looked at her quizzically. "Don't worry about the ranch," he said. "Fay's turning Hobbs's spread over to you and Jody."

"Oh, my . . . !" Crystal turned to him, shocked. "Jody'll never accept such a gift!"

Narrowing his eyes, Stillman smiled ironically. "I have a feelin' he's not gonna have a choice."

Still overcome, Crystal stared off. "All that land . . . my God!"

Stillman chuckled and wagged his head. "You two are gonna have your hands full, that's for sure," he said, patting her knee. "You'll need you a passel o' kids just to keep the house clean!"

He stood and started down the stairs.

Behind him, Crystal said in a voice as tight as razor wire, "My father killed Mr. Harmon, didn't he?"

Stillman turned and sighed. He hiked his jeans and sat back down. "I'm afraid so, girl. I'm sorry."

"Are you sure?"

Stillman sighed again. "Not entirely. But I found a .45/70 slug and a split-rear hoofprint, not to mention a pint jar. I don't think it was Hobbs's men. No cattle were stolen."

Crystal nodded, resting her elbows on her knees and lacing her hands together. She said dully, "Pa always kept a .45/70 Springfield in his saddleboot, and that old mule's had a split rear hoof for as long as I can remember."

There was a long pause.

"He should hang," Crystal said, her jaw ridged with anger. "And burn in hell."

"He's already in hell," Stillman said. He gazed at her sincerely. "I know because I was nearly there once myself."

Crystal threw her arms around his neck and sobbed. Then she pulled away, wiping tears. "I best get back to Jody."

Stillman watched her walk down the hall and turn in to the bedroom. Then he went outside, and took a slow, thoughtful walk to the Decker.

It was dawn, and the main doors were open. Two old men smoked in the lobby, drinking coffee and discussing the storm. A fire popped in the lobby's big fieldstone hearth. Stillman asked for Fay's room number at the front desk and walked upstairs, feeling heavy with exhaustion.

He knocked on the door. Fay opened it, wearing only thin panties and a man's gray undershirt. Her raven curls flowed down her slim shoulders and curved around her breasts.

She smiled, eyes flashing.

"Oh, Lordy," Stillman growled. "I do believe I found heaven."

"Get in here," she ordered, swiping his hat from his head. "We have some catching up to do."

EPILOGUE

One month later . . .
Jody spurred his buckskin up the saddle and stopped beside
a cedar. Holding the reins in his gloved hands, he surveyed
the valley below.

The Johnson cabin and corrals sat ghostly gray in the
cold opal light, behind a veil of falling snow. Hard, icy
snow mounds patched the yard. A shed door slapped its
frame. A thin ribbon of smoke curled from the cabin's
chimney.

Spying movement, Jody slid his gaze to the east side of
the ranchstead, where a red fox was trotting away from the
trash pile, a sheepish cast to its gait.

Jody drew his Walker Colt from its holster, weighing the
old beast in his hand, and made sure all six chambers were
properly loaded, then clucked to the horse and rode down.
Several pigeons flew out from the two open doors in the
barn loft, wings flapping like wind-buffeted sheets.

Keeping his eyes on the cabin, his hand on his holster,
he stopped at the corral, dismounted, and tethered his horse
to a rail.

A cat meowed. Jody looked around. A liver-colored puss,
hair matted and ribs showing, ran from under a trough. It

curled around his ankle, stiffened its tail, and purred. He reached down and stroked the half-starved creature, then crossed the yard to the cabin.

He walked up the three half-rotted porch steps, shucked the Colt, took a deep breath, and shouldered open the un-latched door. Clicking back the revolver's hammer, he looked around. It took several seconds for his eyes to adjust to the semidarkness.

To his left, against the wall, Warren Johnson lay on a bed covered with a rank-smelling buffalo robe and several deerskins. A slop bucket sat nearby, filling the room with a nearly palpable stench. The man's rheumy, swollen eyes were open, staring at Jody.

"Good day, 'breed. Been expectin' ya."

Jody stood in the open doorway, gripping the pistol firmly in his hand. He swallowed and licked his lips. "Did you kill my father?"

Johnson reached for a jar on an upended crate beside the bed. The covers fell down his shoulder, revealing a pumpkin-sized lump where his liver should have been. He tipped back the corn liquor, set the jar down, and pulled the covers up to his neck. He gave a shiver and let it settle.

"You got a burr under your ass, 'breed," he said dryly, with a grin.

Jody stared at the man coldly. "Did you kill my father?"

The rancher stared at him dumbly.

Jody said, "Ben Stillman found the print of a split rear hoof and a .45/70 shell casing where Pa was killed. Your mule's right rear hoof is split. I've seen a .45/70 Springfield in your saddleboot." He paused, and swallowed. "Now I'm gonna ask you again—did you kill my father?"

Johnson stared at him with faraway eyes, as though he hadn't heard a word.

"Goddamn you!" Jody thumbed backed the hammer and

shot into the wall behind the man. "I asked you a question!"

Johnson did not react to the splinters flying around him. He asked calmly, "You still diddlin' my daughter?"

Jody stepped forward and pressed the Colt to the sick man's forehead. He gritted his teeth and narrowed his eyes, trying for all his worth to pull the trigger. His hands shook uncontrollably. He bit his lip until it bled.

Johnson reached up and wrapped both his hands around the barrel, steadying it. He closed his eyes. "Come on, boy—you can do it! Pull the trigger!"

"You killed my pa!" Jody cried.

"Pull the trigger, 'breed!"

Jody held the barrel to Johnson's head for several more seconds, tears rolling down his cheeks, willing himself to shoot. Over and over the man begged him to pull the trigger.

Then Jody lightened his grip, and Johnson's hands fell away. Jody looked at him. For the first time there was fear in the drunkard's eyes.

"What are you doin', boy? I killed your pa!"

Jody drew a ragged breath and sighed. He released the hammer and lowered the pistol. He regarded the fear in Johnson's face, and smiled weakly.

"I ain't doin' you any favors, old man."

Then he turned and started for the door.

Behind him, Johnson yelled, "Where you goin', 'breed?"

Jody said nothing. He left the cabin and walked toward his horse.

Johnson's voice rose shrilly behind him. "Shoot me, goddammit, 'breed!"

At the corral, Jody gathered the cat off the empty trough

and clutched it to his breast, ignoring the epithets spewing from the cabin.

"*I killed your pa, you goddamm half-breed son of a bitch!*"

Jody mounted his buckskin, stuffed the cat in his coat, clucked to the horse, and retraced his path through the snow.

Johnson's tortured wails echoed behind him.

When he reached the saddle's crest, he saw Crystal waiting there atop her filly, her rabbit hat snugged low on her forehead, her eyes wide and questioning. Jody rode up to her and halted his horse. He pulled the cat from his coat and handed it to her.

"Let's go home," he said.